IMAGINE
THAT

Also by Barbara Kastelin

THE PARROT TREE

WHEN SNOW FELL

A BAD LOT

HOTEL BELVEDERE

IMAGINE THAT

SHORT STORIES

All the best
Barbara Kastelin

BARBARA KASTELIN

Matador
Unit E2 Airfield Business Park,
Harrison Road, Market Harborough,
Leicestershire. LE16 7UL
Tel: 0116 2792299
Email: books@troubador.co.uk
Web: www.troubador.co.uk/matador
Twitter: @matadorbooks

ISBN 978 1803136 592

British Library Cataloguing in Publication Data.
A catalogue record for this book is available from the British Library.

Printed and bound by CPI Group (UK) Ltd, Croydon, CR0 4YY
Typeset in 11pt Aldine401 BT by Troubador Publishing Ltd, Leicester, UK

Matador is an imprint of Troubador Publishing Ltd

For my daughter, Pascale

CONTENTS

DO MIRACLES HAPPEN?

If you drive out of Palermo along the coastal road east and, in the fishing town of Termini Imerese, turn right onto a minor road which snakes up a hill, you come to a village called Maiale. Don't give up. Keep wriggling on up, to where the view opens to show, beyond the flanks of vines, orange and lemon orchards, the azure Gulf of Termini Imerese. At the foot of the mountain Pizo Conca, you enter a village, the sign of which depicts a square tower with three white doves flying around it. The village is called Colomba del Castello. The castle at the top of the village is long gone, and only the original foundations of the chapel remain. Whilst the castle was left to crumble, wiped out by the mishaps which befell the Spanish Bourbons ruling southern Italy and Sicily, the villagers contributed to the restoration and preservation of the chapel, erecting a fine stone bell-tower.

Along one side of the churchyard still stands part of the original dry wall, having withstood weather and earthquakes. It appears again here and there further down, demarcating the private gardens of village dwellings.

★

Father Benedict and the village carpenter stood beside the church and gazed into the sky. Three white doves circled the bell-tower.

'Those are direct descendants of the original three birds – a holy trinity,' said Father Benedict.

'Ah!' responded the grizzled carpenter. 'I can feel the vibrations of the last three thousand years.'

Frescoes in the church depicted battles, and the pews were made of intricately carved castagna wood. Foreigners were attracted to Colomba del Castello to admire the church, the old wall, and a few gravestones made posthumously and doused in lime, purporting to mark the burial places of viceroys and their ladies. A booklet with the history of the reigning families could be purchased for two thousand lira pushed into the slit of a sturdy box.

Luckily, tourists get hungry and thirsty faster than any other people, and the only restaurant halfway up the cobbled road to the church catered for their culinary needs, often more than they bargained for.

When Giovanni and Feliciana had bought the place and wanted to call the restaurant La Colomba, the priest objected. They were his doves, his historic right, and the easy-going couple understood. They went to church to make amends for their flagrant forwardness, and became an important part of village life. Their restaurant offered Italian specialities and was named Girasole, or Sunflower, a name which did not offend anyone.

The restaurant had a few metal tables out on the pavement next to the cobbled road, which offered views up to the church and contact with village life. The sunless interior had wall mirrors and a large picture of Van Gogh's *Sunflowers*, ceramic pots with felt sunflowers, and a carved, wooden sunflower head lying flat on a sideboard. The head was actually a dish filled with loose sunflower seeds, a creation the carpenter had made to order. Any client who guessed the exact number of seeds was offered a starter of *mozzarella alla griglia* on the house.

To the rear of the restaurant was a covered pergola, a large space with ten tables and umpteen chairs, all high-backed with straw seats. From the rim of the rush-covered roof came the music of wind chimes.

On Saturday evenings, Romeo, the younger brother of the carpenter, was contracted for three hours to play the guitar and sing to customers, O *Sole Mio* winning every time.

Beyond the pergola, three steps down, extended the garden which was given over to vegetables and herbs. At the end stood a section of the historic wall.

To the right, a waist-high metal fence separated the garden from the neighbours' property, on which stood a converted barn. The neighbours, Rosa and Antonio, reared chickens, which regularly ended up on the large, stoneware plates on which Feliciana served her food.

*

Anke's fishmonger's van came up from the fish market in Termini Imerese, as it did twice a week. She drove like Phaethon and hooted as she went, to herald her approach.

In front of Girasole she stopped. They were regular customers.

3

Anke opened the back of the van and patted the flank of a seabass, laid out on ice in a row with others.

'Caught early this morning. You can't do better. Was feeding off blooming seaweed. Late spring time, the best season for mature fish with muscle meat.' She held the fish head right in front of Feliciana's face. 'The eyes not yet blind, he is smiling at you, Feliciana. You have to buy and grill it for someone. Such a beauty.'

Feliciana looked at the down-turned mouth of the fish and shook her head. 'A worthy fish, I agree, but customers seem to be off ordering large fish. We're lucky if one of them chooses a mullet from the menu.'

'There is this fad called vegetarianism. No meat, no fish. You must have heard.' Anke put the seabass back with the others, so she could cross herself, saying, 'Your restaurant is spared more than others. Imagine a steakhouse!'

'Try the seabass on Father Benedict,' said Feliciana.

'He does buy from me, but only ever fish gut.'

'To keep his doves in the tower.'

Anke got back into the van and drove off, one of the back tyres free-wheeling in dry earth. Feliciana had to wipe the dust out of her eyes with a handkerchief. Up by the church, the fishwoman hooted the horn to wake the dead in the churchyard.

Feliciana turned round and, to her pleasure, saw a group of tourists making their way up the road. It was a reasonably warm early June day, but the way they panted and coughed... She pulled the sign for beer and soft drinks further out where the sun hit it. Then she went into the house to check the larder and fridge, ran under

4

the pergola and covered most tables with washed and ironed gingham tablecloths.

At the fence stood Rosa. 'Looks like you will get busy today,' she shouted. 'I saw a large group of them halfway up to the church.'

'God willing!' Feliciana shouted back, while putting out menus.

'Come over here, I have to tell you something,' coaxed Rosa.

The women knew each other well. They had both moved to Colomba del Castello on marriage, within a few months of each other. That had been almost a dozen years ago but, alas, neither woman had become pregnant in all that time.

Feliciana crossed her herb garden, taking care not to trample on any plants. At the fence, she noticed Rosa holding her belly.

'It is right for me to tell you now. I am with child. In five months. End of October.'

Feliciana could not help hot tears welling up. 'You are blessed. I am happy for you.' Her voice quivered.

'Will you need a chicken for the tourists today?' down-to-earth Rosa went on, as if the miracle of her pregnancy was incidental, while in Feliciana's life this was a constant torture of deprivation. 'Tell yourself that, if I got pregnant, you will too. You are years younger than me.'

'Only three, to be exact,' said Feliciana. 'To get pregnant you need sperms for insemination. And the days you ovulate, you have to really go for it. Giovanni is not the man one orders to pull down his trousers.'

'Mine is only too happy to. Men, huh?' Rosa rubbed her abdomen. 'You can be godmother to this boy.'

'How do you know it is going to be a boy?'

'I don't. What I know is that, right now, I will twist the neck of a plump chicken for you. A gift.'

'I don't need pity.'

'It's not charity. It's corn-fed chicken meat.'

Both women laughed at that. There was a bond between them, the bond of the earth they shared, as there was a bond linking all the villagers.

Fourteen guests sat under the pergola. Five years ago, they would have eaten two seabass at least, several osso bucco, and chicken cassatas. That June Saturday, the guests ordered risottos with mushroom, salads, and salads again. Even the brave one who ordered spaghetti carbonara had to have it without bacon. What was happening in the world that the people of Colomba del Castello did not know about?

'When I offered them desserts, they recoiled. "There is milk and cream in desserts," they objected. That comes from cows. And they are animals,' said Feliciana to Rosa at the fence that evening.

'I read an article about this,' sympathised Rosa. 'Anything coming from animals, even chicken bone broth, is now out.'

'Don't tell me this is the end of traditional cooking in restaurants,' said Feliciana.

'I guess we have to adapt,' replied Rosa. 'Herbs, fruit, vegetables can be eaten without having to slip into the confessional and tell Father Benedict "I have sinned and eaten an egg".'

'Unbelievable.' Feliciana shook her head. 'I am not going to tell Giovanni about what you've just told me. I fear he would become rude to customers.'

'Capitalise on your herb garden,' said Rosa. 'Cut out the more expensive meat dishes and replace them with bullshit about mushroom stems marinated in wild ramson sauce, which is widely known to revive passion.'

'Is it?'

'Who knows? And then charge double.'

'I love you,' said Feliciana simply.

'Even now I am having a baby?'

'Of course,' said Feliciana, turning away. It did not sound convincing.

'It's not all going to be cherry lollypops and knitted booties, you know,' said Rosa. 'For starters, I have to rest a lot to avoid a miscarriage at my age. The doctor called it a geriatric pregnancy.'

'You are thirty-eight.'

'And you are a businesswoman growing herbs, while I will have to be a nursing mother for months.'

'I grow the herbs to enhance dishes with new flavours.'

'I saw a book in a shop in Palermo when I went for my check-up: *Spices, herbs and other wonders we find in nature*. I opened it at random and there was a picture of a tree, and a recipe of how to use its sap in soups.'

Feliciana lit up with interest. 'Really?'

'I'll buy it for you,' said Rosa. 'You will put Colomba del Castello on the gastronomic map!'

Feliciana smiled and immediately frowned. 'I must go and help Giovanni tidy the kitchen.'

'It's Sicily.' Rosa spread her arms. 'There is no hurry.'

Back in her kitchen, Feliciana collapsed into a chair. Giovanni's hand came to her neck, a cool hand against a hot neck.

'This is the worst day of my life, and it is St Anton de Padova's day,' she said vehemently.

'I know the tourists were difficult, but they were Danish,' said Giovanni. 'Soon, the French will come and things will get easier.'

'Rosa is pregnant,' Maria blurted out and was immediately assailed with sorrow. Her head sank onto the table, her forehead knocking against it hard, as if she did not care about her head any longer.

To this, Giovanni found no words. He left the kitchen.

'I would give anything to be Rosa,' she whispered to the tabletop right next to her mouth.

*

The heat of summer came to Sicily.

On one ordinary Monday, a man who was unaccompanied entered Girasole. 'Table for one?'

He had dark curly hair, trimmed on either side, but left wild on top of his head. His eyes were dark blue, and he ordered lamb with herbs.

Feliciana beamed and rushed into the herb garden with the kitchen scissors.

After he tasted the food, he called her to his table, saying, 'This was unusual. Have you by any chance used Allium Ursinum?'

She nodded. 'Wild cowleek is in season, and ramson is budding.'

'You know your herbs,' he admired, and congratulated her on the taste she had produced. 'I am a bit of a botanist, writing a book about it at the moment: *Botany in Cooking Worldwide.*'

When Feliciana offered to buy the book, he said, 'It will only be published in the autumn. I need to do more research. My next trip will be to the Middle East, where they use the resin of the Commiphora Molmol tree to enhance lamb stews. Apparently, it has been done since biblical times.'

'And you will make this secret known to every woman who has a kitchen?' said Feliciana.

'Do I detect a problem for you with this?'

'Herb gardening is my strength, my everything,' she said. 'I have nothing else. At my age, I am still not a mother.'

At the door, after having paid, the botanist lingered. He reached out and touched her arm. 'I will buy a young Commiphora tree and send it to you. It will probably be a Commiphora Myrrha, which is the hardiest species. You will find out how to use its magic.'

She did not thank him. She turned away because Giovanni was watching.

'Don't flirt with customers.' Giovanni almost jumped at her when the dated Volvo drove off. 'He is too young for you. You make a fool of yourself.'

'You are the most jealous man in all of Sicily.'

'I am the alpha male in Colomba del Castello.'

'It is my time of ovulation, Julius Caesar.'

'I'm going to buff up the copper pans and, that done, Antonio will come round for a few drinks.'

'Fine.' Feliciana climbed the stairs to the bedroom. 'Get drunk with Rosa's husband. What do I care?'

★

A month later, an ungainly parcel was delivered by the postman. 'It smells, it feels odd, and sand is drizzling from the wrapping,' he complained. 'Perishable food is not allowed to be sent by post.'

He went on, but Feliciana was already sprinting through the restaurant and out into the garden to unwrap the package. There was Arabic newspaper wrapped around a plastic bag with sand mixed with reddish earth, and a miniature tree, no taller than the length of an adult seabass. The label on its immature stem read *To be planted in full sun.* In brackets, *Desert plant. Wounds by prickles can get infected.*

She noticed a few buds of thorns starting to appear from the trunk and some branches, but they were soft still. A picture was slipped into the package showing the mature Commiphora Myrrha tree with light-green, narrow oval leaves. Feliciana was so exhilarated that she fetched the shovel and started to dig a hole in the ground, there and then. She chose a place next to the old wall at the bottom of her garden, where the sun hit it most hours in its journey through the zenith, and where the wall, retaining heat, would bounce the heat back to the tree.

Giovanni came down the garden and looked at the plantling. 'Is this a bonsai?'

10

'It will grow to...' she checked the sheet, '... maximum three to four metres high.'

'Useful fruits or berries?'

'Sap, the blood of the tree.'

Giovanni gave a sharp laugh. 'In about twenty years' time, if that thing takes and grows.'

'Patience is required,' she said. 'Be good.' She bent to the little foreign tree standing straight in the newly dug patch. 'Grow and bring us happiness.'

'Should you not rather water, than talk to it?'

'It is a biblical plant from the Palestinian desert.'

He shook his head and traipsed back to the pergola and into the house.

Feliciana remained, standing still amid the scents of her garden. The sun was slanting and giving the tree its own timid shadow against the old wall.

'Maybe Jesus's crown of thorns was made of Commiphora branches,' she said to the garden, which was starting to be overtaken by dusk after a glorious July day.

*

Next door, Rosa grew larger, the pregnant bulge sitting high, which she interpreted as being a boy. Antonio, who was a teacher of music in Maiale and several other schools in the area, was asked by Father Benedict to teach him to play the organ. The current organist had reached ninety, and too often his playing was erratic.

'Our priest can't conduct Mass and play the organ at the same time,' was Feliciana's objection.

'Never discourage a human from learning to play an instrument,' was Antonio's opinion, of course.

Later, when Antonio came over for a beer with Giovanni, he elaborated on the organ lessons. 'Father Benedict really goes for it when it comes to Bach fugues. He wants the throttle pulled out to full so he can thunder on. He is turning our church into a boom box. The doves will flee to a quieter place. He plans to give an evening service, which will be more like an organ concert. I hope you will come, and encourage others to attend the event next Sunday vesper time.'

★

Three months later, the community nurse visited Rosa to make sure her pregnancy was progressing healthily. A date for the birth had been calculated by the midwife on her date-wheel. Villagers visited Rosa and brought baby clothes of children who had outgrown them. There was even a gift of a yellow pushchair with Minnie Mouse on the seatback. Antonio frequently came round to have a beer with Giovanni and drown his fears. He called Rosa hysterical and demanding. She had made him buy an expensive Perego baby carriage in royal blue velveteen, which she cleaned every day.

During one of these male bonding sessions, Feliciana overheard Giovanni. 'My wife has become weird as well. She nurtures an ugly, prickly tree, talks to it, feeds it sand from the building site up the road, and claims it lived at the same time as Jesus, and in the same place.'

'Women need babies, whether they are human,

12

animal or plant,' concluded Antonio. 'Men need mates and beer.'

In mid-October, Etna produced an earthquake. It was only a small burp. Some sensitive people felt it; others heard the small bell ping twice in the church tower. With history came legends: a bell starting to ring on its own portended disaster or death.

It was part of their lives to have an active volcano on their island. In the church, was a wooden board onto which earthquake dates and strength had been carved ever since the large one in 1693, when sixty thousand people had died.

At the end of October, the community nurse drove up and, shortly after that, the ambulance arrived next door. Feliciana just had time to run and grab Rosa's hand on the stretcher to wish her all the best with birthing, before Rosa was loaded up and taken to Palermo.

★

After the birth, Antonio came to the fence shouting for Giovanni. 'I'm a father! A boy. He will be called Marco after my grandfather.'

Giovanni invited him over for drinks, but for the first time Antonio declined. 'I wish I could, but I am knackered after twenty-one hours of Rosa's labour, and it would be a disaster. Besides, I have promised Rosa.'

'A baby,' said Giovanni, 'will change many things in a man's life.'

'Don't scare me more than I already am,' said Antonio. 'That son of mine has a head like a shrivelled old red apple.'

Feliciana fled upstairs to her bed, where she pulled the duvet cover over her head to blot out the ungratefulness with which the men seemed to react to a baby. If it were hers, nobody would be allowed to talk about shrivelled apples. If she had a baby, people would have to whisper and admire, and stand back faced by the miracle. If she had a baby, she would pray to the mother of God every day. With that devoted attitude, why did she not deserve to have a baby? Had she done something so bad to make the angels ignore her most ardent wish, month after month?

The wind got up in November, and Rosa could be seen pushing the Perego pram through the narrow streets of Colomba del Castello, the retractable hood up and the face guard buttoned in place, as if she protected her son, not just from stormy weather, but from the eyes of villagers.

At the beginning of the new year, Rosa still hid her baby in the covered pram. People started to gossip. Was the boy deformed, perhaps? Why did Father Benedict baptise the baby on a Tuesday morning without the bells ringing or any godparents attending?

Rosa turned a deaf ear and moved on.

When, by Easter, not even Feliciana had laid eyes on the now six-month-old boy, still being wheeled in a pram for infants, she came to agree that something was not right, especially as Antonio did not come round for chats with Giovanni any longer.

To Feliciana's pleasure, the Commiphora tree had grown pleasingly tall and a lot more sturdy. She did talk to it every day. Tourists started to arrive, and Girasole was busy. One guessed the number of sunflower seeds correctly and got his starter for free. Later, Feliciana confessed to Father Benedict that she had manipulated this, that she did not actually know how many seeds there were. That particular hesitant customer asking for a small bowl of pasta and a glass of water had worn a wooden cross under his tired old jacket, over trousers which were frayed at the hems, and his shoes had holes in their soles. She had assumed he was a pilgrim and could do with some free food.

It wasn't a sin to be charitable to someone in need. Father Benedict let Feliciana go without having to say any Hail Marys. What she did instead was go next door with the intent of finding out if she could help Rosa with her hidden-away baby.

At the door, Rosa dithered. 'It is inconvenient. Marco is asleep.'

'I came to see my future godson, and you can't prevent me. I thought we were friends.'

At this, wordlessly Rosa let her step into the living room. Feliciana went to the pram, fear knotting her throat. Only after an intake of breath did she dare look at Marco, a smooth-skinned beautiful boy who was propped up by several pillows into a reclining position. He did not look at her, but emitted a little cry like a moan of distress.

'Hello, little Marco. You are a darling boy.'

His lips parted, his eyes were wide with fright, and his left hand started to move erratically. Rosa pushed Feliciana gently to the side and bent into the pram, caught the moving hand and lifted it up to her mouth to calm it with a kiss.

15

'I love you so much,' she said in tears. Marco was looking at his mother's earring. 'Sweet little boy,' she crooned. The child still looked fixedly at the gold hoop. Rosa took a biscuit out of her apron pocket and held it close to him. 'Biscuit,' she tempted. His hand reached out but smacked the side of the pram instead, again and again.

'My darling boy.' She bit off some of the biscuit and held it close to his lips. His red, bruised hand kept smacking the side of the pram. Rosa gave up.

Before letting Feliciana out of the house, Rosa confided in her. 'He has been diagnosed with cerebral palsy, spastic cerebral palsy.' Tears of frustration and grief glistened either side of Rosa's nose. 'So now you know.'

'Marco is a handsome little boy.'

'I am an old mother,' said Rosa. 'It has something to do with it. A spastic child is a life-long commitment of hardship, patience and unrequited love.'

Back in Girasole, Giovanni wanted to know what she had found out. Feliciana just cried, but managed to utter, 'Marco is a most beautiful child. With soft, curly dark hair.'

'Yeah, yeah, but what is really wrong?'

'His mind does not work like other people's.'

'An idiot?'

Feliciana cried harder. 'Never say that word again if you want to keep me as your wife.'

'Don't be so heavy.'

That night, Giovanni held onto Feliciana tight, for fear of losing her. He made love to her with more passion than he ever had. In the morning, Feliciana, quite dizzy from it, rose from the twisted sheets to go to the bedroom window to cool her body. She was staring out into the garden thinking of Rosa's words, 'Life-long commitment of unrequited love.'

And then a white dove fluttered over the garden.

'A church dove has just landed on top of our old garden wall. That is a sign.' Feliciana crossed herself.

Giovanni propped himself up in the bed. 'Father Benedict got up early to pound the organ. The bird fled.' He made himself roll out of bed. His slippers not cooperating, he padded over to her on sleepy pink feet.

'Down there.' She pointed, but the dove had vanished.

Giovanni's lethargic body turned vibrant. 'Look again, woman. It's not a dove; there is a rabbit chewing on your herbs.'

'Oh, no,' she cringed.

'I'll get my rifle.'

Her drawn-out 'no' was lost on him as she heard him rumble down the stairs, the way he could when he was twenty years younger.

Feliciana saw her husband appear from underneath the silent wind chimes. Knees bent, rifle poised, he advanced towards the herb patch. Alarmed, the rabbit pricked up his ears and ran. One dry shot. The rabbit kept hopping towards Rosa's garden. A silky, cool breeze smelling of rain brushed over Feliciana's face up at the window, and the chimes sounded.

Giovanni, murder on his mind, advanced to the herb patch in a crouching position. He aimed again, even though the rabbit was probably through the fence by now. At that moment, the white dove flew back to land on the wall. The feathers had a blue tinge in the ambiguous early light of sunrise.

Giovanni, in trigger-happy mood, fired another shot. The dove fell off the wall.

Feliciana, downstairs, out of breath, yelled at her husband, while pummelling his chest.

'Stop it,' he ordered, pinching the rifle between his thighs and grabbing her wrists. 'It was less than a chicken.'

'A chicken? It was most probably the female dove of the threesome, Father Benedict's holy spirit.'

'Stop talking nonsense and get me the shovel.'

'Get it yourself.'

They buried the dead bird amidst the roots of the now-two-metre-high Commiphora tree, because the earth mixed with sand was easier to shift.

After that, Father Benedict was seen searching everywhere for his third dove. When he came to Girasole, Feliciana made innocent eyes and lied. 'Not seen, not here. Sorry for your loss, Father.'

Later that day, the Commiphora tree pricked her upper arm and it hurt. She watched a heavy drop of her blood hanging on a long thorn, before elongating and falling. On religious pictures, there was blood on Jesus's forehead as he was nailed to the cross, thorns pressing down on his head.

Father Benedict must have guessed that Feliciana had lied to him. In Mass on the following Sunday, he went on about barren women nurturing their sins because they were overlooked by nature.

'He's going too far over a scrawny pigeon,' Giovanni defended his wife.

'Not your rifle again,' she pleaded theatrically.

'I have to stand up for who I am.'

'You can be someone sitting down as well.'

This time, she had the last word, because Father Benedict started to play the organ.

*

With the heat of a new summer increasing, the high season intensified in Colomba del Castello. Feliciana, preparing zabaglione by dribbling the Marsala into the sluggish mass of egg and cream, found this suddenly off-putting. The day before, she had vomited from an empty stomach in the morning, and her breasts had started to feel tender under the cotton dress. It turned out that she was pregnant. It had happened during the night before the white dove had come and been buried under the thorn tree in the early hours of a new day.

Now the community nurse stopped at Girasole to make sure things were progressing healthily for Feliciana, and Giovanni went next door to Antonio with a six-pack to unburden his fear of becoming a father.

It was calculated that Feliciana's baby would be born around Easter the next year.

The mother-to-be walked on clouds. Looking up to the sky, she kept thanking the angels. She floated through her herb garden and smiled at beetles. She cut into the bark of the Commiphora tree, apologising for hurting it, and used the gum-like sap in her baked vegetable lasagne, together with freshly ground nutmeg, a dish which was much applauded. In the confessional, she admitted to Father Benedict of having lied about the fate of his dove. He was about to reprimand her, but she cut in.

'You called me barren and sinful in front of everyone in the village. I am expecting. You had no right to judge my misery.'

'And you, dear Feliciana, seem to have taken to lying.'

'I don't care,' she said in a singing manner. 'I will have a baby, my baby, my child. I will be a mother. Please congratulate me and promise to baptise my child when the time comes.'

'Go in peace,' was the only thing he could add to her outburst, from behind the latticed partition.

Feliciana had never felt better in her life. She was confident enough to take on the world, criticise the priest. Apart from talking to the thorn tree, she now whispered and sang to the baby growing in her womb. Giovanni could hardly get a word in sideways as he ran flattened dough through the machine to cut spinach tagliatelle.

On 11 April, a healthy baby girl came out of Feliciana's body. Giovanni, the alpha male of the village who had asked to be present at the birth, flaked out when the doctor said he could see dark hair through the enlarged vagina opening. Crumpled up on the disinfected linoleum he lay, white as a sheet and soft as a lamb.

The day they brought the baby home, and hung the sign *Closed for family reasons* on the door of the restaurant,

Mount Etna made the earth shake again. Glasses rattled in the cupboard. It caused the large bell in the tower to swing enough to boom once. People ran outside and looked up at their houses, worried that cracks would appear, the foundations heave and destroy their homes. The news reported that, in the harbour of Termini Imerese, high waves had destroyed several fishing boats.

Anke the fishwoman's van did not toot up the road for several weeks after that.

*

Feliciana named her miracle baby girl Angelina. The baby spent her first summer gurgling and playing with her fingers in a small hammock under the pergola and, after five months, crawling on all fours across the planks. On her first birthday, Angelina stood up and subsequently learnt to walk. Marco, eighteen months older, was still doddling along, ending up on his bottom more often than not. Angelina held out her hands to help him up. She guided him, fetched things for him, laughed with him, never at him. When she was three years old, she went up to tables with families, and gave the children toys which belonged to her.

One day, after Giovanni had moved the tables and chairs to the side to clean the pergola deck, Angelina started to dance in the empty space to the music coming from the radio inside the house. The parents watched from inside. The three-year-old twirled, moved with grace, arms out, head up; she moved as if she were lifted by some superior force, the skirt of her little flower-print dress swirling. In a pirouette, her long, dark curls obscured her pretty face. The love for her daughter was so tight in her chest that Feliciana had problems breathing. At the end of the music, Angelina went over to Marco, who was sitting on the floor, legs stretched out.

'Boys don't have to dance like that to make them feel better,' she said.

'Thank you,' he said, and Angelina pulled him up.

Feliciana thought this was the sweetest thing she had ever witnessed. Angelina took care of Marco, showing infinite patience and understanding. When Rosa arrived to fetch her son, eagerly Angelina offered to dance again.

'Bedtime,' objected Giovanni, but even without music Angelina took off. The tips of her toes hardly touched the ground.

'She is a dancing spirit,' commented Rosa. 'The music is inside her. It is almost frightening.'

'I wouldn't be surprised if the children had sampled sap from the thorn tree. Perhaps the girl is drugged,' mused Giovanni.

'She is not allowed to go near the sap buckets,' Feliciana said, irritated. 'And neither is Marco.'

Angelina made a last twirl before bowing. 'Marco doesn't like the sap,' she said.

Giovanni looked at the child for a moment. 'But you do.'

'It's not honey,' interjected Feliciana. 'And you are not allowed to go near it.'

Rosa, who held Marco close to her legs to give him support while standing, looked at Feliciana curiously. 'Are you growing poisonous things in your herb garden?'

'The gum resin of the Commiphora tree has been used in food and medicine for hundreds, if not thousands, of years,' said Feliciana.

The evening ended with both children promising never to touch the tree buckets, or any of the herbs, again. However, the way children are, once they have discovered something forbidden or scary, they inevitably are drawn back to it.

★

Every year after that brought something special. In the first, a gourmet journalist wrote an article in a French magazine about Girasole's special preparation of dishes, calling Feliciana an accomplished chef whose vegetable lasagne contained a mesmerising culinary secret.

In the second year, the curly haired botanist returned and helped Feliciana fix specially designed collection pots under the cuts in the bark of the Commiphora, which had by now reached three metres with a trunk circumference the size of a slender young man.

In the third, Angelina became six and danced on her birthday in front of customers to the tunes of Romeo's guitar.

'She moves as if she were in a heavenly trance,' said a guest from Milan.

'My darling daughter is an angel,' replied Feliciana. 'That is why I named her Angelina. Would you like me to bring you the dessert menu?'

'When older, she will turn young men crazy.'

'I hope so.' Feliciana smiled with pride.

★

One Monday morning, Feliciana was awoken by an intense thunderstorm. She got up and walked to the window, under which the wind chimes were jingling madly. The sky was an unwholesome dark steel against which Father Benedict's two white doves were performing an air ballet, carried by strong wind. What must it feel like to swoop in a surge of wind like that? She marvelled at the sight.

'Come back to bed, woman,' Giovanni growled. 'It's Monday. Lie-in time.'

'There is something strange going on out there.'

'Did a spaceship land? Are women mud-wrestling?'

'No.'

She heard him turn in the bed. A little later, the noise of his breathing increased. Soon, he would be happily snoring again.

She had slept badly. In the middle of the night, she was woken by the endless dull crying of Marco next door. It had triggered the feared dream which often plagued her during the intensive sleep before waking. It never played out the same way, but it started by her trekking through a landscape of barren earth. When she came to the dark, hidden lake, it was clear nobody else knew about it, otherwise some less-tormented dreamer would have done something about it.

In her dream, she knelt down and dipped her hands in the water, prepared for the upsetting sight. The figure of a woman dressed in languidly swirling wraps appeared, deep in the water, seriously entangled with weeds and tendrilled plants. Yet, she seemed to sail and trail along, like a human-sized veil fish, although there was no visible movement in the water. Feliciana's hands were spread on a sheet of thick glass which covered the entire pond. She panicked. The woman down in the water needed air, to be pulled up, saved. At this point, Feliciana had been awoken by the thunder and drawn to the window.

Now, more awake, she followed the doves which still performed fearlessly amongst the storm-driven clouds. The contrast of their flitting white against ponderous thunderous steel was dramatic. They flew in a pair in a circle, the distance from each other maintained. They turned on themselves and, from the clouds, came a threatening grumble. A flash of pin-narrow, zigzag lightning cut through the dark mass of bulbous clouds.

'Come back,' Feliciana shouted out of the window, her voice trailed away by strengthening wind.

'Who are you shouting at?' Giovanni had moved to sit up in bed.

'The doves flying out there could be speared by lightning.'

'Not on a Monday morning.' He slid back down under the covers.

'Pompeii was destroyed on a Monday.'

'You make that up every time I want to lie in.'

'It was a horrendous disaster.'

'The Neapolitans deserved it. They are liars and cheats.'

'You say that every time I mention Pompeii.'

'Women predict catastrophes. Men don't.'

Trying to ignore him, she concentrated on the outside where the storm raged. The nightdress fluttered at her loose sleeve, as she tried ineffectively to pull the shutter closed, while the wind whistled high-pitched. She tried to locate the doves, but couldn't. Had it been a hallucination? After a minute or two searching a landscape of dark tumult, during which the fear of disaster from her paranoid dream crescendoed, her gaze was forced away from the sky and down to the ground, to her garden.

And there it lay sprawled, snow white on the dark earth – the dove bird slain out of the sky. It took a flicker of electricity in her brain to understand that a bird's body would be much smaller than what she was looking at. What she saw was not a bird but a human, a child. Not wings, but stretched-out pale, naked arms. Her child. The shock and horror of it was so powerful that she could not move. However, she gave a yell as from someone about to die a violent death.

Giovanni, shocked into the moment, jumped out of bed. Man and wife ran down the stairs, butting each other as they went. Their six-year-old had been struck by lightning.

Not far from the steps of the pergola lay the pale body of Angelina, dressed in knickers and a sleeveless nightshift.

'The Commiphora tree sap – that's what she was out here for. You were disobeying orders,' Giovanni said, looking down to the immature body. A crackle and grumbling of thunder answered him.

Feliciana threw herself over the body, searching for the child's mouth with her own lips to breathe air into her lungs. At the same time, with both hands, she reached under and scooped the lithe body off the ground, to press it close against her own, as if to force her warm blood into her child's veins, as if to take the child back into her body where it had been safe.

'You sneaked into the garden to lick sap from the buckets on that weird, prickly tree, didn't you?' Giovanni's shock and grief brought out aggression in him, although his next 'Didn't you' was distorted by the sob which had risen in his chest.

'She is dead,' pronounced the first-responders Rosa had called. They loaded the child into their ambulance. Feliciana and Giovanni watched what was being taken from them, like people who had died inside themselves.

A few days later, the report from the autopsy stated that Angelina, six years old, had not been hit by lightning, but had died of a heart attack. It happened in children who were born with a hole in the heart. The letter was unsympathetically signed *Cordiali Saluti* – 'Yours sincerely' in Italian – and in a PS requested instruction about what to do with the body.

Father Benedict hastened to Girasole after Anke, scooping fishgut into a plastic bag for him, reported that the restaurant owners were catatonic with grief. The priest offered to talk to the carpenter for a child's coffin to be made as fast as possible. The body would be brought back by ambulance the next day.

'White and shiny.' Feliciana said that she wanted only the best. 'The prettiest the carpenter ever made.'

When it came to size, they had to guess.

'Better err on the larger size,' suggested Father Benedict, 'so we will not have to break her legs.'

Feliciana fainted on the sofa.

'Poor woman,' said the priest, who was asked by Giovanni to leave.

★

Angelina lay in the silk-lined coffin, looking like the sleeping beauty in the book she had liked so much. Her cheeks were still flushed by circulating blood and, in her small hands, folded over the lace of her bodice, lay the silver cross on a chain her mother had worn around her neck. The curls of the dead child's dark hair were draped around her head, and the curved dark eyelashes made shadows on her cheekbones in the neon light of the undertaker's viewing room. Part of the ample white skirt of the dress, bought for the baptism scheduled in two weeks' time, showed wet and discoloured from the tears of the heart-broken mother, having buried her weeping face in it, seeking to feel the body beneath the artistry of the undertaker's presentation.

Angelina had lived. She had made of Feliciana a mother, and not just a woman who once existed, grew old and decayed. Angelina had kicked against the inside of her womb. Surely, there was nothing more miraculous in life than that?

'I would feel better if she had been baptised,' said Father Benedict, closing the lid of the lacquered coffin at the undertakers. 'Parents often wait to commit to this ceremony because they are busy with other things. And then it is too late.'

'Angelina will go to heaven, whatever you say, Father,' said Feliciana. 'Not having had blessed water dribbled on her head does not prevent this.'

'Baptism welcomes a baby into the Catholic faith, which protects them from the original sin they are born with.'

Feliciana stared at the priest. 'And don't you dare say anything undermining at our daughter's funeral tomorrow, otherwise I will fetch Giovanni's rifle and pay you a visit.'

'Anger is the first stage of grief.' Father Benedict warded off the angry woman. As she stepped back, he added, 'The equally painful time after that is mourning.'

'Let's go.' Holding tight to the jacket sleeve of her husband, Feliciana pulled Giovanni away from the closed coffin, Father Benedict and the softly piped music.

What she did not know was that Giovanni had given the priest a nice little bundle of liras for the church committee and, thanks to that, a small grave was being dug at the top of the churchyard near the oldest and tallest cypress tree.

God took her from us too early was carved into the wooden cross the carpenter had made as a temporary solution, until the stone with the statue of a little angel with large wings would be ready to be installed.

Girasole was closed for business. Often hesitating at Angelina's bedroom door, her mother did not have the strength to open it. Feliciana locked the door and was about to slip the key into her bra cup, when she heard a bird twitter. The window in the girl's room was still open. Feliciana opened the door and put the key back into the lock from the inside.

'I don't want to lock you into your room, darling,' she said. 'The bird you heard is a blackbird. Children should know their birds.'

The neighbours understood mourning and, in small ways, showed kindness. Rosa tried in vain to unlock Feliciana from the grip of grief. But it was the discordant crying of Marco, which sounded like a dog abandoned, that tormented Feliciana right back into despair. *Time heals grief* was the saying. Feliciana did not want to be healed, and time had become an enemy. She made a wide circle around Father Benedict.

After a painful year hiding their problem from customers in Girasole, Giovanni made the decision to tackle the problem head on. He bought a television set for the restaurant, so customers could come for drinks and watch sport. It worked for a while because the football Euros were on.

However, when Feliciana watched reality programmes in the morning, it bolstered her denial. Girls of seven were already fashion-conscious. They liked designer jeans, frayed at the knee, and T-shirts with long sleeves off one shoulder.

'We have to get that for Angelina,' she insisted. At first, Giovanni switched the TV off and, later, had the television picked up by the shop to sell for him, second-hand.

A few months later, when Giovanni returned from an errand, all looked normal at home, except for his wife sitting on one of the high-backed restaurant chairs in front of the prickly tree. At first, she did not notice him coming towards her, so involved was she in what she was doing.

Giovanni was already annoyed to find a package of clothes for Angelina ordered from a catalogue, but he had been admonished by Father Benedict and told to be gentle with Feliciana. He therefore spoke softly to her.

'I see you talk to your tree. Does it ever say anything back?'

'It is a holy tree. His aura communicates.'

Giovanni did not ask what an aura was. Instead, he stood behind her and held onto the two carved pinions, as if he could navigate her life into a different direction.

'Jesus, who wore the crown of thorns, did not leave us without guidance, you know.'

He let go of the chair because he was weary of her talking to him that way.

'As Mussolini tried to do to us?' he attempted a joke.

'A spiritual idol, who makes it possible to dream away a painful day-by-day life,' she said. 'Angelina is still here. I can feel her, sometimes almost see her.'

'Be rational, woman,' said Giovanni. 'We lost our child. She had a faulty heart.'

Feliciana reached up in an awkward twist of her arm to take hold of his hand. 'Angelina is not dead. That's all I'm saying.'

'I saw her in the coffin, and so did you.'

★

31

Some days, Giovanni envied Feliciana for being able to believe that Angelina was still alive. His wife lived by how old her child would now be, what she would wear, do, want, while he felt himself getting older every year and just more worn out.

'Today is Angelina's birthday!' Feliciana sounded jubilant. 'She is a teenager. Sixteen, would you believe it.'

For him, his daughter had been dead for ten years and he did believe that.

'I know you never buy her presents, but I have bought her something teenagers call "real cool". It is from both of us.'

It was true; she had asked Antonio to drive her to Palermo and help her buy a good-quality electronic keyboard, which he did with pleasure because he believed that music had a healing effect on human beings. Feliciana did not reveal to Antonio that the piano was for Angelina.

When it was delivered, luckily Giovanni was out. Feliciana asked the delivery man to install it in the child's room, which he did.

'A present?' he asked.

'Yes,' she smiled.

'A pretty good one.' He nodded and left.

When Giovanni returned, he found the delivery note for the piano on the kitchen table. He slammed the door so hard the house seemed to twitch.

Despite the tragedy in the family, tourists still came to eat. The menu was much simplified, though, and only basil was used in the tomato sauces; the other herbs in the garden had become overgrown and tangled. The Commiphora tree bark grew thicker and coarser as a result of it not being milked any longer. At times, often early in the mornings, Father Benedict's new *holy spirit* white dove came to sit on the old wall.

'I wasn't able to buy Nike trainers for Angelina today,' said Feliciana, returning from Palermo. 'The horrid woman in the sports shop said the girl had to come in herself to try on a pair to make sure they fitted properly.'

Giovanni was trembling with nervous anger. 'Feliciana, you know there is no Angelina anymore.' His balled fist was thumping the tabletop. He was living under the strain of doing most of the work to keep the restaurant going. Customers were afraid of his silence.

Marco next door had become a teenager too, and Rosa sent him to a special school where he stayed during the week. He never mentioned Angelina, but kept the hair ribbon she had given him in one of his shoes at all times.

Giovanni decided to adopt a new tactic. He made an attempt to convince Feliciana to add two more dishes to their uninspiring run-of-the-mill menu.

'Baked sardines with fennel,' he suggested tentatively, in an attempt to get her interest engaged, after he had studied the cookbook Rosa had bought in Palermo.

Feliciana remained thoughtful, but to his pleasure said, 'Concordare. Anke is a good woman. She needs income and can sell us fresh sardines.'

'It's the fennel-growing for you I was mostly thinking about.'

She looked up at him, surprised. Just then, the pergola floor started to shift beneath them. Plates intended for garlic bread skidded across the tables. And then they heard the large bell dong, and dong again, up in the church tower, joined by the small bell's continuous tinkling.

'Shit.' Giovanni pulled Feliciana back into the house and through the kitchen, where he unplugged the gas supply to the oven on the way to the walk-in cupboard built under the staircase, the spine of the house. He pushed her inside the confined space and shut the door behind them both. They were silent for a moment.

'This might be a big one,' he said, watching a screw holding up the lamp above them unscrew itself.

'The house will fall on our heads. I want to be in my garden when I die,' she lamented.

'We had this safe room reinforced with a steel frame for just such an event.'

Standing so close, they could feel each other's breathing. They heard shattering of glass, thumping of things falling and, worst, creaking of the structure of the house. Feliciana startled him with her loud yell right next to his ear.

'Angelina! Oh, my God. Go get her down here with us.'

'You can't be serious.' Giovanni circled her body with his arms, which was easy now that she had lost so much weight. 'Angelina is safe where she is. It just happens not to be with us any longer.'

In his strong grip, she twisted like a cat held too long against its will. Her head turned back to seek contact with his eyes.

34

'You still think she is dead, don't you?'

He let go of her, because the determination in her frightened him.

'She isn't,' she continued. 'If she were dead, I would feel it. Any mother would.'

A fresh tremor made them topple sideways, his shoulder hitting the steel-enforced wall, hers against his. Somewhere in the house, an alarm went off. The annoying beeping persisted.

'Our fire alarm,' he said.

'Angelina!' She threw herself at the door, knowing he was master of the key and would not let her out. Instead, he tried to calm her down. Feliciana turned and bit his hand. 'I hate you. I hate you,' she panted. 'Try for once to understand me. I have been your wife for twenty-two years.'

Resigned, Giovanni changed course. 'There must be much damage out there. I need to go and help.' When he tried to open the door after unlocking it, he found the quake had wedged it. He kicked it down. Immediately outside, Feliciana shoved him aside.

'Angelina,' she shouted. 'I'm coming.' She took the stairs.

'Angelina is in the churchyard,' he said with vehemence, 'buried in the earth.'

It made Feliciana hesitate halfway up the staircase. Somewhere in her, it made sense, for she relented and was suddenly eager to go to the churchyard.

When the pair were outside on the cobbled road, they noticed that there was something murky and palpably strange in the still air, as if a deity above it all was

smirking, *'Look what I can do to you insignificant humans.'*
From the town, alarms were ringing. The metal tables and chairs in front of Girasole lay on the pavement. One of the round tables had rolled down the road, like a spindle toy on its side.

Rosa came running to catch up with them, the sleeves of her dress unfastened, flopping around her wrists. 'The church,' she panted, 'is falling down. We need to go and help.'

'We are going there to save Angelina,' said Feliciana almost breathlessly.

Rosa sought the eyes of Giovanni. 'Yes,' he said. 'That is what we are going to do, to make a few things clearer.'

They were disturbed by a rumble, but it was the carpenter, pulling his rack-wagon behind him, the iron-clad wheels rattling on the humpbacked stones.

'The church tower has come down!' he shouted. There was hysteria in his voice. Further back, they saw his brother Romeo running up the road with several of his mates.

The church building appeared to be still intact. The men dived into it through the open double doors.

Father Benedict was sitting at the organ playing scales, each note bouncing off the battle-riddled walls. The tower had not come down, but the large bell had, leaving a wide hole in the church ceiling. It lay on its side in the nave, resting on the backs of the carved pews, the tongue against the cast metal as in the mouth of a dead, giant creature. Large fragments of the roof, and much debris, lay on the pews and on the marble floor.

Feliciana's strident yell of 'Angelina!' made Father Benedict flinch on his organ stool. His eyes, when he turned his head, were dark cavities in the gaunt face. It was evident that the priest was overwhelmed by what had happened. He sought refuge in playing scales, but was drawn back to reality by the cracking of the castagna wood under the weight of the bell. Father Benedict got off his stool and, arms crossed, contemplated the further destruction of his church.

'The bell must weigh at least half a ton. I only brought my small wagon,' said the carpenter.

'We came to make sure Angelina is not hurt,' reported Feliciana, untouched by the priest's problems or the crackling of the wood of the pews. She walked straight through the side door, which was wide open, and into the churchyard, the priest hot on her heels.

When he perceived the upheaval in the landscape of eternal rest, he made a strange sound and slumped against the three-hundred-year-old stone doorframe.

'Pull yourself together,' Feliciana said to a man who certainly had not been addressed in such a way since he joined the Church. 'We need to find Angelina.'

It was the way she spoke to him that reanimated Father Benedict more than the fresh air outside.

'The dead!' screamed a woman from some distance. 'The dead are lifted out of their graves. This is a gruesome day.'

'Leave the graves alone,' shouted the priest, detaching himself from the doorframe. 'Everybody, get out of the churchyard! It is consecrated ground. The dead have a right to rest in peace. Do not go near the graves. This is an order.' Nobody listened. 'An order from God.'

'Rest in peace,' the woman repeated, while standing on a mound of earth. 'The side of the coffin has come off and my husband's head is sticking out.'

'Look!' Feliciana pointed to the cypress, at the foot of which several coffins had been spewed out of the earth.

'Go home,' Father Benedict kept shouting. 'All of you. There is nothing to see here.' He was clearly not succeeding in getting the message across. Villagers were arriving, searching for the graves of their relatives. 'It is illegal what you are doing.'

Feliciana tested her way up the slope to where her daughter was buried. Rosa and Giovanni went with her. They passed two people shovelling, the spades making pinging noises when scraping against stones and giving a dull rumble when reaching the coffin. Further up, Feliciana stepped over an untidy bundle of tattered clothes. With fright, she saw a human arm still in it. The forearm and fingers were gone; the humerus resembled a charcoal-burnt ox rib.

She took a firm grip on the wide skirt she was wearing, which swirled about her ankles, lifted it and stepped over the disturbing sight, forcing her mind towards finding Angelina.

The quake had created a wave, pushing the earth from underneath. Where the wave had ended, coffins showed and headstones lay flat. The small, white-lacquered coffin had been lifted out of its resting place close to the trunk of the old cypress.

'I made that piece,' said the carpenter, who had followed behind them. 'Still looking good after so long.'

'Ten years, four months and two days,' Feliciana rattled off.

'Your pretty little daughter. Now I remember.'

'I want to make sure she is all right.'

The carpenter looked at her, his face creased. 'The guys in their boxes might have been jolted about, but I can assure you they didn't feel a thing.'

'Angelina is very sensitive.'

Father Benedict had caught up with them and overheard Feliciana's words. 'There is nothing for you to do here. Please, go home and stay there.'

'That,' she pointed, 'is my daughter's coffin, thrown up by the shakes of the earth. I want to see my child and kiss her for a last time.'

'I forbid it.'

Romeo spoke up. 'What harm can it do to let this woman see her daughter again?'

Father Benedict lifted the wooden cross, hanging on a chain fixed to his belt, as one winches up an anchor. He held it tight in his hand before he spoke again.

'What was once her daughter is now a decayed corpse, a stinking cadaver after ten years in the ground.'

Gently, Rosa touched Feliciana's shoulder. 'Father Benedict is right. It is better to remember Angelina the way she used to be.'

'You have your son. I lost my daughter. Here in this box is the proof that I, too, was a mother once. If she smells, I don't mind. If she looks haggard, I don't mind. I feel I can have her back for a last caress.'

39

'You do remember the funeral,' the priest tried with desperation to get to Feliciana. 'Ashes to ashes, dust to dust?'

'I don't remember.' After saying this, Feliciana realised that she had just lied to the priest again. Vaguely, there came back to her the memory of a moment when the wind held its breath as they stood around the dug grave, watching the little white box being lowered into the dark forever hole on two straps. Marco had tried to force his little hand into her clenched fist.

'She will not play with me again.'

The memory was too hurtful. The truth-telling voice had to be silenced.

'I was forced by my husband to go to that funeral,' said Feliciana, 'but I never gave up my belief that Angelina is still alive.'

'We know your troubles,' said Father Benedict. 'It is not easy for Giovanni, either.'

'He is a heathen. I have a right to see my daughter again. God is asking me to do this.'

The priest hesitated. 'I don't think so.'

'God lifted her coffin out of the earth to offer me a last goodbye.' Feliciana turned to the carpenter. 'Now someone open it, please.'

'That small corpse has festered in a musty grave for ten years,' said Father Benedict. 'There will be nothing much left of her. I have to say that to you, because it is the truth. I also want to protect you from a shock. A putrescent corpse is a shock for hardy people. One who used to be your child could drive an unstable woman like yourself into total mental chaos.'

'He is right, dear Feliciana,' Rosa tried again. 'Your pretty Angelina's remains are now a macabre sight.'

'She is still my daughter. Remains mean that something remained. I have a right to see her and reassure her.'

'Let's leave the churchyard, all of us now,' suggested Giovanni. 'There might be aftershocks.'

'I'll stay with her.' Feliciana put both hands on the coffin, proprietorially.

'Let's be generous,' said Romeo. 'Her daughter is still in the expensive coffin she paid for.'

'Shut up.' The carpenter pulled the chisel out of the leather belt he was wearing, pushed it under the ornate lid and applied his weight. With a complaining creaking, the nails gave.

The lid was peeled back.

Giovanni turned away and looked up at the cypress tree, as if it held the answer to his confusion. Father Benedict bent and lifted the seam of his cassock to hold it against his nose, thus exposing two legs in grey, woollen, knee-high socks. The carpenter made to leave at a trot, as if he feared being blamed for something about the construction of the wooden box. Romeo took after his brother, in a skip hop, which was badly coordinated due to the unevenness of the ground. The frightened men left the carpenter's wagon behind.

As those who remained were stepping back, Feliciana went up close to the open casket.

'You shouldn't be doing this,' Father Benedict could not prevent himself from saying.

Fearfully, they had no choice but to watch Feliciana,

41

who bent right into the coffin at the head end, and to hear her kissing whatever was left in there.

'Enough,' ordered the priest. 'Come away from there.'

'No. I want her to sit up so you can see her. She is perfect and beautiful.'

'For God's sake!' The priest lost his patience. 'You are insane. Stop molesting the dead. There are laws about this. You…' he added, with a flick of the hand, 'close that lid right now. Now!'

Feliciana lifted her head out of the casket. 'My darling Angelina is not dead.' A smile spread on her pale face. 'I told you. Come and see.'

Father Benedict dropped his cross to dangle at the end of the prayer bead chain. Hesitantly, he advanced on the open coffin. After a while, he encouraged the others to come and see as well.

In the coffin lay a six-year-old child, sleeping like a princess, although the white lining had tarnished and showed tearing. There was still colour in the dead child's cheeks, and a glow to her skin. Her eyes were closed, the long, dark eyelashes had grown more curved, the black hair around her head had become abundant. An oxidised silver cross lay in her small hands, folded over a decayed lace baptism bodice. A sweet scent of flowers emanated from the body.

Giovanni cursed crudely and then turned to the priest. 'She is not still alive, is she?'

Father Benedict could hardly formulate words in his emotional state. 'An incorruptible in my churchyard,' he gasped. 'It's too much. It's too much.'

They watched him wring his hands.

'A saint!' he further enthused. 'An incorruptible body. A saint, a saint in my churchyard!' he shouted, waving his arms. 'Perhaps I am getting ahead of myself.' His head dropped.

Giovanni tapped the side of his head with a finger.

'The Catholic Church has to pronounce her a saint and canonise her,' continued the priest. 'Tests will have to be done. I have a friend in the Vatican. His name is Cardinal Pappalardo. He believes in a more intellectual or even scientific approach to the Catholic faith, whereas I embrace a belief which is full of mysteries and miracles. Of course, the Pope will have the last word should this be a canonisation. An incorruptible…' He took off again joyfully, even performing a little jig.

'I'm confused,' Giovanni grumbled.

'Because you don't believe,' said Feliciana, shaking her head at him.

'What is an incorruptible?'

'A saint,' said Father Benedict. 'A human being so virtuous and special that death refuses to decay its body.'

'Feliciana, we are going home.' Giovanni hitched his trousers up at the belt. 'I've had enough. Come along.'

'We need to take Angelina with us. She can't stay in the churchyard.'

'Don't start that again.'

'You do not understand. Our Angelina will be eternal. She will inspire Catholics around the world. Millions will be praying to her, lighting candles. The saints' calendar will be amended. I told you that Angelina was not dead. Now, go ahead and ask Antonio to lend us Marco's old pushchair and then bring it up here.'

43

'Pushchair?' Giovanni had not expected this word.

'The yellow one with the Minnie Mouse picture.'

'Minnie Mouse,' he repeated slowly.

'I'll get it myself.'

★

Twilight wrapped the upheaved churchyard in its uncertain light. People had gone, leaving the jolted dead to their long-ago-decided fate. Romeo and Feliciana lifted the body of Angelina out of the casket. The silver cross slipped from the enlaced fingers. Feliciana picked it up and put it around her neck again.

They seated Angelina's body in the pushchair, making sure her arms were in her lap so they wouldn't become entangled in the wheels. Triumphantly, Feliciana pushed her daughter down the cobbled road to Girasole, singing *Il coccodrillo come fa*. The North Star showed clearly in the dark sky.

Giovanni opened the door to them and made a move backward in fright.

Feliciana manoeuvred the pushchair into the dining room of the restaurant. 'We have to get her up to her room,' she said. 'I can't do this by myself.'

Carefully, Giovanni enunciated, 'Does she need supper?'

'No, stupid. She is going to be a saint.'

He poked Angelina's naked feet with his shoe. 'She seems pretty dead to me. She is not going to smell or anything?'

'She will never smell. Except for the scent of the

44

incorruptibles, which is that of lilies.'

That night, Giovanni was disturbed by the thought of Angelina's body in the house. By two in the morning, he was still not asleep; worse, from her bedroom came the playing of the keyboard. He held his breath. It was soft music, but definitely real, for there was nothing wrong with his ears. Was his child dead or alive? Not bothering about slippers, he pushed himself out of bed and crept out of the room, being careful not to wake the sleeping Feliciana.

In Angelina's room, he saw the face of the child on the bed, white as marble in the light which came from the full moon. The piano against the wall continued to play, keys depressing without a hand doing it. Giovanni realised that it could play by itself, because it was electronic, and the curtain brushing over it must have started it up. For, if not, this was too spooky for him to deal with.

★

Three weeks later, Feliciana received copies of the correspondence which had gone between Father Benedict and Cardinal Pappalardo, both men excited about the case. Angelina's body had to be brought to the Vatican.

Feliciana packed to go to Rome. She wanted to do this alone, called it a pilgrimage, a journey a mother and daughter did together.

Anke offered to drive them to Palermo Centrale for the first train to Rome. From the door of Girasole,

Giovanni watched as Feliciana pushed the child, strapped into the yellow pushchair, out into the sunshine. Anke came out of the van and fell to her knees. She grabbed Angelina's skirt hem and kissed it several times, eyes closed in religious ecstasy.

'Perhaps Angelina will be made the patron saint of fisherfolk,' said Anke. 'Shoals will fill our nets.'

'Holy cow,' Giovanni said to himself. He closed the door to blot out the sight. The sun was rising.

★

Late that same day, Feliciana was back. She threw the folded yellow pushchair into the corner of the corridor.

'They were rough with Angelina and then kept her. She was such a good girl during the trip. She sat quietly in the train, sleeping. A passenger commented on how silent she was. I told her the child died ten years, four months and twenty-three days, and about six hours ago.

'At the taxi rank in Rome, there was a kerfuffle. People were fighting for taxis. Angelina lost one of the new shoes I had bought her for our pilgrimage. She tilted out of the pushchair. It caused her eyes to open. The taxi driver said she looked scary and drove us to the Vatican, wanting to get rid of us. The friend of Father Benedict had people come and touch the girl. Angelina stared ahead of her. I noticed that the white of her eyes had turned pink, and a red vein showed. I became frightened she would become alive or decompose, just when two physicians came and looked her over, before carrying her away from me for a thorough physical examination.

46

According to Cardinal Pappalardo, people cheated and embalmed bodies, claiming them to be incorruptibles. I had to wait in a room for a long time.

'When the cardinal came back with a surgeon, they said they had to examine the organs of Angelina. I objected to her being cut open. According to them, I had no more rights over her; a saint belonged to the Pope, or some such nonsense. They did not care how I felt. They set upon me, asking hundreds of questions. Did Angelina have a talent? Did she hear voices? What did she love to do? I hold them how beautifully she danced. They did not like that answer. How was she with children, animals, people? I told them how kind she was to Marco. They liked that.

'When they asked whether she had been a devout Catholic, I told them she was six years old. They asked whether she was obedient, and I told them she was, except for licking sap from the Commiphora Myrrha tree. "Myrrh?" one of the doctors kept repeating. "Myrrh is the main ingredient in embalming. And you say she ate this?"

'I defended Angelina, telling them she knew she wasn't supposed to, but that it had a sweet aroma and was a great temptation for a child.

'Again, I had to wait for a long time in that boring room. When the surgeon came back, he seemed excited that every organ inside the child was untouched by decay.

'Eventually, the office closed and they sent me away. I was already out on the piazza, when Pappalardo came running with the pushchair. "We don't want His Holiness the Pope to fall over it in the corridor," he said.'

Giovanni, who had listened to the account in silence, got up and opened the door to whoever was knocking at that hour.

'It's almost midnight,' commented Feliciana, and switched on the light in the dark room.

Father Benedict came in. 'Anke told me you were back,' he blurted out, without any greetings. Without being invited to take a seat, he pulled a chair away from a table and plonked himself on it.

'I came to give you the marvellous news,' he continued. 'After you left Rome, there was a meeting with the Pope about Angelina. Pappalardo called me. Angelina has been pronounced a true incorruptible. Imagine: Saint Angelina of Colomba del Castello. My church, my church! Pappalardo believes Angelina will be made the patron saint of spastic children! She will sleep in a crystal casket in the cathedral of Leon in the north of France.'

★

On a rainy November day, a man wrapped in a see-through plastic raincoat over a dark suit arrived at the closed Girasole. Invited into the dining room, he dripped on the floor.

'Cardinal Pappalardo,' he introduced himself. Shortly after that, Father Benedict arrived, closed his umbrella and more rainwater was on the floor.

Feliciana invited them to sit at a table, brought bread to dunk into virgin olive oil and mopped the floor. She watched as Father Benedict's hand cupped the cardinal's arm resting on the tabletop. The village priest had said they had known each other well.

'Guests?' asked Giovanni, coming in.

'Wait!' shouted Rosa, entering the restaurant with Marco through the pergola door. Chairs were moved, people squeezed up. 'I noticed the Vatican number plate,' she explained.

On Marco's wrist was knotted the discoloured hair ribbon Angelina had once given him. Feliciana smiled.

'Is Angelina in Leon, France?' she asked the cardinal. 'My husband and I plan to visit her for Christmas.'

'Brandy,' croaked Giovanni and plonked a bottle onto the table, before handing out balloon glasses he had carried unsteadily on a tray.

'Not for Marco.' Feliciana took the glass away from the boy.

The cardinal started to speak. 'It is four months since you brought Saint Angelina to Rome. You have a right to hear first-hand what happened to her.'

'Thank you,' Feliciana whispered.

'The canonisation examination showed no tampering with the outer aspect of Angelina's body. I am quoting from the physician's report, although "since she was exhumed, there was slight deteriorisation in the extremity body parts", like her toes and her fingertips. The telling factor about incorruptibility is the eyes. Hers are limpid, with a cornea as healthy as if the nerves feeding the eyeballs had been intact during the time in the grave.'

Feliciana took a large gulp of brandy.

'The Pope at first hesitated. His Holiness does not

want to make the mistake of pronouncing a saint which falls apart in front of praying believers.'

'What was the Pope's final decision?' asked Giovanni. 'He does have quite a peculiar job.'

'The young eyes,' Pappalardo continued, 'looked right into His Holiness's soul, he told me. No saint so far had their eyes open. This, in itself, His Holiness thought was a sign. But...'

There was a pause, during which the cardinal pulled a piece of paper from his breast pocket. 'A report the examining surgeon forwarded to me.' Unfolding it, he read. 'Due to the signs on the toes, it was decided to autopsy the organs in her body.' Marco started to cry. 'Every organ I examined was in prime condition. No sign of decay anywhere. Not even in the intestines, where body decay begins.'

'An incorruptible,' Father Benedict enthused. 'A miracle. I knew it.'

'An internally incorruptible, according to the doctor.' Pappalardo doused his friend's enthusiasm. 'The Pope has put the announcement on hold and suggested burying Angelina again for twenty years and seeing what happens to her body then.'

'We'll long be dead by then,' objected Feliciana. 'Just when she came back to us intact, a darling daughter perfect in every way, a kind obedient child.'

'Sometimes she was bad,' said Marco.

Frowning, Pappalardo looked at the boy.

'She liked the honey from the tree she was not allowed to touch,' said Marco.

'Children, you know.' Feliciana shrugged her shoulders.

'Interesting,' said the cardinal. 'There is an addendum to the surgeon's letter about Commiphora gum resin, which was mentioned in the first interview with the mother when she brought in her daughter. Now, I made some relevant studies for my doctorate about alchemy, which became biochemistry. The mother's mention of the sap reminded me: it was used for embalming.'

Concerned, Father Benedict looked at the cardinal. 'You, my friend, are a cynic and seek truth through facts. There are no facts. God creates miracles. Facts are fabricated by humans.'

'Look, Benedict,' the cardinal said with a benign smile. 'We've had many such differences. Let's just concentrate on this canonisation.'

'In which you don't want to believe.'

'If they don't know what they are doing, where does that leave us?' asked Giovanni.

'Angelina is a saint,' stated Marco. 'I know it. I know it here.' He patted his chest.

Pappalardo and Father Benedict got up to leave.

'You came to put our tortured souls to rest, and all you did was upset and confuse us,' complained Feliciana.

'You got a phone?' Pappalardo asked, to which Feliciana nodded.

'Calling God?' Father Benedict asked under his breath.

The conversation the cardinal had with Rome lasted for some time.

'It will cost,' said Feliciana.

When the cardinal came back to them, he was beaming, which gave him a holy aura. 'Angelina has been pronounced a saint for children with brain damage. She will definitely go to Leon Cathedral. They are working on her saint's day. Some shuffling has to be done.'

'It *is* a miracle. God chose Colomba del Castello, and we will become world-famous!' Father Benedict, who did not drink, poured himself a brandy. He already looked flushed as he brought the glass to his lips.

'Before I leave for the Vatican, I just want to say this.' The cardinal got up from his chair. 'Jesus, on his birth, was offered gold, frankincense and myrrh. What does a baby do with such gifts?' He started to pace, as he was thinking aloud. At the dish with the sunflower head, he dipped his hand in and let the seeds run through his fingers. 'On the third day, Jesus was resurrected. His body was intact.'

'Oh, my God,' fretted Feliciana. 'Mary might not have had much milk in her breasts to feed baby Jesus, seeing she had so little to eat herself. And there was the edible gift of myrrh after the three kings left, which tasted like honey.'

BOUGHT ONLINE

10ᵗʰ Birthday – Milton Keynes

A red balloon, tied to the garden gate, bobbed in the
wind. It had the number ten on it. Today was Arthur's
tenth birthday. Washed and brushed, he was inside their
small semi-detached, waiting for three lots of parents to
bring three of his 'friends' from school. Actually, they
were just bullies.

There was also Uncle Rupert, who had said he would
show up – a scary enough presence to frighten anyone.
Mother thought he was a darling to drop everything
to come to his nephew's birthday. She always said that
Rupert appealed to women. And Arthur did not say,
'Obviously, to you as well, Mum.'

Arthur was a shy boy. He had got over the affliction of
stammering, which had been his ever since he had learnt to
speak, but he still suffered from an inability to pronounce
the letter R. His parents said it was called 'rhotacism' and
lots of children had it. At school, he was mocked all the
time. He had to prepare what he was going to say, because
words with Rs in them tripped him up. *All right* had to be
OK. It made Arthur a reticent, almost silent, child.

Once, Uncle Rupert had swiped the back of his

head. 'Try harder,' he had shouted. 'Everyone can learn to speak properly. It's not *wocket* science.'

Better keep away from the uncle, and please Mother by helping in the kitchen with the sandwiches and the expensive cake, bought specially. His peek into the box revealed a blue sports car made of sugar with a marzipan steering wheel. Bought, not made, because today he was ten.

Only two of his torturers were brought by their parents; the third, thankfully, had something better to do, which the mother explained on the phone as 'feeling under the weather'. What did that mean? The weather was really all around us, so we had no choice but to be right in it. Arthur did not say that either, and not just because there were too many Rs.

Arthur knew that he was mistreated by life, and his response was a reverse technique – to change people's attitude by distributing kindness. He helped his tormentors with their homework, gave them sweets which he had hidden from his mother, and stayed after school with the teacher to sort out the classroom. He had a need to defend the weak and make people happy.

For the birthday, Dad had organised a sack race because he'd found old coffee sacks on Amazon. It was lame, but why not? Uncle Rupert joined in by putting one of his legs in a sack. Arthur was roughly knocked over by one of the boys, but he laughed with the others. It was his birthday, and they could all be in the small garden because it wasn't raining.

The winning boy in the race was given a wrapped present prepared by Mother. *Oh, God!* Arthur cringed.

What embarrassing item will be revealed? It was a pencil case with a picture of Spiderman on it. Arthur sighed – not a disaster.

Back inside, waiting for the appearance of the candled cake and the singing, Uncle Rupert felt the need to give a speech. He was, after all, the one who had dropped everything to be here.

'I'll be short,' he started, but actually, coming from him that was wrong, as he was a really tall uncle and would stay that way.

He said that he was proud of his nephew, which was a lie. He said his younger brother was lucky to have Arthur as a son. He mentioned Mother (Arthur saw her push her bosom forward) who protected and guided her son. This was the most valuable thing a child could have. Wasn't Arthur named after the king who taught his knights about justice and bravery?

Uncle Rupert was probably better at giving speeches to his company employees. He started to sing, 'For he's…' However, Mother over-sang him with *Happy Birthday* while Dad, who had listened to instructions, carried the flickering cake into the room.

Arthur felt almost sick at that moment. They did all that for him, thinking he deserved it when he didn't. He wasn't King Arthur on a steed. He did believe in justice, and defending the weak, but he harboured a dark secret which he had never dared confess to anyone: he was absolutely not brave. So not. A great problem in his life was the dog next door – the barking which made his ears ring, the rattling of the chain which restrained the devil disguised as a Rottweiler. His nightmares were full of saliva-glistening teeth, the dog's mouth open to take chunks out of his body. When he left the house on the way to school, and Mother had closed the door after him, the beast would charge the wire fence separating the gardens. The snarling came from the underworld; the jolted fence rattled; the liquid in the beast's eyes was pure lava. The devil had already managed to chew through two links in the fence. A few more and he would make himself tubular, fit through and devour Arthur.

At the end of the birthday party, just as the parents walked away with their sons, and Mother was still waving, the balloon on the gate came undone and rose in silence, up, up and out of reach. The number ten became smaller and smaller until, in the clear blue, the red dot floated away and finally disappeared.

25ᵗʰ Birthday – Milton Keynes

Fifteen years later. The pink wall-to-wall carpet was still in the entrance of the small semi-detached, and so was the picture of the Zeppelin on the wall. Arthur, however, had grown into an adult of medium stature and few words. Not making it into college, he had nevertheless found a job which suited him. It was thanks to his father, a dentist who worked in the healthcare sector. From nine to two in the afternoon, Arthur worked in the files department of the local hospital. It was downstairs in the basement, windowless and stuffy. Long, tall and heavy filing racks were ranged close together, and each rack could be accessed by operating a metal wheel which moved all the racks and opened the required space. Many thousands of beige cardboard files were shelved.

Arthur's job was to systematically take them out and fix any loose letters or reports into the file in the right place by date, before transferring the tidied information of the file onto microfiche. The hospital was going paperless. The process was slow-going, as there were only two of them doing it, and they had no direct contact with anyone else. At the other desk in the room, with her back to him, sat Helen doing the same job, but she was dealing with the newborns, while he had not made it backwards through the dead patients yet. He wasn't allowed to read details in the files, but it always interested him what happened at the very end of a human's life: the last record in the file to be fed into the computer – TOD, Time of Death, as if that detail mattered to anyone. For the family, he or she was dead forever.

Helen, who had looked up his file, knew it was his birthday and had bought him a jam-filled doughnut – three actually, two of which she kept for herself. Arthur, who had respected the rules and not read her file, guessed that she was in her late fifties. He had let her have the new ergonomic chair, with the adjustable back and castor-wheels, because she was overweight. She sat legs apart, because her fat thighs tended to stick together. She claimed to suffer from asthma and had an inhaler she only used when the supervisor came downstairs to check on progress, thereby proving to Arthur she did not actually have asthma. He did not know why she made this pretence; perhaps it was attention-seeking or a defence mechanism? However, he was kind about it and did not challenge her. One good thing about her was her name, Helen Anne Smith. Nothing to stumble over in that.

On working days, Arthur was home by three o'clock. He still lived *at* his parents' and not *with* them, a nuance he pointed out to himself. The 'at' was a downstairs bedroom with its own entrance, and a loo/sink nearby which his parents had adapted to include a shower enclosure. After getting off his Vespa, he would wheel it through the wooden side door into the garden, where he chained it up. Every time, he remembered the neighbour's dog which had terrorised him. New people had moved in, lovely neighbours who did not have a dog.

'I've made it to 35.24.60,' Arthur informed Helen, rattling his trolley past her desk.

'Doing anything exciting tonight for your birthday?' she asked in an upbeat tone of voice.

'Can't be bothered.'

'That's a shame. My niece, Gemma, is staying with me for a while. She doesn't know anybody here. Why don't you two have a celebratory drink in The Queen and Duck this evening? Surely you have other friends who can join in? I'll offer you all a round.' She lifted her handbag from the floor and started disembowelling it.

Arthur did not say thank you, did not wait for her to produce the money. He pulled the trolley into reverse for a three-point turn and parked it close to his workstation, where he unloaded the grubby furry files onto the desk and sat down on his speckled grey chair, on which was a cushion to support the lower part of his spine.

Helen said only one more personal thing. 'I'll send Gemma to the pub for seven. She won't mind if you and your friends don't turn up.' An odd thing to say unless you knew Arthur well, but she *had* worked with him for the last three years.

He knew her too. In the next couple of hours, she would ask him to help with a computing problem. It was her way of validating her generous move towards him, for now twenty-five pounds lay on his mouse pad. He would have helped anyway; he always did. He even cleaned her screen regularly with computer wipes he bought.

Later in the afternoon, Mother stretched her head into Arthur's room, after knocking and not being invited to enter, and gushed, 'Happy birthday, darling. Dad and I were wondering whether you might go to a pub tonight to celebrate with colleagues?'

Arthur ignored her.

'Oh, darling.' She came further into the room. 'You didn't think I would get in balloons and buy you a cake, did you? You are so grown-up now, but I still love you. I only have this little thing.' She was now within arm's reach of the bed on which Arthur rested his back against the headboard. 'It's a pair of leather gloves to wear on your Vespa when the weather is bad.'

Suddenly, he remembered that one of the schoolboys had not come to his tenth birthday because he was under the weather, and then he thought of the red balloon.

Mother took his silence as a rejection. Shyly, she put the present on the bedcover at his feet and slipped out of the room. Arthur heard her run into Dad outside the bedroom door.

'Is he going to the pub with mates tonight?' he heard Dad ask.

'I don't know,' she said in a slow, tired voice. 'I don't think he has many mates.'

'He works in a hospital with over a thousand employees. He is twenty-five today. Why can't I have a normal son?'

Arthur tore open the door and stood glaring at them. 'I am normal. I am like anyone else. I am going to The Queen and Duck at seven to meet a girl, and others will join us.'

'Hallelujah!' Mother clapped her hands.

'Who is the girl?' asked Dad.

'Norman.' Mother's voice was sharp. 'Don't jinx things.'

'It's an innocent question. For the first time, he mentions a girl after two and a half decades, so…'

'Let him rest and get ready for tonight.'

Dad dug in his pocket and paid out two tenners, thought for a bit and added a twenty pound note. 'Have fun on me.'

Arthur did not say thank you.

'Well, who would have thought?' Dad said out in the hallway.

It was interesting, pondered Arthur, what people said as they left a room or a situation. A little bit like what they said before they died. Back on his bed, he leant against the headboard, turned and looked at the velour-upholstered wood.

'Headstone,' he said. 'Never thought of that before.' He then lay flat, eyes closed, hands joined on his chest.

★

At around seven, perhaps it was by now ten past, Arthur was annoyed to see Helen loitering in front of the pub, fingering leaves on a bush. He turned back to the Vespa.

'No, no, no.' Helen ran after him. When she caught up, she said, 'Gemma is inside the pub waiting for you.' This was said without panting or fighting for breath, therefore she definitely did not have asthma.

Unwillingly, Arthur walked back to the pub. Helen did not follow him. He yearned to be back in his room, playing computer games. On one's birthday, wasn't one allowed to do what one wanted? At that moment, a car passed in the road, loud thumping music coming from it. It was full of youngsters, a girl shouting out of the back window, holding onto a pair of white balloons which caromed crazily against the on-wind. Is that what they wanted him to be part of? Arthur did not believe in that. Just drunken bitches out getting wasted.

He was torn between being polite to Gemma, and the dread he felt at having to do what he was forced to do. Borrowing the moves of a confident bloke, he shouldered the door, one thumb in the belt of his jeans. He knew the inside of the establishment from having come here with his parents and, once, with Mother's sister, Barbara – a relative with a name he refused to tackle. The pub was not busy; he felt exposed and inhibited. How had he let himself be manoeuvred into this?

'Arthur!' a female voice shouted.

Damn. Gemma had stood up and was waving her whole arm. Now everyone knew his name was Arthur, and everyone thought he didn't deserve that name.

He made a few steps, took his thumb out of the

belt and pretended the 'Arthur' had been directed at somebody else. That was a short relief, for more 'Arthurs' were shouted.

Gemma was not a younger version of Helen, the way he had imagined. She was young, svelte and had straight white teeth in a wide, smiling mouth, just the way his father liked them.

'When you saw me, you wanted to leave right away,' she said. 'Is it me, or didn't you want to come?' There was a long silence as he sat down at her table, and they looked at each other in an unfocused way. 'Helen did say you were shy.'

He looked around him, as if seeking help.

'My aunt who works with you? Helen?'

He sighed as an answer.

'They won't come and serve us at the table.'

'Do you think they have Dr Pepper?' he asked.

'Probably not,' she said. 'Let's start with mojitos. My treat. It's your birthday.'

He cut in. 'When will people stop pushing money at me?' He pulled the handful of crumpled notes from his trouser pocket and threw them on the table, where they slowly uncreased.

'Wow,' she said, and her already short nose puckered up to very short, almost piggish. 'With that we can get sloshed.'

'I have to work tomorrow.'

'No, you don't. Tomorrow is Saturday.'

'That depends.'

'That is a fact, not a choice.'

'I have another job. Online. Work from home.'

'All right, then, you go and get the drinks, Mr Bill Gates.'

He returned with her drink and a shandy for himself.

'Cheers,' said Gemma, raising her mojito. However, as she tried to drink from the glass, the straw was in her face. Decisively, she pulled the straw out, put it on the table and drank with gusto. 'Tell me,' she started, and he tightened his muscles ready to defend himself, 'what do you think of Meghan Markle?'

'Nothing.' And here the inevitable was going to happen, the being told what he should think.

'I think Meghan is only interested in herself, married poor Harry to advance her acting career. Now she has taken him away from the Queen, who was so good to him when Princess Diana died. Somebody should save Harry from manipulative Meghan.'

'Whoever you're talking about,' he said, 'saving a man from any situation involving a woman sounds fair.'

'Don't you know who they are?'

'I know the Queen, and she should have the last word in every situation.'

'Precisely, but she is being bamboozled by Miss Minx. This will end badly, don't you think?'

'Maybe. Maybe not. I don't know what you are talking about.'

'Then you choose a subject, OK?' The 'OK' was spoken with irritated speed.

An older man carrying a large box came into the pub, but Arthur did not see him as his back was turned to the door.

'Did you hear me? You bring up a subject we can

talk about.' Gemma grabbed one of his hands and, thus linked over the table, she smiled at him while crushing his hand in hers.

'Aha!' A male voice shouted right next to Arthur's ear. 'My brother was right. He is here with a bird. All is not lost.'

'Uncle! How…?'

'Your parents told me. Won't you introduce me to your beautiful girlfriend?'

'No.'

'May I join you? I bear a gift.' Once seated between the couple, Rupert put the wrapped box on the table where their hands had been joined.

'You know what they say: large gift, large…' Gemma immediately flirted with Rupert. 'Is it a time machine?'

'Oh, I wish,' said Uncle Rupert. 'For, if it were, I could travel back to when I was young and irresistibly sexy. Your dress, by the way, is fetching on you.'

'Probably wouldn't be so good on you.'

Rupert laughed, relaxed. 'You are not just attractive, but bright and funny. Where did you two lovebirds meet?'

'Guess,' she played on.

'It's a blind date,' Arthur said dryly. 'And I wish I were blind, and deaf for that matter.'

'A cheerful birthday boy, isn't he? Do you want another mojito?' said Rupert.

'I would like one with lime and more rum,' replied Gemma.

'Then come with me to the bar and teach that ape behind it to do it right.'

'Arthur wanted a Dr Pepper.'

Rupert laughed again, loudly and unselfconsciously. 'You are precious. Why don't you and I go to another place I know? This pub is one click up from an old people's home.'

Arthur watched Gemma pick up her handbag, eager to go. Then he saw her and his uncle leave the pub, Rupert holding the door for her as she smiled coquettishly up at him.

'Thank God for that,' Arthur said to his spread hands on the tabletop, hands which were all his again. In the end, he had to walk all the way home, because the large present did not fit on the Vespa. And, after that walk, back to fetch the Vespa.

★

The next day, Saturday, Uncle Rupert was invited for lunch because he wanted to have a talk about his nephew's future.

'That's me?' said Arthur, giving Mother back the drying cloth. 'I don't want a future. I am going to the zoo.'

'You stay where you are. Dear Rupert tries. As your father's elder brother, he feels responsible for us.'

★

Sitting in Dad's chair at the table, Rupert started his attack before Mother had even had time to put the tuna salad down.

'At twenty-five, Arthur, you realise that one third of your life has gone by.'

Mother handed around the bowl with oven-heated, pre-baked rolls.

'Twenty-five, fifty, seventy-five. That should do for a professional life.'

Ah, that was what this was all about: Arthur's menial nine-to-two job.

'You have to choose the rails on which you will roll towards your goal, otherwise you will end up on a side-track and hit the buffers.'

Mother was so fascinated, or frightened, that she knocked over her wine glass. A bit of welcome distraction ensued with the mopping up, the apologising and refilling of the glass, before Rupert resumed his attack.

'Filing in a hospital cellar leads nowhere. You are not really qualified for any medical job, are you? As you know, I own a distribution centre and run it, all of it, taking care of seven companies who sell their merchandise online. Shops are closing in high streets all over the country. People buy online. The warehouses are the new giant shops. I insure them, look after the staff, the packers, the drivers' fleet. You name it, Rupert is the man in the invisible eight hundred thousand square foot Aladdin's cave.'

'Why invisible?' asked Arthur's father, who often did not listen to what people said because he was fascinated by their teeth. Being a dentist, he had an excuse.

'You must have driven past,' said Rupert. 'It's a gigantic building, but it's painted green at the bottom, beige in the middle and sky-blue at the top. It creates the optical illusion that it isn't there.'

'That's clever,' Mother admired.

'It wasn't my idea,' said Rupert, showing a seedling of

humility. 'But it easily could have been.' He trampled it to death. 'Now, in this warehouse of mine is a company called *Awbrey's*. They sell designer clothing, luxury fashion for men. Beautifully made stuff – expensive, of course. The royal household buys from them.' As nobody said anything to that, he went on, 'The issue is how to get the online orders to customers. I have a fleet of vans. *Awbrey's* are currently looking for a young and conscientious driver to cover Buckingham and surroundings. The pay is good, and you'll get a van and a computer. And what I am working on right now is company contribution to a pension. One of my jobs is to make sure the vans are serviced and cleaned. One happy family. I believe I have just found the driver *Awbrey's* is after.' Uncle Rupert looked straight at Arthur. 'You do have a clean driver's licence?'

'Why do you have scwatches on the side of your face, Uncle?'

Instinctively, Rupert reached up to his cheek. 'It's nothing. I was working last night after our drinks in The Queen and Duck. I fell asleep, and the pen I held in my hand gouged along the side of my face.'

'Looks more like…' Mother stopped talking after noticing her husband's furious eyes on her. 'Anyway,' she tampered it down, 'maybe you have a cat?'

'A crazed panther, more like,' said Rupert. 'You do drive?' he challenged Arthur, changing the subject.

'He drives a Vespa,' said Mother.

'But he has a clean driving licence?'

'Yes,' came from Arthur. 'I don't use it much, as I don't have a car.'

'That,' Rupert beamed, 'will change soon.'

67

'I don't know Buckingham.'

'There is satnav in the van, you ignoramus. There is also Uncle Rupert, who will make sure you don't get into a muddle. You, Arthur, are a lucky boy.'

Arthur thought back to his tenth birthday, when Uncle Rupert had said the exact same thing and then the balloon flew away.

'Tell me...' His uncle was on a roll. 'What are the contract terms of your current job?'

'I work through the hospital employment bank. No terms.'

'Splendid. Give in your notice Monday morning, and I'll make sure your new job will start a week from then.'

'So soon?'

'Time is money. Besides, after two years delivering *Awbrey's* merchandise, you'll get twenty per cent off buying their remnants. Are we on?'

All eyes in the room were on Arthur.

'I guess it is time for me to move on. And I like the idea of giving nice things to people to make them happy. I don't ever want to cause harm to people, or play any part in causing them pain or unhappiness.'

'Great,' gushed Mother. 'That girlfriend of yours does you a lot of good.'

'Admirable,' said Rupert. 'In many ways, King Arthur was considered a knight in shining armour.'

★

Arthur browsed through *Awbrey's* website. A casual sweater was in the two hundred and eighty pounds range;

68

a scarf, just a normal-looking scarf, ninety-five pounds. It had to be a rich neck around which that would wind. As for the coat in the large box he delivered to Stowe on his second day, the man who answered the door had paid four hundred and fifty pounds for it. Only coats and sports jackets were packed into boxes; the other items, folded, fitted into padded envelopes of different sizes. Easy and efficient.

Arthur was given a T-shirt and a windbreaker in the colours of the company, which was a muted sage green with a white 'A' planted on the back. The discreet unmarked van was also in the company green and ran on diesel. In the evening, he was allowed to drive home in it. He parked it in front of his parents' house, worrying it would rust when it rained.

*

April came and Arthur had done this job for three months. By now, he was almost familiar with the lie of the land in Buckingham. What he liked most about the job was that he could do it alone. Nobody pestered him. The only grunts were from the packers who loaded up, and then a few words to identify the customers. 'Please sign here.' They scribbled their names on the tablet he held out to them – illegible, most of the time. 'Thank you,' they said, looking pleased, before they closed their doors. Arthur felt elated, like a knight-errant doing good deeds.

As promised, Uncle Rupert was helpful to him. So far, only two incidents had upset the delivery routine.

Once, a packet had been badly sealed, and the recipient at the door stated that whatever he had ordered had been tampered with. It had to be driven back to the warehouse, fixed and redelivered, which caused mayhem on the computer system. The other had been when Arthur drove over a nail near some roadworks, and his right front tyre deflated. He called Rupert who, true to his word, sent two blokes to change the tyre. Other than that, the job had gone smoothly. Arthur knocked on doors, rang bells, handed over the packages, as he was asked to do.

It was a more satisfying job than sitting in the basement with Helen and the thousands of files of sick or dead people – Helen, with whom saying goodbye had gone so badly that it would remain imprinted on his mind forever. He had told the work bank that he was quitting and, immediately after that, informed Helen. A lightning-and-thunder conversation ensued. Helen took it personally and was deeply hurt. Arthur tried his best to point out that she, like him, was free to leave whenever she wanted. She saw herself doomed to stay in the basement.

He had walked away slowly, so that she did not interpret it as abandonment. However, even before he was out of sight, Helen had another fit of anger. She ran up to him.

'I have been good to you, even though you didn't deserve it. I trusted you to be kind to my niece, and look how you treated her. She came home at two in the morning in a state. Sex took place. *Rough sex*, she said. *Total maniac*. She tried to fight you off with tooth and claw. How dare you take advantage of an innocent young girl? Behind your annoyingly calm exterior is a sexually twisted man. It's just as well you're leaving. I wouldn't have been able to work with you any longer, the way my niece was bruised between her legs. I made sure she got the morning-after pill.'

Arthur had accepted her anger, not really understanding what it was all about; anyway, that was now in the past. He marvelled at the concept of him having a past. Thanks to Uncle Rupert, he had 'bettered his life', as his mother kept saying. He earned more, and his father suggested he bought a car. On a Vespa he travelled alone; with a car, there were bound to be situations where he had to give people a lift. He did not like this idea.

Clocking in each morning at the warehouse, he never knew what the day would bring. The only sure thing was that he was not allowed to leave until five, in case of what they called a VIP last-minute order. This left him little free time to play with the cool 3D printer Uncle Rupert had given him for his twenty-fifth birthday.

It was a grisly Friday afternoon, and Arthur had his last delivery to make before the weekend. The package was in the back of the van. He started to enter the address in his satnav, and *Buckingham, 10 Park Avenue* came up. He tapped *Select*. That was easy. The device calculated the route, and on the map Buckingham Park appeared as a large, kidney-shaped green space.

Park Avenue. He turned left into it. Smart houses, a posh area. Well-to-do people who could afford to wrap themselves in *Awbrey's* most exclusive.

Number 10. It was well marked by a plate fixed to the pillar at the entrance gate. So often, house numbers were hidden under ivy or behind a tree which had grown too bushy, or were even absent because the house owners were lazy. Today, on the thirteenth of April, Number 10 even had private space off-road in front of its double garage. Arthur relaxed. He climbed out of his van and grabbed the padded parcel. He pushed the gold-tipped wrought-iron gate. It squeaked a tad. On pebbles, he walked to the arched porch and searched for the doorbell. There seemed to be none. The fancier the houses, the fewer doorbells available.

Arthur lifted the door knocker. However, before he could tap it down, a salvo of furious barking started up. Arthur pressed the soft parcel against his body. The oak door started to rattle as the barking intensified, turning deeper, more dangerous, that of a killer dog. In a frenzy, the beast jumped against the door. All the fears and agony of Arthur's childhood took hold of him. He lifted the knocker, but failed to use it, as his hand shook so uncontrollably. The animal seemed to sense his weakness. Arthur's heart raced. He could not just leave the parcel in front of the door and run back to the van. That was one of the first never-to-dos as a delivery man. The parcel had to be given into the hands of the right people every time. Into the hands, into the hands.

Adding to Arthur's despair, the devil disguised as a dog also ordered the sky to start raining. The water pelted down and ran along the house, dripping from the porch arch. Not daring to get too close to the door, Arthur had

72

no choice but to stand out in the rain. This drenched the parcel – another thing that was never allowed to happen.

Inside, the dog was going berserk with frustration, smelling Arthur through the narrow gap at the foot of the door. Where was the beast's owner? And if there was one, was he really stone-deaf? Or were bloody pieces of his body strewn around the house?

The barking stopped. Arthur forked the wet hair out of his face. Water dripped down his neck and ran along his back, inside the *Awbrey's* windbreaker.

'Hello. Anyone home?' He summoned the courage to knock, jumping back immediately. The dog's yelling was accompanied by claw-scraping, or perhaps it was the teeth. How thick was this door? How long would it take for the beast to chew through it and jump at his jugular?

Just when he was ready to give up, he heard a woman's voice shouting, 'Dinner!' Oh God, a demented house owner on Park Avenue was feeding delivery boys to her hound. She shouted again, and this time it sounded more like Dillon. Dinner or Dillon, the dog did not calm down. The woman had courage. A fight between her and the dog started up. The door was bashed from time to time as if bodies were thrown at it. The dog barked, the woman shouted; there was the jingling noise of a chain. More barking, louder shouting. A stroke of lightning cut into the dark sky.

'Parcel!' Arthur yelled into the thunder.

A lock was activated. The woman must have won the fight, so far. Arthur protected his body with the parcel. The door opened a crack. The dog growled and tried to force his muzzle through the crack.

'Sorry about that,' the woman said. She opened the door a little more. 'We're training him.' One of her hands was on the dog's collar, twisting it. It seemed to force the dog's eyes out of their sockets. A pendulant saliva-string hung out of the corner of its mouth. 'He is only a puppy,' she said, and smiled at Arthur encouragingly.

The devil. Was there any evidence that the devil was ever a puppy? Now it could see Arthur, it displayed its full set of teeth, molars clacking together, catching air rather than the trouser legs of the young man standing just too far away to be reached.

'Parcel for you,' insisted Arthur. The woman looked stressed, under untidy locks of hair hanging into her ageing face. Any moment now, she would get fed up and shut the door. Then it would be package not delivered…

'A rainstorm. How unpleasant,' she said.

Arthur checked again the now-wet package, and clearly read *10 Park* on the stained label. He was at the right place.

'Sorry about the dog,' she said. 'He's quite a character.'

As he could not use the tablet, he asked for her name. 'Weston.'

That's wight. That's cowect. That's twue. Arthur mentally discarded the options before alighting triumphantly on, 'That's it!' He gave the parcel into her hands.

'It's wet,' she commented with irritation. *Not as wet as I am*, thought Arthur.

'Thank you,' she said finally and, mercifully, closed the door.

Arthur expected another salvo of insane barking, but it was so silent that he could hear the rain falling onto

74

the pebbled ground. Driving off, he felt worn out by the experience. Over the bridge, he stopped at a lay-by and relieved himself into rain-glistening greenery.

By the time he reported back to his overseer, with the last delivery done without a hitch, Arthur felt almost proud. He had managed to face and survive his fear and panic, and done the job. The devil who had appeared again to test him had been silenced. Arthur had not faltered or given up. Nor had he peed into his pants the way he used to do as a child. Arthur had lived up to his name, perhaps for the first time. *Thank you*, she had said and, for a moment, liked him. He was giving to people, improving their lives, making them happy.

He even chuckled on the way out of the overseer's office.

'What's funny?' she asked him.

At the door, he twisted round. 'The devil started out as a puppy. People don't know that.'

★

Diane Weston opened the package. The inner wrapping revealed that it was a piece of clothing from *Awbrey's*. She exhaled with surprise, and pulled out an olive-green man's sweater.

She searched through the packaging and found an oblong envelope in which was a description of the item, boasting that it had been knitted in Scotland with six-ply Shetland wool, with instructions on how to care for it on the reverse. Stapled to it was a receipt in case the item did not fit and needed to be exchanged.

'Beautiful,' she admired, holding the sweater against her body in front of the downstairs mirror. Someone had paid two hundred and forty-five pounds. That put into the shade the present she had bought for her husband, whose seventieth birthday was the next day. Spencer didn't want any fuss made of the occasion, but their daughter and son-in-law had invited them for supper, which was a wonderful idea, because Spencer doted on his two granddaughters. Diane folded the soft sweater and, instead of slipping it back into the packaging, she put it into one of the smart gift bags, which she always kept for re-use. *Who has sent Spencer such an expensive present?* she wondered.

★

On the day of the birthday, Spencer woke up and grumbled, 'Damn it. Today, I am officially an old man.'

'Seventy is not old,' his wife countered, thinking it was actually scarily old. The cemetery adjacent to the park was packed with seventy-year-olds. She had once walked through it and come away in tears.

Dillon was at the bedroom window, barking at passers-by.

'I hope he calms down when he grows older,' Diane said. 'He really scared the young man at the door yesterday.'

'Why are young men at our door?'

'Ah,' she smiled. 'A surprise.'

'I made it clear…'

She silenced him with a kiss. 'Happy birthday, darling.'

'I don't want to be seventy. Once you hit the seven zero, you fall apart.'

'My mother became eighty-seven and stayed young and together until the end.'

'Yeah, but she was a bitch.'

'Whatever. Come downstairs and look at the present someone sent you.'

At the kitchen table, Spencer pulled the olive-green sweater from the gift bag. 'I know that bag,' he said.

'It's the one I use and re-use because it's attractive,' said Diane. 'The present was delivered in a brown, bubble-wrap envelope.'

'So, the pullover has nothing to do with the bag, or with you?'

'The pullover is from *Awbrey's*.'

'Am I supposed to know who that is?'

'*Awbrey's* – you know, the exclusive menswear company. Look, that's how much it cost someone.' She showed him the receipt. 'Two hundred and forty-five pounds.'

Spencer looked uncomfortable, as if the knitwear on his lap was crawling with worms.

'Pure Shetland wool, six-ply.'

'Good quality.' Spencer bounced his hand on it. 'I'll give you that. Stupidly expensive, though. Who would spend that much money on me, just because I am a seventy-year-old fart today?'

'I don't know,' said Diane. 'There was no card or letter, but somebody knows you well enough to choose a sweater in your favourite colour, in the right size and just in time for your birthday.'

He looked at her. 'You didn't do that, did you?'

'I don't shop online. I don't know how to.'

'Was there really no card with it?'

She shook her head.

'You opened the parcel and threw the card away with the wrapping. You always unwrap things carelessly. Remember the instructions you chucked out, and I had to work out how to put together that IKEA desk?'

'This time I didn't. A young man arrived with a van, and brought the parcel to the door. He checked our name and, satisfied, gave me the parcel.'

'The young man who was frightened by our dog?'

'The very one. And,' she continued, 'there is no card, because it is probably meant to be a surprise.'

'A good bottle of wine is a surprise,' said Spencer. 'A two hundred and forty-five pound handwoven *Awbrey's* sweater is something different. Come on, spit it out. You must be in cahoots with someone.'

'I swear, I don't know. Here, my small present. A token really. Nothing much.'

He lifted the lid of a leather-bound compass and looked surprised.

'For walks,' she said, 'and your interest in map-reading.'

'At my age now, all I need to know is whether it will be up or down.'

Spencer's mobile rang. He answered it. 'Thank you,' he said and, from the inflection of his voice, Diane knew that the caller was their daughter, Judy. 'As long as it is just supper with you and no fuss made.'

'Thank her for the sweater,' Diane prompted.

'I got my present from you,' he said. 'It's too much. It is wonderful, far too good for me, but thank you both for it. You should not have. It is too expensive, and you have the girls to consider and not your old man.'

Diane watched as her husband said, 'No? Really. Really? No, really. See you tonight.' He slipped the mobile back into the breast pocket of his shirt, the only style of shirt he wore nowadays.

'Anything wrong with the kids?' asked Diane.

'She did not buy me the sweater,' replied Spencer. 'And she believes firmly that Karl didn't, either. If he had, she would have known.'

'Your sister, then.'

Spencer considered this for a second before rejecting it. 'She has no money. And she doesn't like me enough for that.'

'A sister is a sister.'

'How close are you to your brother? Maybe he forked out for a sweater for me.'

'Harvey? Never. His wife left him because he is so mean.' Diane leant her lower back against the range cooker, as she did when she needed comfort and warmth, the cooker being her ultimate lover.

'Someone from your work bought the sweater,' she said. 'A woman. How about the one who recommended the dog breeder to us?'

'Accounting Annie? No way. She doesn't even know where I live, or how old I am.'

'The neighbour, then. Douglas.'

'Why on earth would a stranger buy such an expensive gift for me?'

79

'You told him when we met up in the park that you would be seventy today. In fact, you also told the check-out woman in Sainsbury's, the cleaning lady and the electrician who came to fix the lamp in the porch. Our neighbour always stands close to you when we meet. Have you not noticed? Perhaps Douglas from number twelve is gay and fancies you?'

'Now you're giving yourself away. It's you. You bought this sweater and are playing games now.'

'Haha, I am such a funny person. The gift comes from someone who knows you intimately, but it isn't me. Hand on my heart.'

'It has to be my son-in-law,' Spencer concluded. 'He's got money, he's got taste, he is a nice guy.'

'Well then, you can thank him at supper tonight.'

*

Judy had cooked coq au vin for dinner. They sat at her dining table once the grandchildren were settled upstairs, story-telling over. And then the five-year-old came down again in her pyjamas; she could not sleep because granddad had said he was a kangaroo, when he wasn't.

Spencer took the child on his lap. 'I am a kangaroo because I have a pocket in my shirt, in which is not a baby kangaroo, but my mobile phone. If it's not in there, I'll never remember where I put it. A kangaroo mummy, if her baby is not in the pocket, how can she find it?'

The child understood the problem, and agreed that her grandfather was a funny sort of kangaroo.

When Judy served dessert, Diane kicked Spencer under the table.

'Ahem,' he cleared his throat. 'Thank you for my birthday gift.' Spencer reached out and gently tapped his son-in-law on the shoulder. 'Most generous of you. You spent a great deal of money on a gift for me when I am on my way out. You shouldn't have.'

Karl looked at his wife for help.

'I must say,' Diane came to the rescue, 'the *Awbrey's* sweater you bought Spencer is a piece of knitted art. Spencer is a bit overwhelmed by your generosity, but likes the gift, of course.'

'What sweater are you talking about?' asked Judy.

'The olive-green sweater your husband bought me online and had delivered yesterday,' said Spencer. 'It will be perfect for our trip to Norfolk next month. May in England can still be tricky, especially near the coast.'

Karl lifted up both arms in a gesture of surrender. 'It wasn't me. Honest.'

'Can we drop the subject?' said Judy. 'Who wants seconds?'

'Whatever elegant bashfulness you display today, I want you to take on board that I am moved by your generous gift,' replied Spencer.

'Mother.' Judy rose from her chair. 'Into the kitchen now, please.'

Karl turned to his father-in-law. 'I know I should have bought you something, but I am very busy at the moment.' Karl squirmed. 'If you want me to buy you an *Awbrey's* sweater, I will do so.'

Before Diane was entirely in the kitchen, Judy

exploded. 'What is it with Dad and that sweater? We haven't bought him anything. We thought inviting you tonight would be like a sort of gift. Now Dad is upset that we didn't give him the expensive sweater and we, especially Karl, have to suffer. Anyway, I wouldn't have let him buy it.'

'Darling,' started Diane. 'I don't know what to think. I was there when the sweater was delivered. There was no card. Karl has money and taste, so...'

'Not you as well! Get off our backs. Dad has got Alzheimer's in one birthday swoop. This pressure about a gift we should have bought him is sickening. Right now, Karl is overwhelmed at work. In fact, we've got to pull out of the trip to Norfolk. You, Dad and the green sweater can go alone.'

'Judy, please, no,' said Diane. 'I've been counting the hours until then.'

'If you don't know how to cancel our family room in the hotel, I am happy to do it for you. Let's go back to the men before Dad tortures Karl to death.'

The women returned to the dining room.

'Look!' Karl, flushed by now, was shouting. 'I haven't given you a bloody green sweater, nor a blue one or a red one. If you want me to have done so, buy one and I'll reimburse you. End of.'

Judy winced, as she saw Karl tilt the red wine bottle to fill his glass up to the rim.

'By the way, Dad,' she faced her father, a bluish vein throbbing on her temple, 'you and Mum will have to go to Norfolk by yourselves. We can't come. We're too busy. Sorry.'

'Too busy buying pullovers online,' joked Karl, on whom the wine had had an effect already.

★

'That did not go well,' said Spencer to Diane as they drove home.

'You noticed.'

'Of course I did. But I still don't know who...'

She cupped her hand over his mouth. 'I've had enough about that sweater. Now they are not coming to Norfolk, I won't go either. You, the dog and your sweater can go by yourselves. That's what Judy said to my face.'

Spencer parked the car in front of the double garage. The neighbour's security light came on, and the neighbour came out of his house.

'Evening, Douglas,' said Spencer civilly.

'Here is the line between our driveways.' Douglas pointed. 'It's called the boundary between us. Your bins are always over the line, and they stink of your dog's shit.'

'Come into the house,' said Diane, pulling her husband by his sleeve. 'I think Douglas has had a few too many, as well.'

'Drunk? Me?' The neighbour had heard her. 'If I were seventy today, I would not go around accusing people of not having bought me an expensive pullover. I told him already on the phone this afternoon that I did not buy him a sweater, and that I am not sorry about it. I will never buy him a sweater, no matter what tactics he uses on me. From now on, park your rubbish on your land or I'll complain to the council.'

Diane slammed the oak door shut when they were both in the house. In the kitchen, Dillon barked. From the study came the ringing of the landline phone. Spencer went to the dog, Diane to answer the phone.

When they met up again, she said, 'That was Accounting Annie.'

'Calling me at home at this time of night?'

'It is only just gone nine,' said Diane. 'But, did you call her during the day about the sweater? She sounded distressed. Apparently, she has put it to your company that you have… erm… are… erm…'

'What?'

'Showing signs of old age.'

'No brown spots on my hands yet.' He held them up.

'Mentally, more like. She is sorry, but they will probably ask you to retire gracefully.'

'I'm only working three days a week, and I am not gaga yet. How dare Annie suggest that? Management, the way they are, will pick it up and retire me with a gun at my back tomorrow.'

'Annie did say she was sorry about that, and also about not having thought of buying you a pullover for your birthday. She is apparently aware that dark green is your colour.' Diane stroked the dog, whose tail tapped the kitchen cupboard, so happy was he that they had come home.

'When I find the one who bought me that sweater, I'll strangle him,' said Spencer.

'More like a her. This is the moment to open up,' Diane said. 'Are you being unfaithful to me?'

'Stone the crows. A few hours ago you accused me of being gay with our neighbour, and now I have a lady lover.'

'In the first puff of sexual attraction, women do crazy things for men.'

'I haven't been in that situation,' he said.

'You are now,' replied Diane. 'She, whoever she is, fancies you, and you haven't even noticed because you are insensitive and lack insight into women. For you, they are just mothers and cooks. She, who wanted to spoil you with that gift, probably doesn't even know that you are married, or that I exist. Nor that you have a daughter with a husband and children, who are now not coming with us to Norfolk, or ever again anywhere else. Thanks to that floozy who sent you the sweater.'

Spencer was dumbfounded by her outburst. His eyes swivelled, which they only did when he was highly charged with a problem to solve, like the putting together of the desk for which she had thrown the instructions away, because she thought they were just advertising.

Spencer poured himself a glass of cooking brandy, because his house was declared a non-spirit drink area by her. He tossed it down and made a grimace.

'Don't you think you've had enough alcohol today?' said Diane.

'A woman,' he said. 'Do you really think there is a woman out there who would go so puffy because she was in love with me?'

'You tell me. You're the one who is unfaithful.'

'And what do you mean about the kids not coming to Norfolk with us? Judy said they were too busy.'

'See? You don't understand anything that matters to women, never have, never will. To which we can add increasing dodderiness. Every week, you will get worse.'

'What has got into you, Diane? Why are you so nasty all of a sudden?'

'We lost our kid's trust and love, now and forever.'

'Stop weeping. You've upset the dog. Look, Dillon's crawled under the table.'

'I knew something awful had entered my life the minute I saw that green sweater, which is so not us...' sobbed Diane.

'I can't cope with this melodrama,' said Spencer. 'I need logic. For instance, what have you done with the wrapping in which the sweater was delivered?'

'I threw it into the bin, the one our neighbour was so upset about. Been picked up this morning, Friday, yellow bin day.'

'My sister,' Spencer said, out of context.

'What about her?'

'She is the one who sent me that gift. I know she doesn't have extra money, but she loves me.'

'Call her then and thank her, so we can put this behind us.'

Spencer, with his glasses forward on his nose, punched the numbers on his smartphone.

Sinking into a kitchen chair, arching her spine for a while to relax with relief, Diane heard Spencer say, 'Hello, Totty. It's your brother.'

He wandered out of the room to talk in private.

This brother and sister relationship had not always gone smoothly. Shortly after the wedding, where Totty had played the role of his best man in a tux as a joke, which did not really work, Totty had divorced and moved to Cornwall, which was too far away from Milton Keynes to keep up contact. Totty's name was Dorothy, but her younger brother, when aged five, had shortened it and it had stuck. She had nursed their father during his last months, which was generous of her. Totty had brusque manners, but her heart was in the right place.

Spencer returned. The mobile was back in the kangaroo pocket. He looked done in.

'I had a fight with her,' he said. 'A serious fight like never before. We won't see her again, I don't think. After my dad died, I suggested he was dressed in his favourite green sweater in the coffin, but Totty wanted him in his best suit. The vicar said that normally best suits were put on the dead. We argued then, and I remember saying that the green sweater defined Dad. Anyway, she wasn't the one who bought me the sweater. She took my mere suggestion as an insult to her. In her mind, it instantly brought up the problem with the corpse in the coffin. It must have festered in her, for she yelled over the phone, saying that I should go to hell and more unpleasantries, one being taking you, Diane, to hell with me.'

'This is turning into a nightmare,' said Diane. 'Out there somewhere is someone who wanted to please you, someone who knows you well. Who is that someone? We shouldn't have given away the ouija board Totty gave us for Christmas that time,' she added pensively, while Spencer found that worth a short laugh.

Diane shot him a sharp glance. 'This is no laughing matter. It is unbearably stressful. Every step we make piles on more disasters.'

'I'm scouring my brain, believe me.' Spencer paused. 'There might be just one last, but unlikely, possibility.'

Diane blinked tiredly.

'Hamish, my golf buddy.'

She came to life. 'Why didn't you come up with that before? Of course. Golf, sport, green.'

'I haven't actually seen him for about six months,' continued Spencer. 'He's been off sick. I don't know much about his private life, but he lives on Crescent Way in a house named Putter. That's all. Apart from the fact,' he added, 'that he is uncharacteristically generous for a Scot, always pays for everyone's drinks at the bar.'

'That's it. You've solved the problem.' Diane dance-stepped across the kitchen. 'Why didn't you think of him before? Tomorrow morning, we'll go and thank him. We'll stop somewhere to buy flowers on the way.'

'Blokes aren't keen on flowers.'

'They'll be for his wife.' Diane took a deep breath. 'Honestly, I don't know how I put up with you. Old, you're twice as painful as you were before. Many people our age separate. I wouldn't mind moving into one of those easy-care flats with balconies overlooking the river.' She pushed forward her bosom and tossed back her head. 'Maybe I still have a chance in the single older adult bracket.'

'What brought that on?'

'The penny has dropped.' She stopped hopping around to warm her backside against the AGA again. 'You bought that pullover for yourself, didn't you? Because it is so expensive, you don't dare admit it. You'd rather put us all through hell. Making us miserable and destroying every relationship with family, friends and neighbours. Spencer, I am talking to you. For once, be honest with me. It was you, wasn't it?'

'No, it wasn't. I wouldn't have chosen a green one because of my Dad, who, in the end, wore his green sweater in the coffin. It made him look greener than he already was.'

*

The next day, after picking up a bunch of tulips from Waitrose, they parked in front of Putter on Crescent Way.

The door of the white-rendered house was opened by a frail-looking woman, whose short, straight, white hair looked like a hat over her pale face.

'Golf friends of Hamish,' she eventually took on board and stepped aside to let them into the narrow corridor. It smelled of mould.

They took seats on the sofa in the north-facing front room. Spencer checked his new compass, while the mistress of the house fetched her husband.

Hamish appeared, leaning heavily on a stick. The sparse hair on his head was tousled, like that of a small child woken from sleep in the afternoon, sweaty and confused. His large feet in slippers glided along the floor as if in furry boats.

'What brings you here?' he said, when he recognised Spencer.

'Long time no see,' Spencer replied.

Hamish made it to the other sofa, into which he let himself fall backwards after battling with his stick. 'After my heart attack,' he began, 'my mean consultant said NO to golf for the foreseeable future. That term can be negotiated, can't it? Nice of you to come and see me.'

His wife came into the room, pushed the lamp to the side and put the tulips in a vase on a side table.

'Jake came to see me yesterday. Well...' Hamish rolled his eyes, 'swaggering in and then berating me for half an hour.'

'There's a rumour at the club that he will be our next president. You'd better get into shape and come back to help us out,' Spencer said.

Hamish tried to cough, but gave up on it, as if it required too much energy. All he managed were a few dry, weak cackles.

'Hamish has to rest. Doctor's orders,' said his wife. 'Stress and agitation have to be avoided. You have to deal with the problems in the golf club on your own.'

'Don't listen to the dragon. I'm allowed out of the cage.' Hamish, hunched in his seat, appeared old and broken. 'Five hundred steps a day.'

'Small steps, near the house and well wrapped. The wind is chill,' his wife clarified.

'What do you do to pass the time, apart from that?' asked Spencer.

'Yeah, what do I do? I watch television soaps and spend time on my computer, catching up with friends and acquaintances.'

'I tell you what he does most of the day.' The wife resettled the tulips in the vase by holding them under their heads and bouncing them up and down. She wiped her hands on her skirt. 'Hamish orders things online. Things we do not need. Things which are undesirable. In other words,' she now focused on her husband, 'wasting the money we don't have.'

Diane shot Spencer a meaningful look before asking, 'Does he order things for his friends?'

'I am sure he does.' The wife still answered for him. 'He's at it for hours.'

'If you remember, it was you, dear, who asked me to find a suitable birthday present for your cousin, because I had the time to search,' Hamish defended himself.

'And you know what he found and ordered?' Her head was bobbing up and down. 'A stuffed squirrel wearing a flat cap and holding a shotgun.'

Hamish cackled and glanced at Spencer, who tried hard not to show glee. 'The stuff that is for sale on eBay is unbelievable.' He stopped talking and pointed his finger at Spencer. 'Didn't a little bird tell me you just had an important birthday? Now, finally, you're one of us seventiers. Sorry I couldn't raise a glass with you on the day. Thought of you, though. Another one hitting old age.'

'Thank you, Hamish, for having thought of me on my birthday,' said Spencer. 'Your gift arrived and is more than I deserve.'

'Another stuffed squirrel!' The wife's voice had risen. 'What have you bought online for this… your friend?'

'Nothing,' replied Hamish. 'Now I realise, I forgot

91

to order something. What did you say you would have liked me to buy you? I completely forgot, even though I knew the date of your birthday. I forgot completely. Sitting here with her all day long, only allowed to walk to the post box and back supervised by her, makes me lose my grip. I am sorry, old man. I will make it up to you. Whatever you say, don't thank me for something I have become unable to do any longer. One heart attack, one chest pain… actually it felt like heartburn, and the stretcher, the ECG, and muesli from then on. I am doomed. If I cannot even have the pleasure of shopping online, then what is there left? I open, I search, I click. I give them my card details and someone I know gets something from me, even though I'm now crippled. But I am obviously too gaga to plan in time to send gifts to people who matter. How long have we played golf together? I am useless. You can throw me onto the discard heap.' Hamish started to shake. It looked as if someone had plugged him into the mains.

'Calm yourself,' shouted the wife. 'You are not allowed to get upset. Stop it. This friend here is not worth it.'

'How would you know? And how is it your place to judge?' Hamish replied. 'Just because I am crippled, you are taking over, owning me. I can't have a life like this. It is…' Hamish slumped sideways. The frightening thing was that, inert, his two hands still vibrated.

'Dear God, he is having another heart attack!' exclaimed his wife. 'I'll call 999.'

*

In the gigantic warehouse, Arthur was paged to Uncle Rupert's office.

'Uncle,' said Arthur, sitting down on the chair. 'You wanted to see me?'

'Don't panic, my son,' Rupert said, even though Arthur was not his son. Rupert did not have a son. His wife had left him. 'Separated,' Mother had said. The same word she used when she made mayonnaise.

'I am satisfied with your work,' Rupert went on. 'And so are those working for me who supervise you. The nail in the tyre was not your fault. On Friday the thirteenth of April, sixteen hundred, you were assigned to deliver for *Awbrey's* to Buckingham. Do you remember the job?'

'Yes, Uncle. Clearly.'

'There has been a complaint. The customer did not receive his order. *Awbrey's* confirm the wrapping, labelling and loading into the van. After that, it's up to the driver, which was you. Tell me about it.'

'I delivered to Buckingham, 10 Park Avenue, and gave the parcel into the hands of Mrs West.'

Rupert checked on his computer screen. 'The order was to go to Buckingham, 10 Park Road West.' Rupert looked straight at his nephew. 'A road is not an avenue. You were unlucky that the customer's name was Weston. The "on" sort of gets lost when one pronounces it.'

'Forgive me, Uncle. I only want to bring people happiness,' said Arthur. 'Won't happen again.'

'Don't beat yourself up about it. Glitches happen. *Awbrey's* are insured. No harm done.'

THE NEW BENTLEY

The villa was rendered in stark white, prominent in its position on the slope above Lake Geneva. The city of Geneva stands at the western end of the lake, where the Rhone flows out, and the tall water spout defines the view. Suburban housing extends back along both shores of the lake, the north side favoured by international civil servants for the simple reason that the UN Palace, International Labour and World Health Organisations were built on that side, and the only bridge to get from the other side is chronically congested.

In front of the white villa, English expat Charles Worthington paced in a peculiar fashion. He wore cotton trousers and a Dior casual shirt. In his Italian loafers, he performed large steps on the pebble-covered driveway, as if he were avoiding patches of quicksand.

'Thirty-five metres,' he pronounced, when he got to the hedge. It was July in Switzerland, and the foliage luscious.

Kate Crick, Worthington by marriage, shorter in build than her husband, was under the pillared porch. 'What are you measuring?' she asked, having watched her husband's odd behaviour.

'Capacity for parking cars off-road. Four large cars fit onto our drive, without having to do any juggling. And that doesn't take the double-garage into account.'

To the side of the house, next to the swimming pool, was a home gym, and its basement was the garage, accessed by a steep ramp.

Not interested, she turned to enter the house.

'I need a coffee,' he called out to her.

She hesitated, sensing that he would have recourse to the tiring old game of dependency. Sure enough, he scuttled up to her. She felt his body heat as he pushed against her with come-on nudges. Dogs do that to communicate with humans; Charles thought it was sexy.

'Just a teeny-weeny espresso,' he whined.

Together, they went into the hall with a galleried staircase and on into the kitchen, a large bright room in which removal boxes took up much of the space. On the quartz worktop, items which she had already unpacked were lined up, as if in a shop display.

'We've got to make more progress with unpacking.' Charles kicked an open box, on which was scrawled *kitchen* with a marker pen in Kate's handwriting.

She lifted an item from it, unwrapped it and produced the coffee machine. 'When I packed up the bungalow, I thought of prioritising,' Kate said, with some pride.

'And the coffee pods? Did you have the good sense to pack those with the machine?'

She opened one of the top kitchen units and felt around on the shelf.

'You didn't,' he said, almost keeping his glee in check.

In her head she heard, *You stupid woman.* She blinked it away. 'I have the tea caddy handy,' she offered.

'Kate,' he said, pulling himself up onto one of the swivel barstools. 'Can we get rid of your mother's little pansy-decorated tea caddy, please?'

'What's wrong with it?'

'It was good enough while I was a minor functionary, and we got a small house in a crappy location. Now that the *sainted* World Health Organisation has finally understood I deserve diplomatic status, things have to change. For starters, here we are in a five-bedroom house with swimming pool and heated outdoor terrace. There is even a view of Mont Blanc on its rare appearances.' He swivelled on his chair. 'Geneva is a snob city,' he went on. 'Probably the most coveted place for the elite.' After a pause, he added, 'Worldwide.'

'Why?' she asked, taking a mug which had already been unpacked.

'Because salaries are generous. Diplomats have status. A CD on the car number plate means privilege. First Class plane travel, best tables in gourmet restaurants, balcony seats in the grand theatre. Do I need to go on?' He twisted his head her way. 'Now, Charles Worthington is one of them.'

'We've already been here for three years, and I didn't have to put up with any of that grandiose behaviour,' grumbled Kate.

Charles, head back, face up, not to the ceiling but to some benign divinity, repeated, 'I made it. I made it.'

'To snob city.' Kate ended the refrain.

She made them both a cup of tea from the pansy

caddy. Charles at the breakfast bar sipped it, but it wasn't in his favourite mug. Luckily, he did not comment on it.

He broke the silence with, 'V8, 6.75 litre, turbo. What do they have in common?'

Kate shrugged. 'Telegraph crossword clues?'

'The Bentley Mulsanne's latest model. Just come out. So much in demand that many of them are being made in Germany.' Charles paused. 'How long do you think the waiting list is?'

'People have too much money.' Kate picked at the end of the brown tape, holding together a packing box.

'You're doing it all wrong.' He approached with a bread knife, with which he cut through the tape between the cardboard flaps. When he prised the lids apart, Kate gave a yelp. 'Our dining room curtains!'

'Why did those have to come?' asked Charles. 'This house already has curtains – curtains designed by a professional interior decorator. It used to be occupied by the French Ambassador, did you know that?'

'I don't know,' she said. 'I wasn't always there to supervise the packers.'

'We have been upgraded, and are expected to behave accordingly,' said Charles. 'Your part-time work with Swiss Animal Protection is not an option any longer.'

'I don't agree.'

'You bring animals home. It is against the lease.'

'Only once, or maybe twice.'

'As we speak, there is a sick cat in a playpen in our downstairs visitor's room. It meows, it poops, and for weeks you have syringed formula into its mouth, neglecting your duties as wife to a senior international civil servant – me.'

'Thank God the kitten poops,' said Kate. 'We were afraid his organs had failed. The poor thing was found looking for his mother, which had been killed by a car. He is doing well. Soon he can go to be adopted. We called him Juri,' she laughed happily, 'because we found him on the Route du Jura.'

'I will have to buy myself a Bentley,' Charles said, ignoring Kate's story. 'The French Ambassador drove around in a Jaguar F-Pace. By the way, has their maid been in touch with you?'

Kate shook her head. 'But someone came to the door yesterday. Her name was Mariella Gruber. She is the wife of Jerome Gruber, who works at the WHO with you.'

'Jerry Gruber. A local employee. My junior by about ten years. A most irritating man. His job is PR, and he gets to choose who goes in front of the camera when WHO opinions have to be voiced. This month, he chose an Argentinian twice, because the UN Secretary-General is Argentinian. He has never chosen me. I don't even get to be quoted in newspapers. This is now going to change. In my allocated parking space in the WHO basement will stand a new dragon-red Bentley. And should I ever drive over a cat with kittens, I will reverse and drive over them again.'

Undisturbed, Kate went on, 'Mariella Gruber brought an invitation to welcome us to the neighbourhood. A thoughtful gesture.'

'We don't live close in any way,' replied Charles. 'We

are on the sunny slope flanking Lake Geneva, while the Grubers, as I recall, live down in Morlan.' He read the invitation Kate held out to him. '*We would be pleased to request…* And they misspelled our name. I am not going to Gruber's home. He is odious: tall, pale with a thin nose, and metal-rim glasses. And he has a limp from some skiing accident.'

'It could be interesting to learn more about how the local Swiss live. We meet so few of them.'

'Not one single time did he put my name forward for a live interview.'

'I told Mariella that we would be coming tomorrow.'

'You can bring her your mangy kitten as a gift.'

★

The lunch invitation was for twelve-thirty. Charles and Kate walked down the road towards Morlan. Charles, cradling two bottles of excellent champagne from his well-stocked cellar, was dressed in a grey and white striped blazer with brass buttons sporting anchors.

Kate, walking behind her husband because of her heels and the uneven pavement, carried pansies planted in an oval zinc pot. She had dressed in a blue prom-style dress. The cloche-cut skirt swirled about her well-shaped legs. Around her neck was a blue velvet band, onto which she had sewn artificial red roses – two of them, nestled against her chin, the vivid colour contrast setting off her long, dark hair and pale skin.

The couple entered Morlan. Water splattered into a stone trough in the cobbled village centre.

'Number thirteen, Rue de la Fontaine,' said Charles, who had memorised the address on the invitation, and he turned up a steep, narrow street.

'Pretty,' Kate said, looking up at the houses either side. 'This one has a faded painting on it. It must be very old.'

'Well, this piglet-pink one doesn't and is number thirteen.'

At one short, sharp cough from Charles, the door was opened by a woman of about forty. Her shoulder-length, prematurely greying hair was propped up to the side with a comb, revealing her left ear. From it dangled what looked like a pottery rabbit. Seeing the Worthingtons, Mariella hesitated. The rabbit became inert.

'Come in,' she finally suggested and stepped aside.

Charles and Kate squeezed passed her into a narrow corridor. As they emerged into the living space, Charles handed the champagne bottles to his hostess.

'My goodness,' she exclaimed. 'Two of them. You want those to be drunk chilled. I'll put them into our chest freezer for a while.'

'Please don't...' The rest of the objection remained unuttered between Charles's tight lips.

'Easy.' Kate's hand gently touched his clenched fist. 'Two, three hours and it will be over.'

It was clear that Mariella was not used to entertaining.

In the living room, there was an eared easy chair facing glassed patio doors; a crutch leant against it. Outside, beyond the patio, was a lawn leading to a tall hedge which separated the garden from that of the house backing onto them.

A hand reached round the side of the chair to catch hold of the crutch. Jerry pushed himself out of the seat to greet his guests. Kate watched the painful manoeuvre and felt an urge to assist.

Charles had given an unflattering description of Jerry. The man who stood before them in slippered feet had blond curls, bright blue eyes, and a warm, sincere smile. Jerry was years younger than Charles, about five feet eleven, slender of build, a good-looking man with a strong, well-defined face.

'Don't let these people stand around. Make yourself useful,' said Mariella, speaking to her husband as if he were not hampered by infirmity. 'Open the French windows. It is warm enough to sit outside. I wiped down the furniture this morning.'

Jerry found it difficult to both manage the crutch and push against a stuck door. Charles watched as if the sight entertained him.

'Ruddy doors.' Jerry gave up. 'I need to get my hammer and chisel. French windows were not part of Swiss village houses in the eighteenth century.'

'Let me.' Charles pressed his foot against the bottom of the doorframe and then threw his right shoulder against the door. With a bang it flew open.

Remaining politely calm, Jerry said 'Thank you', and invited them to install themselves outside. The rectangular table was covered with a wax cloth, and there were plastic garden chairs, as well as a hanging rattan egg chair.

Charles headed that way, muttering, 'When you get wax cloths, you're in the third world.'

Before stepping outside, Kate looked around the

living room. On the mantle surround was a collection of cards. *Happy Birthday Jerome, forty-five today. To Jerry, life begins at forty-five.*

'This is a birthday invitation. You should have told me,' Kate said to Mariella, who brought in a wooden board on which was laid out charcuterie.

'Jerry didn't want it to be mentioned,' replied Mariella. 'His sister Corinne is coming, though. She is an artist, sculpts, and is starting to make a name for herself in Switzerland. I thought it would interest you. WHO gossip tells me that you paint.'

'Only animals for charity greeting cards. Charles wants me to paint his portrait. That is definitely beyond me.' Kate giggled.

'Corinne mostly makes charming, small things.' Mariella reached up to touch the dangling rabbit. 'Like this.'

Once they were all sitting outside, the sun appeared from behind a large cloud. It became instantly warmer. Mariella smiled broadly and distributed large linen serviettes. Charles shook his out to unfold.

'Almost pillowcase-size.'

Mariella gone, Jerry thought he had to explain. 'She is nervous about today.'

'Here we are.' Mariella returned. 'Finger food.' She put two plates onto the wax cloth: a scalloped serving dish with meat patties, decorated with fan-shaped gherkin slices, and another dish with short, plump sausages speared onto large slices of tomato with cocktail sticks. No champagne had yet appeared, or any other drinkable substance, and conversation lapsed.

103

The hostess, possibly aware of the awkwardness, turned to Charles. 'Tell me, what does a WHO employee do? Jerry is hired to promote the image, I understand that, but how about the others?'

'The others?' replied Charles. 'From nine to five, they pass round that day's memo. The one who gets caught with it at five o'clock has to do something about dengue fever in Namibia, or cholera in Lesotho.'

'Are you one of them?'

'I'm not interested in bugs. I came to the job from health security administration. But we have heaps of scientists, biologists and virologists – people who crawled through bushes in uncomfortable countries for years.'

Mariella nodded. 'World health, that is quite a responsibility.' She looked at her husband. 'Jerry has never travelled outside Europe.'

'I wrote a paper on Tabanidae, horseflies,' Jerry defended himself.

Charles put his half-eaten patty on the serviette to be able to talk. 'We know about your paper on horseflies.'

'It had more importance than you all realise.' Jerry went on, 'In 1974, there was a diphtheria epidemic in the alpine villages of Eastern Switzerland: a serious reproach to the hygiene level of our rivers. I found the link between horsefly bites in cattle, and their infected urine polluting the mountain brooks with diphtheria. Horseflies don't sting; they scissor-cut through the skin and into the flesh, and the blood becomes infected.'

'Jerry here reveals depths of which I was not aware,' said Charles. 'All he is asked to do now is promote the work of the WHO, and put me in front of a news camera from time to time.' Charles's bulky body nestled in the cane egg suspended from a bowed metal frame. Pushing his foot against the ground, he started to swing.

A red-haired woman, wearing pink dungarees over a rust-red roll-neck pullover, jumped out of the house onto the terrace, singing *Happy Birthday*. A sizeable red bow gathered her hair into a ponytail. The toes, displayed in her open sandals, were painted in a range of glossy colours.

After a third chorus, she ran out of puff. 'A gift for my birthday boy brother.' A knitwear thing unravelled to turn into a macramé three-tier plant-hanger. Holding it up, she explained, 'The top is for a small vessel of wisdom. The water passes down, carrying the earth's wisdom, to the plant at the middle level, and then, grown in power, to the last and largest.'

Charles watched as she threaded the 'vessels', upside-down ceramic skulls, into the macramé pockets.

'Jerry, you will have to block the mouths from the inside. Otherwise, the earth will push out through the teeth,' Corinne said, satisfied with her offering. 'I made the skulls. My art is sculpting.'

Kate clapped her hands in delight, possibly at the singing, or the wisdom of the pots, or the sight of the woman – Charles really could not tell. Kate led the dungaree person onto the small lawn.

'Mariella told me about your talent in sculpting. Do you take commissions?' Kate whispered.

Corinne nodded.

'I would like you to make a bust of my husband. The one sitting in the egg. It has to be a surprise.'

105

'Difficult,' Corinne whispered back. 'If at all possible, I will need photographs of his head taken from all sides. Talk to my brother. He owns a good digital Canon.'

Charles watched as Kate left the side of the woman to sidle up to Jerry. They, too, whispered flirtatiously. Kate's hand movements were animated; a pink colour had come to her cheeks. Where was the champagne he had brought? He needed some alcohol to help him get through the ordeal of this lunch.

Corinne approached his egg seat. 'Can I get you another sausage on tomato?'

'I am still hungry, but not for food.' Charles offered Corinne a salacious smile.

'If you think you are irresistible, think again.'

He raised his eyebrows. 'Whatever you say, Miss Made-of-Steel.'

'OK, I can see that this will end with a fight.'

'The sooner the better,' said Charles. They glared at each other. 'I bet you get turned on when dominated.'

'Keep wondering about that. You are too old for me.'

He reached out and grabbed her wrist. She gasped and tried to free her arm. The cane seat shook.

'Leave me alone. You're hurting me.'

'Foreplay,' he said, pulling her closer to him.

'Your wife.'

'Kate is busy flirting with your brother. He limps. She is a sucker for creatures who are mangled.'

'Jerry is not mangled.'

At that moment Jerry approached, a camera in front of his face. Click went the shutter.

106

Charles brushed his hand over his hair. 'I had my eyes closed.'

It was unbelievable that Jerry was taking pictures of this pathetic event. Pictures of him, mostly. Only him, it became clear, when Jerry pointed the camera at others but did not press the shutter button. Instead, he asked Charles to step out of the egg chair so he could take profile pictures. This must be for work. Charles smiled. Finally.

'I'll take many more, if you don't mind,' said Jerry reassuringly, giving Kate a wink.

Charles relaxed. All was well. The pictures were being taken to prepare his appearance in front of news cameras. Best angle, pleasing appearance. Charles adopted the facial expression of a man who cared deeply about world health.

'You look like a constipated ostrich.' Corinne destroyed the benevolence on Charles's features.

Angry, he retorted, 'You dress in stupid clothes, you make stupid pottery skulls, you talk nonsense. You are a rebel in a teacup. Artist, my foot.'

'My flying cow sculpture is in the Zurich Museum of Art,' replied Corinne. She amended it to, 'Well, outside, at the back, on loan.'

'Wearing romper suits at your age does not make you an art personality.'

'Imagine what your striped Harrods jacket does not make *you*.' She emphasised the *you* aggressively.

They were interrupted by Mariella. 'The dessert is meringues, but I am afraid the meringue shells have not risen. I have to do them again. It will take some time.

So sorry. Perhaps, with this interlude, you could go and look around Morlan? Calvin used to preach sermons in our church.' The hostess, flushed with embarrassment, fled back into the house.

'Interested in Calvin?' Corinne asked Charles.

'The Reformationists were killjoys,' replied Charles. 'Why don't you and I explore the upstairs of your brother's house? There are some fireworks between you and me which we need to detonate.'

Her body language instantly showed defence. Was this to protect her brother's abode, or to ward him off?

'No worries,' he said. 'It'll do me good to see where Calvin prated.'

Disappointed, she jutted her pelvis forward. Her shoulders relaxed and her eyes, on him, became velvety. It became inevitable that they should go inside together.

He closed the door behind them in what was clearly the main bedroom of the house; Mariella's dove-grey dressing gown hung from a curved hook against the inside of the door. Corinne ran at the double bed and, with a leap, clumsily landed on the patchwork cover.

'Are you a man with sexual over-evaluation?' she asked, when Charles bent over her.

'Probably not, as I don't even know what you are talking about.' She had just succeeded in diminishing his euphoric sense of sexual adventure. 'What I am is a man of action.' He grabbed her and pushed her further up on the bed cover.

She lay, her head turned sideways, her red hair freed from the ponytail. 'This quilt is a fake, made of polyester,' she complained.

He took his shoes off and was working on his trousers to make them slide down his legs.

'It takes three hundred years for this stuff to disintegrate.'

'We don't have that much time right now,' he breathed at her. 'We'll have to reappear downstairs soon.'

He unclipped her dungarees and pulled them off. He helped her force the tight sweater over her head. Underneath it, her skin was damp. She unbuttoned his shirt, and he took it off. Charles debated with himself whether this was the right moment to take off his briefs.

Doing women, he thought, was an occupation for men without intelligence. He lowered himself over her and started to stroke her head, his fingers getting entangled in the ample, odd-smelling hair.

'Is this going to take long?' she enquired.

'No, no.' He checked his erection. He could take his briefs off; he was good. He leant close over her, trying to find the way into her. She loosened her legs to fall open more, and he succeeded.

It did not take long.

'Got tissues?' she asked.

He reached back to the bedside table and pulled a single-ply tissue from a cardboard cube.

*

Kate, who had first offered help with the meringues, which was declined, wondered how she should occupy the interlude. Charles had gone upstairs with Corinne. All the signs of that outcome had been there from the beginning, watching the two of them sparring. It was often like that with Charles and women he met for the first time. She did not mind any longer. Corinne could make herself useful by sculpting his head. Charles tired of his conquests as fast as he made them.

Kate went into the house. Mariella was not in the kitchen, but the bowl and the carton of eggs were on the work surface. From behind a door leading off the kitchen, she heard someone moving around. It turned out to be a small utility room, so small that only a washing machine and a sink unit fitted, with cupboards above. Towels hung from a drying-rack.

Jerry was leaning against the stainless-steel sink in which were Charles's champagne bottles. Hot water was running over the thick green glass. Kate picked up the crutch from the floor.

'Charles would probably not like what I am doing to his Veuve Clicquot,' he explained, 'but ice was just about to form in the bottle. Mariella left them too long in the freezer.'

'You can do with those bottles what you like,' Kate said. 'I don't care.'

'You are not a bit like your husband.'

'I take that as a compliment.'

He turned the tap off. 'He will never know,' he said with a twinkle in his eye.

'He will never know,' she repeated.

He let go of the sink and grabbed the crutch she held out to him, her other arm at his back steadying him.

'You are caring,' he said softly. 'I like that about you.'

'I mostly care about suffering cats and dogs.'

110

'And I resemble a poodle?'

Embarrassed, she stared at the wedding band on her finger, before she cleared her throat. 'Actually, more like a golden retriever with your blond hair.' Then she dared to look straight at him. 'It must have been a serious skiing accident.'

'That's what everybody assumes. In fact, I was kicked by a cow in Fribourg. She was plagued by horseflies – a different story.'

'We'd better show up outside again,' Kate fretted.

'As long as there will be another time for me to be with you alone.'

'You are flirting with me,' she said, pleased.

'I am too clumsy to do such a thing well,' said Jerry. 'Normally, in the presence of a beautiful woman, I just make a total idiot of myself. That is not my only shortcoming. Charles thinks I am not up to the international civil servant snob-mob.'

'I think...' she began, but stopped. 'It's not important.'

'You are the sort of woman to whom I would like to tell everything about me.'

Just then, they heard Mariella in the kitchen, shouting for Jerry. There was an edge to her voice.

Jerry lifted a bottle of champagne out of the sink and started to dry it, using a towel from the rack.

'The meringues have risen,' Mariella called out. 'We can have dessert.'

'I'm in here,' Jerry responded and limped past Kate in the tight space. 'Woof woof,' he whispered, before disappearing into the kitchen, one hand moving the crutch, the other swinging the bottle by its neck. 'The champagne ought to be drinkable now,' Kate heard him explain his absence to his wife.

Kate decided to count to one hundred before leaving the utility room.

★

The next morning, before Charles drove off to Dresden in the seven-year-old Renault, a car that would not be returning, Kate had not made him coffee or shown any warmth towards him. She did not even say, 'Drive carefully,' which was the minimum line for a wife. Instead, she had attacked him for his behaviour the previous day.

'I know you mess with women, but this time you have gone too far.'

'Look who's talking. What about you and Jerry, whispering and giving each other flirty looks? Can you tell me what he did with the champagne I brought? When he finally brought it out, it was tepid. That idiot has no clue.'

'I knew you would seduce that crazy Corinne from the moment she walked in. A grown woman coming to an adult lunch party in baby-pink dungarees? Don't tell me she reaches your inner child.'

'You liked Corinne as well, sidling up to her, whispering, giggling.'

It was true, it occurred to him. During lunch the day before, Kate had behaved out of character. Normally reserved with people, she had displayed great intimacy

112

with Corinne and Jerry, engaging them in intense conversations. It was probably Jerry she had been trying to seduce, using his sister as an accomplice, and the whole charade had been to pay Charles back for going upstairs with Corinne. Kate didn't know the first thing about seduction or sex. Charles pressed on the accelerator and drove down to the motorway along Lake Geneva. On his return, the Bentley pedal would provide a whole new experience, he thought, and felt happy with life.

*

The next day, sadly, it rained. Water prattled onto the shiny dragon-red bonnet, but silent windscreen wipers showed him the exit sign to Morlan with clarity. He had made great time, Dresden to Morlan in nine hours. He reached out and patted his Bentley on the dashboard.

'Well done,' he said. Charles was a happy man.

And the day became even better when he saw Corinne walking along the pavement. She wore a raincoat, and an umbrella in the shape of a sunflower protected her head. Her gait was slightly askew, due to a heavy bag in her left hand.

He tried out his car horn. The elegant noise it produced made Corinne look his way.

'Hey,' she shouted and put the bag down. He brought the car to a stop, and she approached. 'What a fantastic car,' she admired. 'It suits you. Honestly, it does. As if you belonged to the Royal Family. I have never known a man who could afford a Rolls Royce.'

'It's a Bentley.'

'Same thing.'

He decided not to go further with that. Instead, he asked her, 'Where are you heading in this weather?'

'Up to your house, actually. I am late, and they will not be pleased.'

'And what is in the bag?'

'Clay. Don't force me to say more. They asked me to keep it a secret.'

'Who are they?'

She sighed and shook rain off the umbrella. 'Your wife and my brother. We didn't expect you to be back so soon. They will feel under pressure.'

'Jerry is in my house, with Kate?'

'Has been there yesterday and again since early this morning. Doing art takes time.'

He ignited the motor, indicated and pulled away from the curve, to drive through the village and up the hill to his house. In the expensive rear-view mirror, he saw Corinne trying to run after him – an inelegant sight, as the heavy bag was in the way of her moving legs.

In front of his house, he stopped the car at the head of the ramp down to the garage. He felt the uncomfortable violence of his heart. In the gym above the garage, all the lights were on. That's where Kate was having sex with Jerry. He imagined the scene and thought about the lame leg, but drove away the thought before it became more graphic. Angry with him about Corinne, Kate had wasted no time and had used his absence to bonk Jerry yesterday and again today. Calling it *doing art* was no embellishment of the sordid act. Jerry Horsefly was in there right now, the two of them not expecting him back yet.

114

Indeed, he saw Jerry at the window, naked, certainly down to the waist. Then Kate joined him. She had a cloth, a flannel perhaps, with which she wiped along Jerry's neck and over his shoulders, slowly, sensually. Aroused, Jerry stretched his neck, moving his head to the side. Kate stopped caressing him with the flannel, and went with one hand into his hair, letting her fingers play in it. As she turned her back to the window, Charles realised with a gasp that her back was bare. She turned; the little that covered her breasts was nothing more than the top flap of an apron. They were playing dirty games: the little maid in the short apron to be taught a lesson. Charles felt like crying. Suddenly, Kate looked outside, at the Bentley, and straight at him.

At that moment, Corinne caught up with him.

'Up that hill,' she panted. 'You could have given me a lift.'

He popped open the passenger door. Still rasping, she climbed onto the fawn-coloured calf-leather seat.

'Just to catch my breath. I need to get the wet clay up to them.'

The side door, next to the garage door, opened and Kate came out, still in her apron.

'My bloody wife is in love with your brother,' said Charles. 'His infirmity turns her on like catnip.'

Kate, in front of the garage, made desperate moves with her arms. They were not those to express her joy at the sight of the most beautiful Bentley ever, but her dismay at him having come home early and interrupted sex with her limping lover.

'What is this?' Corinne fingered on the console

between their seats, while Charles's foot tapped the brake pedal. The Bentley started to roll. It gathered speed down the steep ramp.

'The handbrake!' shouted Charles. Two and a half tons of car smashed into the garage. Between the car and the garage door was the body of Kate.

★

'Can you talk?' Charles, with a black band around his upper arm, sat in a chair near the bed in the Geneva Cantonal Hospital. The patient in the bed was Corinne, her head and face mostly hidden under gauze wrapping; the broken nose had a plaster cast on it.

'It's been ruled an accident. New cars don't have handbrake levers any longer; they are just little flip switches. It just needs a flick to release the brake, but only if the brake pedal is touched at the same time.' Charles justified the tragic event. 'I wasn't aware of touching the brake pedal. It was subconscious, with that slope in front of us.'

'I flicked the switch, but I didn't know. And the car started to roll...'

'Only five more minutes,' the nurse said into the private ward.

'You have five minutes to tell me what was going on in the gym over my garage.'

'Kate commissioned me to sculpt your head, and she wanted to help,' explained Corinne. 'Jerry took pictures of your head as a guide and, later, he sat for Kate to help her with the neck and shoulders. I was bringing more clay to finish the shoulder blades. All three of us were excited about the bust.'

'A gift for me from Kate?' Charles jumped off his chair. 'Damn you, woman,' he shouted at Corinne. 'It's all your fault.'

The nurse reappeared. 'Please keep your grief under control, until someone can help you with it.'

CIRCUS AROLLO

'Why are the nobles at this corrida, when the toreador is known to be mediocre?'

'They're not here to honour Manolo Garcia, but the bravery of the bull he fought last Saturday in Alicante.'

'They pardoned the bull? I've never seen that happen.'

'I did,' said Juan. 'And I hope this is not going to be a repeat. Too painful to watch a man with a weapon unable to bring down a bull.'

'Tell me about it. Details, come on.' Lorenzo looked at his watch. 'Seven more minutes to five.'

The two young Spaniards sat in the shaded area of the Valencia bullring. The arena was packed. The August sun was still high and fried those in the sun who had paid less.

'Last week's bullfight went down the drain from the start,' said Juan. 'In the first tercio, Manolo already showed weakness, and the clever bull was learning fast. When Manolo did the Saint Veronica pass, the bull managed to catch the cape in its mouth.'

'Oh, my God.'

'It got worse. In the second tercio, when the picadors

had already weakened the bull's neck and it had lost a lot of blood, Manolo made a clumsy move, and he was forked up by the horns and tossed off, rolling on the ground. People threw their caps into the arena, shouting and booing. When it came to the coup de grâce, Manolo had lost all confidence; he waved the cape about like an old granny. He had three attempts with his sword. The bull was already trembling on its legs after the second. At the fourth unsuccessful stab, the crowd went berserk. That's when his grace, the Duke, stood up and waved his orange handkerchief. Manolo laid the sword down in the dust at his feet and walked out of the ring. The bull was pardoned.'

'Hombre!' Lorenzo knocked his balled fist on his thigh. 'I missed all this because I was finishing my media course in Marseille.'

At that moment, the trumpets blared. The young men turned their attention to the bullring. The toreador appeared, followed by the picadors. Manolo's waistcoat, jacket and tight trousers were overloaded with sequins, gold and silver threads. He held his head high, showing his Adonis profile, as he graced the crowd with his conceited lap of honour around the ring. Passing in front of the metal enclosure, behind which the *toro bravo* was waiting, Juan saw the toreador's shoulders twitch. Onward he proceeded in the roar of applause, until he stopped and stepped back in front of the dignitaries' lodge to salute. The Duke rose from his seat and saluted back. The ladies remained seated, flitting handheld fans in front of their faces.

A band started to play the *paso doble*. A young lady threw a rose, which the toreador caught adroitly.

'She's my cousin,' said Juan. 'Doña Isabella.'

'I didn't know you had aristocracy in your family,' said Lorenzo. 'Why aren't you ever invited to sit with them?'

'It's a bad story,' replied Juan. 'My mother's family were genteel, upper class, moved in high society. Her sister struck gold and married the Count – Isabella's father.'

'You never told me.'

'No, because my mother didn't do so well. She fell in love with an ironmonger. The family disapproved and, after the wedding, well... they just disowned her. We don't talk about it.'

A loudspeaker announced the *toro*: a five-year-old, weighing 700 kilos. Lorenzo whistled. 'Maybe we're about to see another bull winning the fight.'

The *paso doble* ended, the gate was opened, and the bull, shining like polished ebony, made a leap out of the confined space. A murmur of excitement came from the benches. Manolo waved his cape. The bull charged and pushed it aside with its horns.

'Why is the toreador showing the bull the yellow side of the cape and not the purple?' asked Lorenzo.

'It's one of Manolo's fads,' said Juan. 'It doesn't make any difference. Bulls are colour blind.'

An elongated admiring 'Ah!' came from the spectators. Manolo had goaded, mocked and then tricked the bull with the cape, to wind the beast touchingly close around his body. The adrenalin from the men in the arena hovered in the stagnant heat of the August afternoon.

So far, Manolo had performed the traditional initial moves to test the bull's reactions. Old men observed, their hands gnarled into each other on the parapets – men who had watched hundreds of bullfights and were alert to every single move of the opponents, every snort of the bull, every twist of the bullfighter.

'It seems to me that this bull is intelligent,' commented Juan. 'It goes at Manolo, its head held high.'

Lorenzo grunted. 'Not for much longer.'

Manolo performed the move of trailing the cape over the bull's head, successful with the Saint Veronica pass this time. Then, in a surprise move, he dropped his handsome head in humility and fell onto his knees, right in front of the bull. The crowd clapped and shouted. Manolo was making good for last week's shameful performance.

In the second tercio, the two picadors speared the animal's neck several times. Carmine blood ran down the shiny black body. The picadors dared to jump in close, to plant darts into the bull's shoulder. It was weakened. It stood immobile, the ribbon-decorated darts dangling from its shoulders. It did not understand what was happening to it.

In the last tercio, when the killing came, Manolo's sword caught the sun and shot flashes into the audience. He did well this time; with the second plunge of the sword, the *toro* sank onto its folded front legs and eyed the people sitting all around it, before collapsing sideways, its heavy-skulled head falling into the dust, dead.

The crowd roared with bravos and applause. Manolo lifted his embroidered hat, not to salute, as one only saluted the dignitaries, but to push back his sweaty black hair. Each elderly man in the crowd wished he were young again and in the skin of this toreador.

Mules entered, pulling a wooden plank fixed to their harness with rattling chains. The corpse was loaded on and circled the arena. The crowd shouted 'Bravo, toro!' The mules stopped, and the muleteer cut an ear off the bull to offer it to Manolo as a trophy.

'This guy must have drawers full of ears,' said Juan. 'He is already thirty-five years old.'

The bull gone, the winner, in his bejewelled killer costume, made the final laps around the ring, advancing gracefully in his rhinestone-decorated pumps. Another *paso doble* played. Manolo was reinstated as a hero; the incident of the bull in Alicante, now recovering on a farm, forgotten. The toreador-turned-successful-matador soaked up the adoration. He was a handsome specimen. Facing the Duke and his noble entourage, he struck a pose, yanked down the tight corset over his skin-tight trousers and lifted his head high.

'Look at your cousin, Isabella.' Lorenzo elbowed Juan. 'Just look at her.'

Isabella had defied protocol and was standing, her mouth ajar. One hand was on her breast; the other sent Manolo a kiss.

'She is gagging to touch that tight-muscled ass, and he plays her as he did the bull, jutting forward his goodies,' Lorenzo said. 'Not badly endowed, but nothing like the bull's. Imagine Manolo and Isabella in a hotel room. He, trying to peel himself out of those trousers. She, finding out that most of the goodies are padding.'

123

A statuesque woman behind Isabella grabbed her shoulders and twisted the young woman away from the toreador, who had taken to bowing excessively.

'Isabella is in for a stern lecture from your aunt,' laughed Lorenzo.

'She deserves it, lusting after Manolo like that,' said Juan. 'She may be my cousin, but she's still hot.'

'You're jealous, admit it.'

'What I fancy is the toreador's job,' said Juan. 'If only I could be Manolo, just for one fight. Instead, I've got to go and close the shop. Ciao, amigo.'

'Off with you, dreamer.'

★

Juan Arollo's father owned a hardware store in Valencia, and the family lived in the apartment above. When Juan was a boy, his duty had been to move wheelbarrows and ladders into the shop when it started to rain. Now an adult, he gave the customers practical advice and, after closure, did the inventory.

His baby sister had died before she was one year old. On a rainy day, their mother had enclosed her in the pushchair with the plastic cover, making sure it was tight, and Leona turned blue before she became asphyxiated. Mother brought her to the doctor, who talked about pulmonary weakness. Juan never said anything about watching his sister in the pram, fighting for her life, while their mother chatted to a friend. He had been trained to be a quiet boy, and he did not understand what was happening.

124

By the time he was twenty-one, he was bored by the monotony of a traditional hardware supplier. He suggested they offer a key-cutting service, but Papá objected, saying that the machine was too expensive. Somehow, this had come to the attention of Isabella's mother, and the Countess offered to pay for the machine, but Papá refused. Juan, however, took the money and purchased a key-cutter. This caused a rift between his mother, who thanked her sister for the help, and Papá, who resented being belittled by having to accept gifts from the rich relatives of his wife.

Juan learnt to cut keys, but found few customers. His father forbade him from advertising the service, fearing it would seem that he, father of the Arollos, was unable to provide for his family.

One day, a farmer came into the shop, looking for metal ear-tags for sheep. Juan was dismayed that they did not stock them. However, Papá said, 'We can't stock everything. He can go elsewhere.'

Juan researched these metal bands, which clipped into an animal's ear like women's earrings. He ordered three sizes, for large, medium and small animals, together with rings for poultry legs. That worked well. The livestock owners chose their own stamp; the month and year of birth of the animal could also be embossed into the soft lead.

One day in January, when it snowed for the first time in more than thirty years, a farmer called to order ear-tags for sheep, but wanted someone to show him how to apply them. Papá, suddenly expert, drove out to the farm. On his return, he was in a bad mood and complained that a ram had nipped his leg. Under the circumstances, his wife allowed him to drink two glasses of brandy.

Papá started to shiver with fever. The bite didn't heal, and the whole leg swelled up. Juan drove him to the outpatients department of the Hospital la Salud. A blood sample showed that he had an infection, and Juan was told off for not bringing the patient in earlier.

The leg, tight as a drum skin, turned red, then blue, and the infection spread through the body. Papá died in a hospital ward, he who had never been away from home one single night. Mother and son sat at his bed. She held one calloused hand and cried silently. The last words of the dying man were to his son: 'This happened because you always want to do something risky and grandiose, instead of sticking to selling hardware.'

Juan could not say how sorry he was, because his father passed away too rapidly.

The funeral was held in the Iglesia del Sagrado Corazón. Some of Mother's noble family attended, because he, the reason they had ostracised her, now lay in a casket.

'Look at my new shoes,' exclaimed Isabella. 'Ruined. Damn it.' She had been forced to walk from the church porch to the grave in black satin, high-heeled pumps, which were indeed now covered in mud.

Mother had lost her husband of many years. He had been a tradesman, of peasant stock, and never accepted by the Count. Now with him gone, Mother assumed that she would be welcomed in her sister's family. In preparation for the funeral, she had spent money in a haberdashery, and sewn a new frock for herself and a black suit for Juan, to go with the top hat which had once belonged to the Duke's half-brother, a beautiful piece of millinery that Mother had somehow picked up after her sister's wedding. She had kept it in its original box on top of the bedroom wardrobe, hidden from her husband.

This marvel was now sitting on Juan's head, with a cushioning band fixed inside by Mother's nimble hands, because the hat was too big. Family and friends at the funeral, who would naturally have looked at Juan's face, now only admired the shiny, black top hat. Even Isabella manoeuvred herself close to him.

'You look good in that,' she complimented, during the refreshments in the restaurant near the church. 'Almost attractive.' The wink she gave him fixed itself on him more permanently than any sheep's ear-tag.

Isabella's mother said to her nephew, 'A bit of spit and rub, and even you turn out to look quite aristocratic. You should wear that hat more often.'

'Thank you, Countess,' replied Juan. 'I will try to find occasions to do so. Not more family funerals of course, that's not what I meant...'

His aunt had already lost interest and moved on.

*

After the loss of her husband, Mother fell into a depression. The Count and his family did not really take her back into the fold; they merely demonstrated civility towards her, which she interpreted as much more than it was. In her fragile self, she had always harboured doubts about her value and abilities. Marrying Papá had made it worse. The family belittled her: 'Imagine, she sews her own clothes.' Overly docile, she had accepted the role of dutiful wife to a lower-class husband. Who was she now? Her sister had made a gesture by giving Juan the money for the key-cutter. Isabella, that female snake, clearly had plans for Juan. Were they hoping to turn him away from her? Was her son not, right now, sitting in the bathtub, wearing the top hat?

Juan was of mixed aristocratic and peasant stock and, from an early age, he had felt uncomfortable in his own skin and needed to rebel with excessive behaviour, not knowing where he fitted in. Soaking in the bath, he stopped imagining being a toreador, having roses thrown at him by his cousin. He pulled out the bath plug. In reality, he had to face the fact that Mother's mental state was deteriorating and he did not intend to become her carer. And the business was in trouble. Customers asked where his father was and, when Juan told them that Papá was six feet underground, too many were going elsewhere. Something had to change in Juan's life.

He met up with Lorenzo in a tapas bar in downtown Valencia.

'Hombre, you look like shit,' Juan was greeted by his friend.

'My life has become crap,' he replied. 'Do you remember the Saturday bullfights we used to go to?'

'I remember the day we went with a group from school,' said Lorenzo. 'The girls ran after the toreador, clawing rhinestones off his clothes as souvenirs, until he looked like a plucked chicken.'

'Those were the days,' Juan said pensively. 'Nowadays, for me, every day I serve in the shop in the morning, drive home to Mother and calm her down, give her lunch, reassure her, and back to the store in the afternoon before an evening with Mother. Same thing all week. I'm going to crack up.'

'Sell the hardware store,' said Lorenzo. 'Invest the money in a different business. Go somewhere else. Do another job. You're only twenty-seven.'

'If I were ten years younger, I could train as a toreador.'

'You would have to be twenty years younger for that. Get off this idea. I have seen an interesting ad in the newspaper which might interest you, though. There is a circus for sale, and I thought of you.'

'I'm not a millionaire who can take on a big top and all that goes with it,' said Juan.

'It's being sold surprisingly cheap,' replied Lorenzo. 'Very soon, circuses won't be allowed to perform with animals. The animal conservationists are fast winning this battle. Maybe that is why the circus has come onto the market.'

Juan dunked a sugar cube in his brandy and popped it into his open mouth, while Lorenzo went on.

'Haven't you heard? The same is happening to bullfights. The Animal Protection League has declared bullfights to be cruelty to animals. They have started to campaign to ban them. The Portuguese found a way for the bull not to get killed. Their picadors are acrobats and often get gored. The Animal Protection League doesn't give a shit about that.'

'I don't want to listen to you,' objected Juan. 'It's all wrong. Our bullfights are part of being Spanish, our historic heritage. The blood running in our veins is linked to that of the bull. The *paso doble* is our military march. We venerate the bulls. How is that cruel? Untamed animals and brave men have always had an important relationship. Neither should ever be afraid to die.'

'Tell that to the women in Birkenstock sandals,' said Lorenzo. 'They sit in offices, munching muesli. They don't stroke the dead bull's body on the way out of the arena, and rub his reeking sweat into their breasts, or elsewhere.'

'What shall I do?' Juan brought the conversation back to his problem. 'I can't stand my boring life any longer.'

'Any luck with your cousin Isabella?'

'Sure, she's going to date an overweight loser who talks about drill bit sizes.'

'Go and find out more about the circus for sale. Here, I brought the ad.'

Juan glanced at the paper. 'Maybe the circus is for sale because they have depressing clowns?'

'Well then, you should fit right in.'

★

The circus was called Maravilla, the Wonder Circus. Juan made an appointment to see the circus owner, Señor Mara.

Driving the jeep out of Valencia, inland and along the Júcar River into wild countryside, Juan eventually came to the farm. The farmhouse was small compared to the barn. At the barn door, the circus owner, in his late fifties, was clearly waiting, perhaps desperate to sell.

When Juan was led into the barn, he realised why it was so large. It had to accommodate the big top canvas, stanchions and coils of rope, all folded and kept off the ground so as not to go mouldy or rust when not in use. Beyond, in the darkness of the place, was a round cage made of high steel bars concreted into the ground, from where two large, luminous eyes stared at him.

'Her name is Bashira,' said Señor Mara. 'She is a Royal Bengal tigress, six and a half years old.'

A thrill of excitement shot through Juan. 'Is the cat included in the sale?'

'You have to refer to her and address her as Your Highness.'

Juan gave a short bark of a laugh. Bashira's eyes narrowed.

'Everything is included in the sale,' said Mara, 'even the contracts with the two clowns, Burly and Toothbrush, the two acrobats, the ballerina and the pair of trapeze artists, plus the support staff, of which there are currently four. Everyone lends a hand. We are one big family.'

The tiger stood up and padded on large, soft-looking paws to the bars, close to where Juan had dared to laugh at her. Her shoulder blades rolled under an amazing striped pelt. The tips of her long, curved whiskers touched the metal. Her whole body twitched. She stopped, lifted her head and continued to glare at Juan, the unknown intruder.

'Is Your Highness tamed?' Juan asked in a strangled voice.

'That depends on the tamer,' said Mara. 'In this circus, it's the ring master, myself. Are you planning to have a go if you buy?'

'Definitely.'

'Her Highness has calmed down since the birth of her son. Before that, her hormones, hombre, I tell you.' Señor Mara fluttered his hand. 'The audience hardly dared sit down.'

'Her Royal Highness has a son?'

'Over there.' In an extension to the large cage, further into the darkness, was a smaller cage separated from Bashira's by a sash metal door, now closed. A much smaller and slimmer tiger was curled up on a piece of canvas cloth, sleeping like a gigantic house cat. 'He is only six months old, but a fast learner. We call him Bambi.'

'Bambi? Bambi is a baby deer.'

'You have no experience with the world of theatre, shows, circuses, do you?'

'I work in a hardware store, selling screws. I've never felt like calling any one of them Bambi.'

'Bambi brings in parents with their children,' said Mara. 'The juxtaposition of dangerous versus Disney animal works. You'll learn. There is the horse, of course, but he is not a performer. He pulls the cables when we raise the top and helps move the stanchions. He's white, so you can tint his mane and tail, and use him in the ring. Fifi, the female trapeze artist, is willing to pirouette on his back, if you are short of acts.' After an awkward pause, Mara looked Juan up and down.

'Young,' he pronounced. 'You are young to take on this responsibility. Wife? No?'

The tigress emitted a bone-chilling, drawn-out roar.

'She likes you,' Mara said happily.

Juan had seen right into the back of her open mouth. 'For lunch or supper?'

'You've got a sense of humour. Clown work, perhaps?'

'No, I've done enough of that already.'

The ring master grinned. 'I was thirty-one when I started this circus company from scratch. A street show with a monkey, two poodles, and my daughter balancing on my out-stretched hand. The circus grew larger, but I made mistakes because I am too cautious. A circus owner needs guts, flair and people skills. Lots can go wrong, all the time, I have to warn you. A large downside of owning a circus nowadays is the bureaucracy necessary with the local administrations of the towns in which we set up. A real bore.'

'How about the rumour of banning circus animals?' asked Juan.

'That's a tricky one,' said Señor Mara. 'The Animal Protection League is working on it. Every circus will be considered individually.'

'Circus Maravilla has to be top on the prohibition list,' said Juan. 'Your Royal Bengal tiger is not exactly a performing poodle, is she? What then?'

Mara pretended not to understand the question. 'Her overheads are big, I admit,' he started, 'but the income from her is also big.' He sighed theatrically. 'Bashira belongs to this circus. She means more to me than my

133

wife,' he confessed. 'That must stay between us. I hope you will grow close to her, too. Few have the privilege of taming such a magnificent animal. I am dedicated to her well-being. While you were driving in, you might have noticed I am erecting a double row of four-metre-high steel fencing around my three acres. There is also a large pond planned, the water of which will be drawn off from the Júcar River and back to it. All that for Bashira and her son. Work advances slowly and is expensive. If I sell the circus, it can go faster.'

'But Bashira will belong to the new owner.'

'Maybe an arrangement could be made for the tigers to have time off on my farm.' The tone of Mara's voice changed. 'Are you seriously interested in buying, or are you just playing me around?'

'I live with my mother in a small apartment above the shop,' said Juan. 'Where would I put the tent, Her Highness and all the other things?'

'I'll lease you the barn on a yearly contract. For the first year, you can have it for free. That way, I will still have Bashira to look after. I will also help you move the tigers, until you are confident enough to do it on your own. What else can I do, retired all day long in this remote farm with my nagging wife?'

'You could stay on as my consultant,' suggested Juan. 'I am new at this and have many, many questions. For instance, what does Bashira eat?'

'She and Bambi eat the flesh of a whole horse in ten days,' replied Mara. 'I have an arrangement with a pet crematorium. I can also introduce you to the training routine of the tigers. It is simple. With time, you will want to elaborate on it. You will want to change acts and the style of the show to make it yours. You are young. I am a worn-out sixty-year-old.'

'How do Bashira and Bambi travel from one town to another?'

'In caged trailers.'

'Are your employees easy to manage?'

'For starters, they'll love you because you'll be saving their asses. After that, your relationship with them is up to your skills with people. Toothbrush is French. Watch his drinking.'

'I haven't signed on the dotted line yet.'

'Let me introduce you to Bashira.' Señor Mara took a key ring from his belt and unlocked the padlock on the double-door trap of the cage.

Juan stepped back. 'Are you insured?'

'That's another thing we will have to talk about. I can transfer my performers' insurance and public liability certificate into your name. With tigers like these, you can imagine the premium. Although, I hear this is now coming down significantly.'

'Sure,' mocked Juan. He then found himself inside a cage with a full-size Royal Bengal tigress. He stepped behind Mara.

'Her Highness has not had lunch yet,' said Mara.

'I've seen the animal close up. Beautiful. Can I leave now?'

'Is that the best you can do?' Mara concentrated on Juan's face. While their attention was drawn elsewhere, Bashira began to prowl closer to them. Juan could smell her strong feral whiff.

'Down!' ordered Mara, feeling the tiger closing up behind him. To the fast-breathing Juan, he said, 'Don't make any sudden movements. Down, Bashira!' he repeated more forcefully.

The animal looked around her as if this order did not concern her. However, at the next 'Down, Bashira', she sat back on her haunches and, when Mara turned slowly to face her, she was flat on the ground in surrender, front legs stretched in front of her.

'Good girl,' praised Mara. To Juan he said, 'Now you can stroke her.'

'I think I'll do that another time.'

'Hold out your hand for her to smell you first.'

Juan tried his best, but his hand was still one metre away from the face of the tiger. Mara grabbed Juan's arm and brought his hand right in front of the animal's face. Juan felt the warmth of the breath coming from her nostrils.

'Nice man, nice man.' The ring master patted Juan's head. 'Now, stroke her head between her eyes, and upwards to the forehead.'

Juan stopped thinking and did what he was told to do. The short fur felt coarse, the skull beneath it hard. Bashira closed her eyes. She had long lashes. She opened her eyes again, and his hand was still caressing her. Juan started to weep.

'It feels like being allowed into the original paradise before man destroyed it,' Mara said softly.

The magical moment came to an end. Bashira stayed in the cage; the men left the barn. Juan dried his eyes with his sleeve.

'I want to do everything I can to make it up to the tigress for having lost her habitat in India,' Juan said emotionally.

'She comes from Bangladesh.'

Mara put his hand around Juan's shoulder. 'Next Sunday, Circus Maravilla will give its last performance in Zaragoza at three o'clock in the afternoon. I invite you to come and see what we have developed under my tutelage.'

'Thank you,' said Juan. 'I'll be there, and after that I will make my decision.'

'Clever young man. You're obviously brighter than I am. You'll do well. See you.'

Juan went back to his jeep, running the fingers which had touched the tiger's fur along his cheeks. A glimpse into paradise. Mara was right.

At home, Mother listened to her son's account of the visit.

'Juan,' her voice was hoarse with hysteria, 'a Bengal tiger is a very dangerous animal, a man-eater. It cannot be tamed. It is born as a carnivorous predator. Don't do that to me. I don't want to have to pick up what's left of you with a pan and brush.'

'No, Mother. You will help me with the costumes of the performers. Circus Maravilla will become the famous Circus Arollo.' He set the top hat on his head and spread out his hands. 'Señoras, Señores y Niños, bienvenidos, welcome, bienvenus, to Circus Arollo. All I need is a black dress coat, spats and a whip. The moustache I will start to grow from today.'

'Help us all,' whimpered his mother, and she crossed herself.

Juan and Lorenzo met up in the tapas bar.

'Guess what,' Juan started.

'You bought the circus? Hombre, that's cool. Now I won't have to run away to the circus. You'll give me a job there, won't you?'

'Publicity. Advertising. You've just done a course in that. Help me get audiences into the tent. For starters, it will be food and a handful of pocket money.'

'I accept, as long as you let me walk the tightrope. I always dreamt of that.'

'OK, you can do that, while I'm learning to stretch my head into the open mouth of a humungous tiger. Life is not going to be boring any longer.'

★

Juan worked day and most of the night through the winter to create his own circus programme, after having seen what Circus Maravilla offered during their last performance. Lorenzo, with whom he met up often, told him that a brand image was most important. Drowning much red wine, they sketched, discussed and made decisions. Circus Arollo would need a grand opening in spring to imprint its existence on people's minds.

Frequent meetings were held in the circus ring to discuss the programme. Everyone present had the right to an opinion. It progressed well. Even the tall, snooty French clown, Toothbrush, contributed. Juan brought in Spanish flair. A mock bullfight was decided on;

Toothbrush was to be the toreador, with Burly made up as a bull. Everything would go wrong for the toreador.

The trapeze number was souped up. The artists would wear Mother's feather-enhanced costumes, turning them into birds of paradise in the coloured spotlights, their long, feathery tails sailing behind them.

Lorenzo worked tirelessly on the publicity. Circus Maravilla had only been known in the north-east of Spain. Lorenzo's ambition was to make Arollo internationally famous. An article appeared in *Paris Match*, four pages with pictures. It compared the traditional family circus with what would be Circus Arollo's style. One photo showed a mother sewing at a table, while a tutu'd trapeze artist performed overhead. There were the clowns, sitting on a swing, laughing and holding onto each other as if they were in danger, three feet above the grass. And, of course, on the front page of the magazine, was a portrait photo of Juan in top hat, dress suit, spats and whip, with a temporarily glued-on handlebar moustache. He was compared to Philip Astley, the eighteenth-century founder of the modern circus and originator of the ring master's outfit. The article called Circus Arollo a unique 'Spanish trend' circus.

Meanwhile, Juan had to work on the tigers. 'Routine is good,' said Mara. 'Tamed wild animals, like children, do best in a structured life.'

And Mara supervised as, every night at ten, Juan entered the cage and unrolled his sleeping bag. Before slipping into it, he took a fat sardine out of his pocket and hand-fed it to Bashira. Five minutes later, she came to ask for another one, and he was ready. He asked her to sit for him and then lie down. When she obeyed, she received the second fish. Then, with puzzled interest, she watched her tamer get into the bag and zip it up. At eleven o'clock, Mara at the barn door switched out the light.

At times, during the night, Juan would feel Bashira's whiskers tickling his face. When he opened his eyes, her head was right next to his. She needed to reassure herself of who he was, and how he breathed.

At seven-thirty in the morning, Juan left the barn to go to the house to get dressed and have a coffee. Bashira eventually accompanied him to the cage door, where he succeeded in making her sit and lift up her paw.

'Have a nice day,' Juan would say to her, restraining himself from throwing his arms around her neck to kiss her, even though he believed that she would let him.

Bambi was an independent little tiger. He slept curled around his *furia roja* football of the Spanish national team, and distributed paw swipes if anyone tried to take it away from him. Juan made slow progress with him. Get too close, and the kitten turned into a spitting, clawing bundle.

Mara suggested it was time to bring Bashira into the circus ring for practice. Once moved from the caged trailer into the performance cage, Bashira was calmly self-confident. She knew the routine she had done with Mara for years; Juan only had to prompt her. After a taped drum roll, she reared up, front paws sawing the air, and roared frighteningly. She jumped over Juan lying on the ground between two drum tables. Throughout these practices, Mara was close to the cage, softly talking

140

to Bashira. On the opposite side was a stagehand with a taser, and another stood at the pull cord of a curtain bunched at the top of the circular cage – a curtain which could drop at one tug.

Winter drew to a close, and they were ready. The publicity had worked, and it felt as if the world, so full of unpleasantness, needed an escape to where clowns gambolled and glitter dazzled. Juan's mother had always liked to embroider and put bits of cloth together, but now... She glowed with pride. Her name was printed in the circus programme. She had appeared on television. She was a new woman.

Mara shook Juan's hand. 'Bravo,' he said. 'I knew you were bright and had the right fire in you. I can retire now.'

'Not so fast,' Juan objected. 'Stay as my counsel until after the grand opening on St Crescentia's day in Valencia.'

The performance was announced as presenting a baby Bengal Tiger to the public for the first time, and as donating twenty per cent of the day's income to the WWF.

★

The big day arrived. St Crescentia was benign, the sky an undisturbed blue. A soft breeze played with the flags on the big top.

Behind this perfect scene was Mara, supervising Bashira and Bambi's safe transport from the farm to Valencia. He had been a generous man throughout and, for this first spectacle, had given Juan his calliope organ, an antique which held nostalgic associations of merry-go-rounds and travelling fairs to everyone over the age of fifty.

Members of the press arrived an hour before the performance. They wanted to interview Juan, to see the tigers, and to poke their noses backstage, until the clowns came running and shooting at them with colour puff guns.

By half-past two, all the seats were taken, and extra benches had to be installed. The national television networks were there with their cameras on dollies.

Lorenzo was highly charged. 'This beats any bullfight,' he enthused. 'Isn't that what you dreamt about? Personally, I don't know how you do it. You are a brave man, Juan Arollo. I salute you.'

'I would salute back, but my hat would come off,' Juan replied. 'So I say: you have proven to be a true friend. Thank you, Lorenzo.' He tucked the tip of the whip handle up against the rim of his top hat.

Three o'clock. The trumpets sounded, the calliope was played, and the thick canvas entrance panel was closed.

Juan gave his handlebar moustache a twirl, straightened the top hat on his head and welcomed everyone.

The trumpet announced the first clown number. The *pasa doble* accompanied the spoof bullfight, in which everything went wrong. It ended with the spear stuck in the bull's bottom, and the toreador on his knees, offering flowers to the bull to ward off further attacks.

As Fifi, the trapeze artist, reached out from the small platform to catch the swinging bar, she fell off, just like that. There was no safety net. The audience shrieked. Somehow, she managed to catch a trailing rope, on which she twirled and swung, while the audience recovered their breath. Some thought that, with all the feathers sewn to her costume, she was probably able to fly. Juan chuckled at the success of the feigned mistake and recovery: an old circus trick, but still a good one.

Toothbrush returned, dressed as a flamenco dancer, keeping the Spanish burlesque mood. 'Her' performance was interrupted by a mouse – actually, a cunningly operated spotlight – and 'she' delighted the crowd by trying to stamp on the mouse in mid-flamenco dance. Frilled red petticoats slipped off one by one, and landed in a circle around Toothbrush's feet. Finally, he picked up the 'dead' mouse and threw it into the crowd. Burly ran around, hurling more 'mice' into the audience; these were little brown bags, sewn by Juan's mother, and filled with sweets.

The painted and stained horse cantered out from the swag-curtained artists' entrance, ridden by a young American trick-rider Juan had hired. In a black bodysuit, she rolled around on the horse's back, did a *salto* and then stood, arms out, while the horse galloped round the ring. Not only did she not fall off, she didn't even sway. Her long, blond hair streamed from her head. The act finished with her picking up a tangerine from the floor with her mouth as she galloped past, and the atmosphere in the tent was electric. The American teenager, hopping off the back of the horse, bowed to Juan, her athletic body in a lean black arc. He tipped his hat with the handle of his whip.

And then came the build-up to the main attraction everyone had been waiting for – the tigers. While some children were chosen to walk around the ring waving flags, the stagehands rushed in with sections of cage and clicked them into each other. The spectators' attention was further diverted from the construction work by Burly, the chubby clown, sitting on a swing high up in the apex of the tent, screaming from fear as he was lowered in fitful spurts by Toothbrush, who was too busy flirting with ladies in the audience.

Once the tiger cage was securely in place and the tunnel from the outside trailer ready, there was a momentous drum roll. In the silence which followed, people craned their necks, twisting their fingers into each other. A tiger appeared behind the sash door, which was raised permitting Bambi to stalk into the performance cage. An admiring 'Ah' went through the crowd. The young tiger took his time, looking around him. He went to the stanchions and rose on his hind legs, his long tail swishing, and showing the pale fur on his tummy. Children waved to him. Bambi dropped down and ran to the other side of the cage, where he did the same. 'Ah' came the reaction from that slice of the tent. He threw a glance over his back and seemed to notice his tail, still swishing. He tried to catch it with his mouth, but the tail escaped. Bambi chased it, increasing his speed until he was running in a tight circle, snapping at air.

Juan entered the cage, crossed his arms and shook his head slowly. Bambi stopped the game and went to

144

stand in front of Juan, who ordered him to sit, flicking his finger down. A soft drum roll came. Bambi sat and pushed his tongue all the way out at Juan. Children giggled wildly; adults smiled.

Juan looked offended and, pointing his whip, ordered the tiger to lie down. Bambi considered this, but then swiped with his paw at the whip. It fell from Juan's hand: what a disgrace!

The children loved it. Some tried to clamber into the ring. Grabbing their clothes, parents held them back.

Juan thanked Bambi for his performance and asked him politely to leave, but the tiger, obviously liking to show off, hid behind a drum table and could not be coaxed into the tunnel. Toothbrush lobbed the *furia roja* football over the cage wall. Bambi and Juan lunged for it, but the tiger got there first. The act finished with Bambi taking a titbit of meat from Juan's hand, dropping the ball to do so. Juan picked it up and tossed it into the open tunnel. In an instant, Bambi was in the tunnel, running after the ball, and the sash came down.

A white sheet was lowered over the artists' entrance. Onto it was projected a film Lorenzo had put together with Mara. Bengal tigers were shown, living free in the mangrove swamps of Bangladesh. A voice-over said that fewer than two thousand still lived in the wild. The film switched to Bashira, pregnant on the farm, and then the birth of Bambi, which Mara had filmed six months ago. It finished with the tigers' recreation park being built on the farm, and was tied in to the contribution to the WWF, which this circus performance was advertised to be all about.

To a new drum roll, Juan let himself into the performance cage, setting the hat straight, twirling his moustache ends and watching the tunnel. Mara, dressed in a red romper suit with white polka dots as if part of the act, took up position on one side of the cage, a stagehand in the same outfit with a hidden taser on the other. No tiger came through the tunnel. A fresh drum roll. The clowns started to clap and slowly the whole audience clapped, shouting, 'Tiger, tiger.'

'Do you want to meet the baby tiger's mother?'

'Yes,' they shouted.

'I can't hear you.'

'Yeeees.'

Bashira was on her way. Juan felt the vibration of the cage. Bashira appeared, crouch-walking through the tunnel. Juan felt dehydrated from fear. In the silence, surely the public could hear the thumping of his heart in his chest. Inside the cage, Bashira straightened up and shook herself. The audience responded with admiring gasps.

Juan announced, 'Your Highness, I adore you. I am your slave.'

One of her furry ears twitched. As the routine had been practised, she hopped up onto a drum table and sat, concentrating on Juan, but still attentive to her old master, Mara, who was whispering to her. She was in a good mood. Her yellow eyes shone clear and were fully open. Her muscles seemed relaxed.

Juan asked her to jump onto the next drum table, by flicking his whip.

Bashira gave him a look of *How interesting is that?*

'Please, Bashira,' Juan pleaded.

She got up and made the jump, and the next and the next, to end up where she had started from. The public applauded. Almost irritated, Bashira glanced back at them over her shoulder.

The next part of the act would involve Bashira emitting an intimidating roar, before jumping down to Juan, prostrated on the ground, and licking his face. But, as he hitched up his trousers to lie down, he noticed that the big top's entrance panel was being opened. *Why this distraction?* he fretted. Everything was in place, everyone inside, and the tiger act could not be disturbed.

All attention, however, was focused on the light streaming in through the opening. A person appeared, a woman with a small dog on a lead next to her. When she was struck by the circus floodlights, Juan flinched. *Isabella!*

'Hi, cousin,' she shouted into the performance cage, coming to a halt right next to the taser man. What he had taken for a dog was in reality a rhesus monkey.

Bashira lifted her head. Her body twitched.

'Leave. Go away and take that monkey with you,' Juan hissed to his cousin.

'It's a gift for you. I bought it from some travellers. The monkey can do tricks. And he came with a blue velvet jacket.' Isabella started to root around in the expensive handbag hanging from her shoulder. 'You are famous now,' she said, pulling out a doll's jacket embroidered with gold thread.

'Go away, Isabella. You're upsetting the tiger.'

'You are much more interesting than I thought.' She turned to the taser man. 'Isn't he interesting?'

'Señorita, go outside, we implore you.'

'I'm willing to date you,' she continued undisturbed, as if she and Juan were alone somewhere having a chat.

The monkey tried to climb up the taser man's red polka-dotted trouser leg.

Bashira gave a growl Juan had never heard her make before. The monkey, having smelled a predator, became agitated. His little head slipped the collar. The audience was confused, wondering if this was part of the act. The monkey tried unsuccessfully to dig itself into the sawdust, and then panicked and stupidly headed for the cage, squeezing through the gap between the stanchions. It did not have time to realise how large the danger was, for Bashira was already upon it, pinning it down under her claws. The animal's high-pitched screeching ended with Bashira biting its head off. The monkey's tail dangled from Bashira's bloody mouth, before its remains fell from the tiger's teeth onto the drum table.

'Well, that's not very nice. I come with a gift,' complained Isabella, 'and that stupid tiger you play with has eaten it.'

The taser man had heard enough. He took Isabella by her shoulders, turned her and escorted her out of the tent, her shoes hardly touching the ground.

There was a mixed reaction from the crowd. Children wept, and some people were threading themselves along the seats to leave in protest. The rest sat, dumbfounded.

Juan lifted a drum table to kick the monkey's chewed remains underneath it, while Mara drew Bashira's attention and clucked, soothingly. The atmosphere relaxed; the public thought the whole episode had been part of the act. Had the mouse not been a fake?

Juan turned back to Bashira, and Mara murmured to her. She jumped up on her drum table, while Juan took position on the ground to wait for her to come down and lick his face.

'Don't do it,' Mara called out. 'She has blood on her lips.'

'I am doing the finale,' replied Juan, 'otherwise we're ending with a flop.'

Mara signalled to the soundman, and a fanfare rang out, bringing everyone's attention back to the man in the cage with the tiger. Bashira lowered herself ominously from the drum table and stalked over to Juan. She placed her front paws on him, before bending towards his face. But she stopped short and, with her hind leg, scratched her neck.

Juan lifted his upper body to see what she was doing. She stopped scratching and jumped at him, knocking him back flat. Pinning him to the ground, she started to tear at his jacket. Juan tried to roll away from under her, but she kept him her prisoner. She growled, and her eyes flashed yellow danger. When Juan noticed her salivating, he knew she would eat him. He fought for his life. He used his hat to protect his face, while his legs kicked against her belly. The taser dart hit the tiger's back.

A stagehand tugged the pull cord, releasing the bunched curtain to drop over the performance cage like a tea-cosy over a teapot.

The audience screamed. In panic, they got up and

rushed towards the exit, stumbling over benches and trampling those less able. Stampede.

Juan's mother, in her sewing corner, sank to her knees praying, the small cross on the chain in one hand, her eyes closed. When the curtain came down to spare the public a gruesome scene, she sighed, 'I told you so,' before fainting.

★

In front of A&E at the Hospital la Salud, a man in a red romper suit with polka dots jumped out of the back of the ambulance. Dr Lopez, on duty with an intern, looked at him.

'What on earth have we got here?' he exclaimed. 'What kind of circus is this?'

'Circus Arollo,' said the ambulance driver, as they pulled out a gurney on which lay the patient, covered in a large white sheet, its two front corners knotted together. As they pushed it through the automatic doors, Dr Lopez followed, shaking his head.

'The patient's still got his hat on.'

In an examination cubicle, a nurse came forward to help. The taser man watched through a gap in the curtains.

The paramedic explained the situation. 'Apparently, a tiger act in the circus went wrong. The ring master had already been wrapped in a sheet to spare the public. We just loaded him up.'

'Haven't you even uncovered him? What happened to first aid?' Lopez sounded stressed.

'It's only a ten-minute drive,' said the paramedic. 'From the size of the body, we reckoned we'd wait for some specialist help.'

'Just what we needed on St Crescentia day,' the intern said sarcastically. Bloodstains had started to expand on the sheet, under which nothing moved.

'It's a top hat,' Teresa, the nurse, was undoing the knot in the sheet, and her voice began to quaver. 'It must be Señor Arollo. Oh God, has he been killed by the famous Bengal tiger?'

'Why would you think that?'

'He always wears a black top hat. Haven't you heard of Circus Arollo?'

'I'm too old and too busy to go to the circus. You two, sheet off,' ordered the doctor. 'Time is essential.'

'I don't dare uncover what must be left of him.' Teresa stepped back.

'Then you shouldn't be in A&E.'

'Don't be hard on the nurse,' said the intern. 'A man half-eaten by a full-grown tiger is not for everybody's eyes.'

'If we act fast, maybe…' Lopez grabbed the sheet and yanked it off the body.

The hat stayed put.

All four jumped back.

On the gurney lay a large tiger on its back, front legs curled, its muzzle wedged into a black top hat.

'The tiger is dead,' announced Lopez, not finding a pulse. 'The animal must have died of asphyxiation. The hat is rammed tight over its face. Help me prise it off, someone.'

'I did have to taser the tiger. That might be a factor,' said the man in the red romper suit.

'How sad. Such a beautiful animal.' The intern stepped forward. The hat came off with a popping sound. Fresh blood showed around the tiger's mouth; the staring eyes were bloodshot.

'You don't see that very often.' Lopez was pensive.

Teresa crossed herself. 'Thank you, St Crescentia. Thank you for sparing Señor Arollo. His circus is one of the best things in Spain. What a blessing.'

'Not for the tiger.' Lopez covered Bashira's body and handed the hat to Teresa. 'Someone had better contact the animal crematorium.'

PANDEMIC

Ignatius was called Iggy by everyone. It sounded like 'eggy', but he did not let it get to him, because the real Ignatius was protected, nestled deep inside. In there was the real him, still alive after thirty-seven years of sublimation, and it had nothing to do with the smell of eggs. Sometimes, it rose up in dreams during which he felt safely surrounded by prosperity and undisguised affection. Sadly, they were only dreams.

Ignatius groaned and rubbed his coccyx. He had been sitting in front of the computer playing patience for over an hour, instead of finalising the report on a multiple vehicle pile-up on the A1. Iggy was employed by an insurance company. Due to the pandemic, he was forced to work from home, which he found almost impossible. Perhaps he could manage it if he successfully pictured himself still at his desk in the cool of his office, its smart, modern décor surrounding him. He couldn't. What made it most difficult was not the unmade, messy bed, but the kitchen pedal bin, its lid held open by pizza boxes, double fries cartons and baked bean cans. He should wash his clothes, the bedsheets and towels; he should empty the bin.

However, an inexplicable lethargy prevented him from doing daily chores.

Iggy clicked the game away. The queen was the wrong colour; the game would not have come out. Instead, he began to read his draft report, but found that he wasn't the least bit interested in its contents. Just then, the shrill barking of a neighbour's dog started up. The walls of River Quay Apartments had to be made of cardboard.

Suddenly, Iggy yelled, 'Shut up!', and to his surprise the barking stopped. Iggy grinned. He started typing. The barking resumed.

Alexa hummed and, in her bland voice, announced, 'Video meeting in ten minutes.'

Iggy had forgotten. Once a month, the CEO, Armel Duke, insisted on 'seeing' his employees who were working from home. Pertinent questions would be asked, and Duke expected some proof that good work had been achieved. Iggy would have to lie about his progress again.

Being 'seen' by the boss entailed preparing a background, to create a satisfactory visual impact. Many opted for bookshelves; some used pleasing pictures. Women often decided on flowers. For previous virtual meetings, Iggy had used drawn curtains as a backdrop, but one of the panels had come off the rod. The only option in the studio flat had to be the wall next to the built-in cupboard, currently very bland, white and empty. Duke's attention would thus be fixed exclusively on Iggy throughout the meeting: bad tactics.

Under the bed was a cardboard box bearing the name

154

of a removals company, one which Iggy had never got round to unpacking since his move two and a half years ago. It contained posters, and he unrolled some to remind himself of what they were. Nothing seemed appropriate.

The dog barked on and on. It was five minutes to the video meeting. Iggy unrolled a poster of Sylvester Stallone in *Rocky*, picked up Sellotape from the table drawer and, standing on tiptoe, stuck the poster to the wall. He adjusted the positions of table, computer and chair, and wriggled until his head and bust were visible in the middle of the screen. The boss would not be able to see that Iggy was not wearing trousers, only a shirt and unclean underpants. The thought pleased Iggy unhealthily.

Once the pandemic was over, Duke would probably fire Iggy. Did it matter? Not much, as Iggy could not see the point of his job. The money mattered though. With his salary, he could just about afford this place, although it consisted of one room only: a studio for which he had to pay too much rent as it had a Juliet balcony overlooking the river.

He got up and went to stand at the waist-high metal balcony. Was this all there was? A barking poodle, and a small section of river which did not flow. It lay still and dark. Leaves and natural debris sat on its surface. It was neither romantic, nor were there any swans, both of which the estate agent's brochure had promised. It was high time Iggy found a way to better his situation and move into larger, more private premises. 'How?' he called out, and it sounded like the howl of a beaten dog.

What Iggy needed was enough money to improve

the dissatisfying situation he was caught in. His ancestor, his great-grandfather Ignatius, had had money and refinement. In Iggy's veins ran the blood of big spenders and snobs. Men and women who did not live in fear of disaster or cower behind insurance cover. With their passing, had all the money gone? Two of them were still alive: his aunts, silly elderly women, Maureen and Adela. They were sitting on some money still, but had lost any attitude of grandeur.

Duke's secretary was online. She announced the imminent appearance of the boss. Iggy ran back to the computer. Behind him, Stallone's biceps shone like basted meat.

Duke's face materialised almost simultaneously with the poster coming off the wall. The paper caught on Iggy's head. He brushed it off and shoved the poster behind him, out of sight.

'When you are ready,' said Duke, the mockery barely concealed.

Someone else in the office had found time to write the report on the accident. Iggy hid a smile behind his cupped hand.

'What have you done about the statistical forecast for next month? It was due to be handed in last Monday.'

Iggy's smile froze. 'Nothing,' was not an option. Iggy squirmed and talked about the impact of increased speeding on roads emptied by the pandemic.

Duke was not in the mood for jibber-jabbering. However, just as his face approached the camera, there was a hiss, a puff, and a vicious green light as the face dwindled to pinhead-size and vanished. Power cut.

Duke would of course think that Iggy had done this deliberately. At the entrance cupboard, he replaced the blown fuse. It was fiddly work. The computer came back on, but Duke had given up. Best of all, the poodle had shut up.

Iggy decided, instead of contacting the office and apologising for the power cut his end, he would pay his aunts a visit. In the face of his charm and determination, surely they would have to relent and make some of their money over to him. 'As soon as possible,' he said as he put on his blue cord jacket.

Leaving home was not allowed, except to deliver food and medicine to people who were sheltering – not meeting them of course; just leaving the goods in front of their doors. His aunts were sheltering, and he bought food for them like the good little nephew he was. As he left, from the non-dog-owning neighbour came the thumping of rock music, mega loud. This stay home torture would last at least three months Boris had said, standing at his lectern in Downing Street.

★

Ignatius enjoyed walking in the fresh air up De Parys Avenue in Bedford. He was carrying a full Waitrose reusable bag. It was April, his birthday month; he would turn thirty-eight. A gentle breeze ruffled his dark blond hair. The crowns of the silver maple giants lining the avenue, which led to the grand entrance into Bedford Park, were a tender green, the spring colour of leaves unfurling.

157

Everything around Iggy seemed to belie the fact that a virus from a bat had spread beyond China and was infesting countries like Italy, where a whole village had been wiped out. A disease which imprisoned so many. It would vanish, as had others before, especially if one followed government directions to wash hands and keep a distance. But, for the moment, Covid-19, as it had been named, seemed to grow in strength every day, according to the news, targeting the vulnerable and the elderly, who had to be sheltered by isolation. It was fascinating to watch the infection graph peaking.

Striding along, the young man glanced at the familiar houses he was passing: number seventy-four with the untidy front garden, number seventy-six with a low wall to a gravelled front. At the next, illogically numbered seventy-seven, an imposing Victorian four-storey brick mansion named *Firecombe*, he crossed the paving stones to a bricked arch over an oak door with a stained-glass inset.

Houses in this part of Bedford had been built in the late 1800s and displayed intricate and proud red brickwork, testimony to the London Brick Company which had moved to a Bedfordshire village and was producing five hundred million bricks a year at that time. Iggy's great-grandfather, after whom he had been named, had been a manager of the works. The man was said to have been a stickler for right angles, straight plumb lines and coved pointing. Some of this perfectionism had spilled into his private life. He liked the number seven, a clean, upstanding, no-nonsense number. *Firecombe*, built in 1877, was intended to become his family's ancestral home. Its site was on the even-numbered side of the avenue, but Old Ignatius would have none of that; his house was to be number seventy-seven – which irritated postmen for years to come.

Sheltered under the porch from the twizzling, winged seeds of the maples, young Ignatius, in his worn, cord jacket, unlocked the heavy door and gazed into the hall; the family history immediately overwhelmed him once again. How could the impact of one domineering man linger, even though he had died forty-five years before his namesake's birth? His presence, the sharp breath of the man, seemed to adhere to the walls and bring out the black and white of the tiled flooring.

Of course, Iggy knew the house rules, laid out all those years ago. The beautiful garden apartment was to be occupied by the head of the family, while the following generation would live on the spacious first floor. The second and third floors were needed to house Ignatius's *objets d'art* and personal things, which were nobody else's business.

After the death of Ignatius in 1937 at the age of ninety, his wife, deprived of strength and initiative, followed suit three months later. Both now lay under a granite slab in Bedford Park's cemetery. *Never to be forgotten* was carved. As if it were an order.

The next in line, Ignatius's son, Victor, moved down into the garden flat with his wife, Marie. Victor was, of course, Iggy's grandfather, whom he got to know reasonably well during the twelve years their lives overlapped. Victor and Marie had been kind to Iggy when their youngest daughter, Iggy's dear mother Iris,

159

slipped away in that horrid, smelly white room in the hospital.

'Cancer took her before she was forty,' Marie cried. Iggy, eight years old, did not understand cancer, except that it was a crab. His life went on quite normally – except, of course, where there should have been a mother, there was nothing.

Now, he hesitated entering the house, because he noticed two new metal letter-boxes to the side of the door, one of them painted bright red. Iggy approached. On one was a label *Tran Nagung*, on the other, *Anderson and Frost*. This was deface-ism! Iggy gulped. Ignatius and Victor would have been livid, and quite rightly, he thought, stepping over the lintel into *Firecombe*, where light streaming through the stained glass costumed him kaleidoscopically.

He put the Waitrose bag down to close the door of number seventy-seven behind him. He slipped the borrowed key back into his pocket. He shouldn't have to borrow a key which let him into a house that ought to belong to him. Ignatius was dead, his son Victor was dead. Victor did not have a son, but three daughters. One of them, his mother, married and had a son – him. The other two daughters never married and now lived in the lovely garden flat, even though the next male in the family line was unquestionably him. How could he claim that right after so much time, during which the selfish maiden aunts would never talk about it, ensconced as they were in luxury, while he...? For Maureen and Adela, Iggy was just an unimportant nephew who could jolly well wait until they were gone.

One winter, when both of them had got flu, he had crossed his fingers. However, tough as old boots, they recovered, became louder and more demanding. Iggy carried around with him deep-seated anger and had for a long time. His doctor suggested he buy an aquarium and watch fish swim around, to bring down his anxiety level.

He reached out and cupped the carved pineapple newel ball at the foot of the wide, oak staircase. Oh, how it had hurt in his tender parts after sliding down the banister! Yes, Iggy had been a lonely boy in this house, while his mother, before her death, had worked as a receptionist at a lawyers' practice, and his father, following her death, had become emotionally absent. Perhaps, if Mother had married a stronger man, things would have worked out differently. Ignatius would use his unabbreviated name, be the head of the family, and not have to buy goldfish.

'Are you coming in, or what?' a grating voice shouted from inside the house. Gingerly, Iggy picked up his Waitrose bag. From the open crack in the door to the garden apartment came the voice again. 'We saw you arrive. We're sitting at the window, you know.'

Iggy walked slowly towards the voice. Head down, he noticed grey dust balls caught in the tassels of the dishevelled and discoloured entrance carpet. New scuff marks were hacked into the corner of the panelled wall. Further along the skirting board, he saw a hole – perhaps mice or rats had moved in? This house was neglected. Somebody needed to be in charge and look after *Firecombe* – which was, after all, the embodiment of his great-grandfather's dream.

The name Ignatius meant *the fiery one*. Iggy pushed his shoulders back. Today was the day he would finally rally his nerves and put his foot down with his aunts.

The downstairs door opened wider to reveal a slender, elderly woman in a pale-pink blouse and floor-length burgundy skirt. Her grey hair was twisted tight into a white banana chignon. Adela smiled at the sight of him. Around her neck was a gold chain with the locket which had belonged to Grandma Marie.

'Iggy,' she exclaimed and made a move towards him. 'You bring us goodies.'

He pulled back. 'No hugging, no touching. Keep your distance.'

'Oh, but you're my nephew.' She looked hurt. 'And you are good to us.'

'That's not important these days. There is still a nasty virus out there.'

'Maureen is just getting herself together after a nap. She is coming.'

She was: behind Aunt Adela, he could see a piece of ceiling detach itself and start to descend. The lift, which resembled a see-through all-body tanning booth, moved slowly. First, blue suede booties appeared, followed by sturdy legs in thick, salmon-coloured tights. Then, an old-fashioned tabard started to show, an apron Maureen always wore over her dresses at home. Her hands appeared, twitching, followed by fat arms, all of this accompanied by the lift's faint drawn-out moan. Making progress, the round chin gave way to a nose, which was red, and red- and blue-veined cheeks and watery eyes. Eventually, all of her was

162

visible, including the tight, white, woolly curls which padded her head.

'Why don't you invite him in and close the door, Adela?' she admonished, still four feet off the ground. 'You know how much I hate conversations taking place in the hallway.'

Adela stepped aside to let Iggy into the apartment. She closed the door and pushed past him, the hem of her skirt running rat-like over his shoe. Iggy could think of nothing better to'say than, 'Was this lift installed professionally? Has an approved electrician given you a certificate?'

'We're fine with it, dearest. It is slow, but we are in no hurry,' reassured Maureen.

'What if it stops halfway through the ceiling?'

'That did happen once, didn't it, Adela? No problem. If there is a power cut or the fuse jumps, there is this red button in the lift right here.' Maureen pointed. 'If I press it, the batteries in this box take over and lower the lift down to safety.'

Controlling his outrage at the existence of this lift, Iggy watched its gentle arrival on the parquet floor. Maureen opened the glass door and stepped out. Then she pressed a button outside the booth and, at the same slow pace, the lift started to rise back up.

'I presume you two are keeping up with the news. I'm still supposed to drop your shopping in front of the door and not go anywhere near you. The virus is getting serious.'

'Unprecedented,' enunciated Maureen. 'Right?'

'Hospital admissions have risen. Most of them are elderly who need breathing ventilators.'

163

'Fiddlesticks.'

Iggy followed the two old women to the living room he was so familiar with, squeezing past the ivory and mother-of-pearl inlaid writing desk, and nearly tripping over the Georgian footstool near the world-time mantel clock. It always surprised him how generous and elegant the rooms were. Old Ignatius had not held back when it came to quality cherry wood flooring and corniced ceilings, and among his exquisite furniture were some unique pieces. The drapes were still the ones he and his wife had chosen and Iggy had hidden behind; the light from the windows had faded them along the crests of their folds. The two enormous curtain tassels, Ignatius had always boasted, came from the ceremonial howdah of a holy elephant. He and great-grandmother had served in the British Indian High Commission after the First World War.

Iggy's contemplation was disturbed by Adela. 'I'll make tea, but we can't have it in the dining room.'

He looked at her, uncomprehending.

'It is chock-a-block with Ignatius's collection of scientific instruments.'

'His belongings are to be stored on floors two and three,' said Iggy. 'What's this about moving things around? You didn't even consult me before you had a lift installed.'

'You will understand. You were always a clever boy.' Adela beamed ingratiatingly at Iggy.

'No,' contradicted Maureen. 'He's none of that. As a boy, he hid behind curtains, broke vases with his hockey stick, and was in awe of Granddad Victor, our father, who was nothing more than a frightened weasel chastised by

Old Ignatius's beatings. The more Victor cringed, the harder Ignatius belted him. When Dad was dead, the undertaker said the scars on his body were a disgrace.'

Iggy counted to ten before he dared to speak. 'Why are Ignatius's collectables down here in your apartment?'

'We needed more space and encroached into the large apartment on the first floor, which is a waste because nobody is using it,' replied Adela. 'Maureen now has a bedroom up there. See, we're resourceful.' She grinned at him with yellowed teeth.

'You have three double bedrooms on the ground floor. That should do for the two of you.'

'It's worse than what we said,' said Adela. 'We needed to move almost everything from the upper floors into this apartment.'

'Does this have anything to do with the new letter-boxes, one of which is red?'

'Mr Tran explained that red is a lucky colour where he comes from,' replied Adela.

'Who is Mr Tran?'

'A nice man. He will help us sell Ignatius's things, which are so much in the way.'

'Oh no he won't,' said Iggy. 'Can't you see you are being bamboozled? You should not make these decisions without asking me first. I have a say, you know.'

If he expected a strong reaction, he was in for a disappointment.

'We don't have to tell you,' said Maureen. 'If you visit, you can see for yourself.'

'Can we talk about this after tea and biscuits?' pleaded Adela.

'We can't have tea and biscuits,' said Iggy. 'The virus is alive on surfaces. No touching each other's things.'

'Don't shout at us,' said Adela indignantly. 'There's no virus in *my* tea.'

'Adela is right. Don't be so boring, Iggy. The Prime Minister is not our teacher.' Maureen eyed her nephew fondly.

'Did I get the shopping right?' He bent and reached into the Waitrose bag. 'Today, I bought you two jars of unusual jams, quince gelée and wild blackberry. Also,' he busied himself in the bag again, 'a pre-cooked steak-and-kidney pie. All you have to do is heat it in the oven for the specified time.'

The sisters glanced at each other. 'We are grateful you do this for us,' said Maureen. 'We made you a new list, if you don't mind. You forgot Adela's statin pills last time, and she's about to run out.'

'No problem,' said Iggy. 'Just a bit more queueing. It gets me out of my small flat. I couldn't get them last time because the system has been up the spout since lockdown. I'll try again.'

Adela looked worried. 'Do you think I will get another stroke if I miss out for so long? Although, I must say, I feel much better without them. Apparently, they are dangerous and can ruin your liver, and then other organs fail. It does give a long list of side effects on the leaflet.'

'You'll be fine,' reassured Maureen. 'You were lucky to get away with a small stroke and little brain damage. The pills are considered widely beneficial if taken in small doses.'

'Still…' Adela fretted, crossing and uncrossing her legs under her burgundy skirt.

'All medication has poisonous chemical elements.' Ignatius felt like saying something soothing and clever-sounding.

'I had a bad turn,' replied Adela. 'That's all it was. So much fuss was made.'

Iggy evaded the continuation of this only-too-familiar conversation by leaving the room with the silver tea tray from the sideboard.

On his return, he opened the nearly empty medicine package he had picked up from the kitchen counter. Pulling from it the folded leaflet, he started to read the small print on the thin paper. *Muscle breakdown leading to liver failure and cardiovascular death especially in the elderly. Keep to the dose recommended by your specialist.*

Adela, who had watched him read, said, 'I only take ten milligrams. Don't look so grim, dear nephew.'

'Good girl,' he said as he sometimes did, to their pleasure. He folded the thin paper back into its intended form and pushed it into the box, which he gave back to her. In a cheery voice, he asked, 'Can you tell me why you always put so many jars of jam on your shopping list?'

'To keep our brains active,' replied Maureen.

'Sugar rushes?'

'Monday is strawberry, Tuesday apricot, Wednesday marmalade and Thursday raspberry.'

'Friday is fish paste,' Adela took over. 'And,' she paused for effect, 'Sunday is chocolate spread.'

'So the quince and wild blackberry I brought today won't fit in.'

'We'll find a way, don't you worry,' said Adela. 'There is still Saturday, which we kept free because it is good to be deprived.'

Maureen butted in. 'See, we still know what is what and where we are, despite the goings-on out there with Stay Home, Protect the NHS and Save Lives. It's funny to watch the sign translator,' she giggled.

'Is it?' Ignatius asked.

'He makes steeples with his hands and then rams his finger through the air,' replied Maureen. '*House* and *Stay put*. When he translates the PPE kit, he goes...'

'Maureen, I know what he does. I see it often enough,' Iggy interrupted.

'Sorry to annoy you, Iggy,' said Maureen. 'You are the loveliest nephew, looking after us the way you do.'

The sisters then sat, side by side on the sofa, their heads to one side like trained parrots in a show.

'I am your *only* nephew.'

'Such a shame your mother passed,' said Maureen. They brought that up whenever they saw him, annoyingly meaning well.

'At least she was spared this unprecedented catastrophe,' said Adela. 'She could have ended up in a home. And, of course, all care homes are death traps these days. The inmates die like DDT-sprayed roaches. On a forklift, their bodies are dumped in mass graves on Hart Island somewhere. Probably in Scotland. It was shown shamelessly.' She shivered. 'Cardboard coffin on top of another coffin and then a third. They'll all collapse into each other.'

'Thank you, Adela. We've all seen it.'

168

'On the subject of DDT,' started Maureen, 'do you think we should drink bleach? The American President said we should try it. His hair is ever so fluffy. We believe he uses hair-straightening tongs. Pulls the front wad through the hot metal rods, and bingo, the perfect snow cornice. Nobody told him not to overheat the iron tongs, though. He burns his head every time. Look how red he is.'

Iggy changed the subject. 'I deduce that, behind my back, you have rented out two apartments in *Firecombe*. It shows disrespect towards me, and disrespect towards Old Ignatius's plans for the family home.'

'It shows initiative,' replied Adela. 'We make money. Maureen can get her dental implants.'

'You don't need money,' replied Iggy. 'Ignatius set up a generous trust for you. With the part you got after my mother's death, you are comfortably off…' Not having time to count to ten, he could not prevent himself from adding, 'Doing nothing all day.'

'We will be working. We will be landladies, won't we, Maureen?'

'You know nothing of that business. It is a bad time. Many tenants can't pay their rent. A great many have lost their jobs, companies are going under. Wherever possible, people are asked to work from home and many have been furloughed.'

'What is that?' asked Maureen.

'Sent home, but still retaining their job and getting it back when lockdown is over,' explained Iggy. 'I work for my insurance company from home.'

'How?'

'Computer communication, video conferencing, virtual contact. Don't worry about it. It does not affect you. You're lucky to have each other.'

'We argue a lot,' said Maureen.

'So, about getting rent?' asked Iggy.

'Would you like some toast with marmalade?' asked Adela. 'It's Wednesday. See, we know without checking the list on the kitchen door.'

'Thank you, Adela, but no. As I am trying to tell you, the Covid-19 virus gets onto crockery and cutlery, everything one touches.'

'We know that,' replied Adela. 'What about if I wore my washing-up gloves? Did you bring us face masks?'

'They're not available,' said Iggy. 'People are urged to make their own with pieces of fabric.'

'Maureen tried, but the pedal of the Singer has rusted. Then she cut up a sock the way someone in Spain demonstrated on TV. Who wants to wear an old sock over their face?'

'I tried using coffee filters, but they kept tearing when I threaded shoe laces into them,' added Maureen.

'We don't need masks. We are...' Adela made a steeple with her hands and then stabbed her finger downward. Both aunts giggled like teenagers.

'Let's get back to your tenants, money. Tell me,' Iggy said in a crisp voice which made him cough.

Four eyes looked at him with alarm.

'Iggy, you have the virus,' said Adela. 'You look peaky.'

'Doesn't he look peaky?' added Maureen.

'A bit like our Prime Minister before they drove him into intensive care.'

170

'Imagine being the nurse who has to clean and talcum powder him.'

'To a professional nurse, he is a patient and not the Prime Minister,' said Iggy irritably. 'Let's get back to your tenants. Tell me about them.'

'Mr Tran asked to pay half-rent until it's over, and then make up for it,' said Maureen. 'His noodle bar is closed. He plays leapfrog with his children or throws them against the wall. It's bumpy up there.' She pointed to the ceiling.

'We don't know how he will catch up with the rent,' added Adela. 'Who will ever want to eat in a Chinese restaurant again?'

'His name suggests he is Vietnamese,' Iggy corrected.

'That's part of China,' said Maureen. 'We've asked him to keep his children in check and to pay for a window cleaner inside and out. The kids stick large pictures of rainbows on the glass.'

'We also told them they are not in China any longer, especially when they go outside and bang ladles against frying pans, shouting and clapping,' said Adela. 'They've got the whole neighbourhood doing it now too. Thursday evenings at five o'clock.'

'Do you read newspapers? Watch the BBC news regularly?' asked Iggy.

'Maureen says a psychologist advised not to watch too much news. It causes depression.'

'We do the Joe Wicks exercises in the morning. Adela knocked over the antique Indian clay pot. Ignatius would have given her a real old spanking. He was hard on us.'

But had a soft spot. Did he not leave you Firecombe and all else he owned? thought Ignatius, but in a spiritless voice soldiered on. 'Tell me about Anderson and Frost?'

'Two ladies,' replied Maureen. 'They're quiet up there on the small third floor, apart from the violin one of them plays. She promised to close the windows. She'll never get the hang of it. Wee wee eek eek, goes on and on.'

'Do they pay?'

'So far.'

'They are key workers.'

'No. They are teachers.'

'Every day, Maureen and I go to the park for our little walk,' said Adela.

'You are allowed one hour exercise a day.'

'We won't go back,' she replied. 'We don't fancy prison. We sat on the bench near the pond, and a policeman came and asked us to move on. I am eighty-seven and had a stroke, and Maureen is eighty-five with bad knees. We need to sit down.'

'He said, "You have been sitting now for over twenty minutes,"' added Maureen. 'He told us that wasn't exercising. The crime rate must be down if a policeman has time to watch us two chatting on a park bench for twenty minutes. What has become of our world? Everything is unprecedented, fur-lined and self-isolated. With all that, we've had the best weather in years. Easter was exotically sunny and warm. Adela, do you remember how Old Ignatius loved egg hunts in the garden? It reminded him of India, crawling through bushes looking for his golf balls.'

'Oh, we almost forgot to tell you what happened on apricot day,' said Adela. 'The gardener came and cut back our bushes. He said gardeners were allowed to work. It's outside and he works alone. As long as he keeps social distancing.'

'It's not social distance we need. It's physical distance,' Maureen corrected.

'Shush,' said Adela. 'I'm talking. He told us that many more burglaries are committed, right here on De Parys and along Park Avenue. It's in these posh houses the good stuff is, he told us.'

'He also announced that he could not come and garden any longer,' added Maureen. 'Probably taking up burglary. Imagine if someone stole our family treasures – the silver, paintings, our precious Monet?'

Iggy turned on his seat to check the wall behind him, where a medium-sized oil painting hung with a bouquet of flowers in a silver beaker. The picture light was not on.

'The bulb is burnt out,' the aunts said. 'How can we find a replacement in this pandemonium?'

'Online,' he said. 'I'll try to find one.' He went to unscrew the elongated bulb and slipped it into the breast pocket of his slack cord jacket.

'Shall we hide the painting somewhere clever?' asked Maureen. 'The gardener saw it from the open door, when he took the tea-tray from us. He'll tell his friends about it.'

'Behind the refrigerator?' suggested Adela.

'Under the spare room mattress,' replied Maureen. 'I couldn't bear losing those beautiful flowers. They have hung here ever since I was born.'

Yes, they have, thought Iggy. 'I have insured it, together with the contents of your apartment and the rest of the house.'

'We owe you money for that.' Maureen started to weep into a handkerchief. 'Monet is not money,' she sniffled. 'Long dead, he cannot paint it again.'

'We used to take the train to London and visit art galleries,' said Adela. 'Now we have to sit here and wait until we cough and have a fever.'

'Iggy, are you really not allowed to drive us anywhere so we can see something different?' asked Maureen.

'That would not be an essential trip, would it?' he replied. 'Everything is closed. People have to do as they are told.'

In unison and standing up, they chorused, 'Stay home, protect the NHS and save lives.'

'Essential?' Adela picked out of the air. 'It is essential that Maureen and I get away from here for a while, otherwise we will become mentally...' She searched for a word. '... unstable. No National Trust open gardens, no picture museums, no culture.'

Iggy pondered this and then looked at them in turn. 'I will think of a way to get you away from here. Many people are driving to picturesque places against the rules of lockdown. As far as I know, none of them have been put into prison.'

The two aunts beamed.

'How adorable you are,' said Adela. 'We will love whatever you come up with. You are the fiery one.'

Most of the fire has been put out by losing out on my inheritance because Mother died, he thought bitterly.

174

Unaware of his mental turmoil, Maureen went on, 'You swooped down our staircase in the laundry basket and didn't mind banging your head against the wall.'

Oh yes, I did mind, he thought.

He looked at the aunts sitting smugly on the sofa for three. Single, and never having had to make a concession, they were now selfish. He would most probably end up looking after them until their end. A DDT care home solution was not an option for them any longer, not after Covid. Now was the time to grasp the nettle.

'I have to ask you something serious.'

The aunts sobered.

'Have you made a will?'

To his surprise, they had made one, handwritten on a piece of paper. He explained that it had to be legalised by a lawyer.

'It is such a simple will,' they objected.

'It should be,' he muttered under his breath. 'Leaving all their worldly possessions to the only surviving relative, their nephew.'

Aloud, he said, 'Simple is often good, but it still has to be made a legal document.'

Adela found the will in the antique bureau drawer. Holding it out to him, she cast her eyes down before looking up at him. 'You will be pleased with us,' she said timidly. 'We know we are doing the right thing.'

Iggy felt the flush of pleasure heat his body. Finally, things would be put right.

In one tidily written paragraph, he saw that they had both left everything they owned to the NHS.

'It was Maureen's idea after watching Captain Tom

giving his money to the NHS just by walking around in his garden. Even the American President sent his congratulations to Tom, who is now famous at his age.'

The nightmare of his deprivation closed in on Iggy. He would never get a penny of the family money, because he was an unwanted limb through which their blood could not run. A tourniquet had been applied to it at the death of his mother.

Having slipped the folded will into his pocket, he threaded his way through the antique furniture course, promising to drop the will in with Bedford's most prestigious law firm, talking as if in a trance. He knew his aunts well enough to realise that they could not be persuaded to give up on this idea. They trampled over rights and hearts, always had and always would.

In the hall again, he decided that he had to do more than knock himself out in a laundry basket; he had to knock them out. This was the precise moment in his life when he had to do something drastic or he would go on as a failure, a man with a Juliet balcony, a slave to his aunts. But 'drastic' did not mean unplanned. He had encountered clever insurance frauds in the years he had worked in the firm, but all the best ones had been minutely prepared. Old Ignatius, he felt, would have been upset at the way things had worked out for Iggy. Some deep sense of identification with his great-grandfather had kept Iggy's sense of purpose.

He turned on his heels and went back to the garden apartment door.

After a peremptory knock, the door opened on both of them.

'Where is the fire, dear? We thought you were gone.'

'I have just come up with an idea where to take you for our little outing. It has a garden, art and lots more.'

His aunts watched him, their mouths slack.

'Why don't the three of us go to France, to Monet's garden, next weekend? The weather is supposed to be good. Saturday morning, we take the Eurostar and stay one night in a small hotel near the gardens. If we leave from here in a taxi, we can catch the eleven o'clock Eurostar. We'd better do this now, before travelling to France is banned.'

'You're the best,' they said mechanically, because they were out of their depth.

'France is abroad.' Maureen woke to reality first. 'It is full of rude French people.'

'Imagine seeing where Monet painted our picture,' Adela said dreamily.

'I have to do some research to find out how difficult it will be because of Covid,' said Iggy. 'You see, travel is not what it used to be. But that is for me to work out. All you girls have to do is pack for a short break. Just a few things. No hat boxes or travel trunks.' He continued more seriously. 'I take it you have passports. You went to Holland three years ago. Can I see them, please?'

'Everyone has a passport,' said Maureen. 'They give you that when you are born.'

'No, Maureen,' replied Iggy. 'They give you a birth certificate when you are born. Go get your passports for me to check their validity.'

'Bully.' Adela smiled at him sweetly and, shortly after, returned with two passports.

'Isn't she amazing?' Maureen said. 'She can find anything. I can't even find the second slipper in the morning.'

'Because, when putting on the first, you push the second under the bed, dozy head.'

'Watch it, you.' Maureen's arm was raised in jest.

'The passports are valid,' said Iggy, 'but you're supposed to have six months left when you travel. Maureen has only four.'

'Either my passport is valid or not.'

'You have a point there. We might get away with it.'

He told them he had to wash his hands before leaving, and headed to the kitchen.

'Better safe than sorry,' Adela said.

In the kitchen, he picked up a Tate & Lyle sugar sachet from the bowl, granulated sugar, 25 grams.

Before he left *Firecombe*, he shouted out to the aunts. 'See you Saturday, eight o'clock. Be good, be ready.'

Back in his studio, he checked his emails, Facebook and WhatsApp, to keep up with his WFH colleagues. As he did so, the computer screen went black again. He cursed before going to the fuse box at the entrance cupboard, where light from the window showed the new fuse had tripped. He pulled it out and held it up.

'You are a fuse,' he said to it. 'Thank you for tripping again and giving me an idea.' Iggy pushed the unit back in. The light came back on.

With intense concentration, Iggy used a craft knife to cut through the top of the sugar sachet. The blade advanced, leaving an untidy zigzag cut. He pried one corner of the sachet open and poured half of the sugar into the sink. From Maureen's statin pill boxes, which he had picked up from the pharmacy but not given her, he took a soft plastic capsule, resembling a bullet, and pulled it apart to let the white powder collect on a sheet of printer paper. He repeated this until the first box was empty – three times twenty-eight capsules. He opened the second box and went on with this job, which required minute handling. When he had finished the second box, he had a heap of six months' worth of statin medication on the paper. One hundred and twenty milligrams of statin sodium, an amount fatal in one swoop to an elderly person.

Rolling the paper into a funnel, he drizzled the powder into the sugar sachet, and then shook the contents to mix the remaining sugar with the medicine. With paper glue drops on the tip of the craft knife, he closed the sachet top and pressed the sides together. It came out crinkled, but held. Only if someone looked closely… He slipped the sachet into his breast pocket.

'Ready,' he said, and threw himself onto his bed. Hands clasped behind his head, he asked Alexa to play Mozart. He needed something to quieten his mind.

*

It was Saturday, early morning, the day of the big Monet garden adventure. When Adela let him in, he put his sports bag down in the entrance.

'It's not sunny today,' Maureen muttered in the background.

He gave them each a mask he had been able to find in a pharmacy.

'I can't wear that. It will make me feel silly,' complained Maureen.

Adela said sharply to her sister, 'Stop being so negative. Today, we can do something wonderful.'

'Something illegal,' Iggy said.

'Really?' Maureen dropped sulky for anxious excitement.

'Tell you what,' he continued, 'here's a packing list I have prepared. Why don't you two check that you have packed everything, while I make us a cup of tea to start this special day.'

'Oh, but...'

'No buts. Off you go.'

As a boy, many times he had seen Grandma Marie make tea in this kitchen. Now, waiting for the kettle to boil, he sneaked into the hall, opened the glass door of the lift and clawed half of the batteries out of the emergency box. He stuffed them into his sports bag. He zipped it up and returned to the kitchen, where he began to swirl the boiling water around the inside of the silver teapot to warm it up, the way Grandma Marie used to do. When the tea was ready, he put the pot on the tray, together with the milk jug and the bowl with the sugar sachets, the tampered one on top.

In the living room, the two of them were still checking the packing list.

'You forgot to put face flannels on the list,' Maureen said, and Iggy realised that she was anxious about the trip.

He poured tea into the cup next to Adela, who sat on the sofa, and held out the sugar bowl. Absentmindedly, she chose a sachet – the wrong one.

He took it back, saying, 'I'll help you.' He then quickly exchanged sachets. He tore the prepared one open. He saw her watch the white granules reach the surface of the hot brew before sinking, his breath withheld. Quickly, he poured a dash of milk after it, in case white particles rose and floated. Her spoon went round and round in the brew, as she smiled up at him. Steam rose from the cup – innocent, thin, whitish whorls which dissolved in the air.

Nothing was said. The spoon stopped clinking against the porcelain. Adela lifted the cup to her mouth and, as was a habit of hers, blew shortly at the surface of the tea, but did not drink. The world-time mantel clock, one of Ignatius's valuable antiques, ticked time away, louder than normal, surely. Adela brought the cup up to her face. The angels held their breath. With a decisive move, she tipped the cup against her dry lips, drinking avidly, thirstily.

Iggy twisted the gold signet ring on his pinkie, a ring he had bought preloved in an antique jewellery shop, one that could have been left to him by a loving ancestor. With time, he and his aunts believed this is what had happened.

With a satisfied sigh, Adela put the cup down after draining the last of the tea. 'In France, we won't get decent tea,' she said.

How fast would the overdose of statins work? How would it manifest itself?

She blotted her nose on her handkerchief. No blood had spurted out. She put the hankie back in her tweed jacket pocket in her normal fashion, except for

181

a questioning look his way. He had to go through this with a much more detached attitude.

Just then, he jumped from fright. Someone had rung the doorbell. The taxi had arrived.

'I see it through the hedge.' Maureen's voice was laced with hysteria. 'We haven't got time to sit around.' She struggled into her raincoat.

'He can wait,' said Iggy. 'Has to wait. That is what taxis do.'

'That's not polite.'

'Maureen,' he said, his hand pressing against her upper arm, 'calm yourself. All is under control. I will carry out the luggage and help Adela into the car, while you, Maureen, go upstairs and change that raincoat for something warmer. Low temperatures are predicted for France. Go, fetch your padded coat, the one with the hood. We don't want to catch a cold.'

'Do we have time for this?'

'I've planned in a lot of extra time. Adela can keep the driver company.'

Maureen went to the lift, giving him a look of 'All right, you know best' over her shoulder.

He helped Adela up from the sofa. There were no deposits left in the tea cup.

He held out the woollen coat for her, picked up the three pieces of luggage and left the house with Adela, while Maureen was ascending in the lift.

At the taxi, Iggy helped his aunt to install herself on the back seat, telling the driver that another person was just coming.

Returning to the apartment, he saw that Maureen

had made it halfway up to the room. He carried the tea things into the kitchen and thoroughly washed all of them, including the spoons.

He put the crockery back, by which time the top of Maureen's head had reached the ceiling.

Through the hedge, he could see the taxi driver twisted back in his seat to talk to Adela.

He went into the living room and played with the elephant tassel. Living here, he would change the curtains and get rid of the carpet. He would buy a modern sofa and easy chairs. He would...

Maureen's head was in the upstairs room.

He went outside to the taxi and apologised for the delay, at the same time telling Adela that Maureen unfortunately was extremely negative about this trip. So much so that she did not want to come any longer. Adela immediately offered to go and talk to her, but he held her back.

'She said she needed time alone to do what she wanted.'

'She already does what she wants every day.'

'See, two days' separation will be a good thing for both of you.'

That made sense to Adela, who was not unhappy to have her nephew to herself.

The upper half of Maureen was in the upstairs room when Iggy got back into the house for the last time. In the utility room, he pushed the fuse trigger down. The light went out in the hall. A shriek told him that it had worked.

On leaving the apartment, he pinned a prepared

notice against the door. *Self-isolating* was written on it. He climbed into the back seat of the taxi next to Adela.

'St Pancras station,' he said.

The driver started the car.

'We can't just drive off and leave Maureen at home.'

Iggy was prepared for this. 'Look, Aunt Adela, Maureen's passport had run out. She was embarrassed about it. It was too late to renew it.'

'You could have tried.'

'As you know, she was not that keen on coming. Was she?'

'No,' Adela admitted. 'Not really.' After a while, she added, 'Not at all, actually.'

The driver drove down the last of De Parys Avenue and the sun came out. Maureen had definitely been left behind. Iggy tried to soften the blow.

'The last thing she said to me was to wish us a happy trip.' He smiled at Adela. Then he hooked the face mask over her ears and folded it out, before pushing the sunglasses to cover her eyes, and pulled the coat hood down over her face. 'Covid,' he said.

The drive to London went reasonably well, apart from Adela being upset that Maureen had let her down. In an effort to take her mind off this, Iggy distracted her with the question of whose photographs were in the locket on the chain around her neck.

'Your Grandma Marie wanted to offer this gold locket to either Maureen or me,' she said. 'After I told Marie that Maureen had an aversion against any jewellery or adornment, she gave it to me. I wish I hadn't lied. If something happened to Maureen while left alone at home, I would feel awfully guilty.'

Iggy reassured Adela that they would take loads of photographs in Monet's garden for Maureen. The taxi driver, in a dry voice, announced that they had arrived at St Pancras and where did they wish to be dropped off?

It was only once Adela was tapping along in the giant building, in which piano music faded into the vast space under the metal-vaulted ceiling, that she complained of stomach ache. She had to go to the ladies twice to throw up. While she was gone the first time, Iggy disposed of the batteries. He peeled his gloves off and slipped them into his coat pocket. When Adela came out of the ladies, he heard her rasping breath behind the vomit-spotted surgical mask. What little showed of her with the hood right over her face had a light-green sheen. He helped her down the escalator to Eurostar departures. After a patient wait in a drawn-out queue, during which she leant heavily against his arm, it was their turn to show tickets and passports.

Next was the security area. Hooked on his arm, she leant heavily against him, moaning in pain.

'I can hardly see,' she complained. At the scan, they took away her large bottle of eau de cologne. She had no strength left to object. All she wanted was to lie down somewhere.

Finally, they made it to the last queue: French passport control. A uniformed young woman, patrolling alongside, gave Adela a keen look and addressed Iggy.

'What is wrong with this woman?'

'Too much standing and waiting,' he said, while

185

peering at the name in the plastic holder on the uniform pocket: *Officier d'Immigration, I. Claudel.*

'Isabelle,' he guessed. 'My favourite French name. Isabelle Adjani.'

She answered with an unsmiling stare. 'Move on,' the inhuman woman ordered. However, watching him support the old woman and encourage her to take steps forward induced her to admit 'Irène'.

'Softer than Isabelle, sexier, suits your style.'

She played deaf. 'Your mother?' A cold finger pointed at Adela.

'My mother died when I was a little boy. This is my aunt.'

'She looks sick. I cannot let you on the train.'

'To tell you the truth, Irène, she had a stroke about eight months ago.'

'What is your destination in France?'

'Paris.'

'Where in Paris?'

'Hospital,' croaked Adela.

'We are seeing a stroke specialist,' Ignatius invented.

'Which hospital?' Irène insisted.

'Hotel-Dieu.'

'Surely that doesn't still exist? Appointment confirmation please?'

'How come an attractive young woman like yourself is an immigration officer, policing innocent people?'

'Proof of appointment.'

'Have pity on us,' tried Iggy. 'My aunt is eighty-seven years old.'

'I can't let you on the train,' she insisted stubbornly.

'You have to have your temperature taken.' Irène stepped back from him and spoke into her headset. *'Embêteur,'* Iggy heard the word she used: troublemaker.

'Irène, please,' he begged.

'Aren't there doctors in England who can help your aunt?'

'Phua. Nothing anywhere near the quality of medical expertise the French nation offers.'

Irène remained puffer-lipped. Encouraged, he smiled at her, giving it that extra little corner twitch he had practised in the mirror years ago.

Adela, feeling left out, begged, 'Can I have a wheelchair, please?'

Irène talked into her headset again.

The queue for the passport control booths progressed fitfully. Each passenger seemed to take an inordinately long time, with much dialogue involved.

A wheelchair was brought: *Property of Eurostar.* Iggy helped his aunt into it. She sat with a groan, and then with a crooked finger coaxed him close to her.

'I've peed myself a little,' she whispered. 'I couldn't help it. My bladder burns like acid. Nothing wet shows, does it?'

'No,' he said without looking at her skirt. They moved a step forward. After that, there was a commotion and nobody advanced any longer.

Iggy realised that the poisoning of his aunt would bring embarrassing physical events with it. What would he do if a load of diarrhoea came out of her? He attracted Irène's attention and asked her to stay put next to his aunt for a few minutes while he went to get something from a shop.

The immigration officer nodded and took up position next to Adela's wheelchair while Iggy legged it to the shops.

When he returned, he carried a bunch of short-stemmed pink roses in a cellophane wrapping. Adela smiled up at him. He held the bunch out to Irène.

'No way,' she reacted, and meant it. She even backed away from him, from the queue, to take up the controlling position, hands on hips, legs apart, out of reach.

Self-assured, he followed her, bowed to her and laid the flowers next to her black leather shoes, as one honours a statue – which she ignored, as a statue would.

Finally, it was their turn at the passport booth. Someone took their temperature with a handheld gadget against their foreheads. A nod. They passed. Their passports were given back.

Iggy looked back over his shoulder and met Irène's eyes. She had not hampered the process. He blew her a kiss. The pink roses lay abandoned on the concrete floor.

The waiting Eurostar looked sleek, like a metallic eel. He helped his aunt up the steps, propping her up and guiding her to the reserved seat in business class, leaving the wheelchair on the platform. All energy seemed to have gone out of Adela.

'I want to go home. This is not fun without Maureen.' Her voice sounded strained, as if she were about to burst into tears.

He promised her that once in Paris everything would become wonderful.

'Paris,' she said dreamily. Then, with a brusque move, her hand clasped her abdomen. 'The pain, the pain.'

The train jolted.

'Iggy!' The hand came off the belly to judder in the air, before being met and held tightly by Iggy's. 'I can't go through with this. I am ill.'

He let go of her hand.

'Very ill,' she rasped. 'Believe me.'

A man with a reddish beard took a seat more than two metres away, on the other side of the aisle.

'Bloody nonsense, this distancing,' he took up conversation with them. 'This virus is an infestation of the mind. The government has implanted it in us, just to get control.'

'What is that man talking about?' asked Adela.

Ignatius checked his watch. Three minutes until departure.

'Did you pack a towel, Iggy? I think I just had an accident.'

Two minutes to departure. 'I'll go and check whether the train is ready to leave.'

'Can you help me to the ladies?' asked Adela.

An announcement confirmed that they were leaving on time. Iggy went to the still-open carriage door. He checked his watch. One minute. The train shook again.

'Iggy!' He heard the loud shout of panic.

The train started to roll; the platform moved backwards. He took a deep breath and jumped out of the train, and then ran down the platform so that Adela could not see him from her window seat.

When he was safe he stopped, breathing rapidly high up in his lungs.

All he could see of the silver eel was its tail with two

round lights like glowing eyes, as the train pulled out of St Pancras. The next stop would be Calais. Adela would be mostly dead by then. Her ticket and passport were in his breast pocket.

He would give Maureen three weeks caught in her lift, five to make sure.

Ignatius walked slowly back to the main entrance. Finally, the worm had turned. He felt relieved of the responsibility of his aunts, which had held him captive for so long. His turn, to have things and be someone, had just begun. He checked over his shoulder for a last glimpse of the train.

To his surprise, the Eurostar had stopped moving away.

A loudspeaker crackled overhead. 'This is an announcement to all passengers. France has closed its border at Calais. For further information, please go to the information desk.'

When it was his turn at the desk, he said, 'I have a friend who left ten minutes ago on the 11.25 Eurostar. I saw the train off.'

'This train has been stopped and will return to St Pancras.'

'Why?'

'An elderly passenger was discovered with symptoms of Covid. It was reported to the French authorities. They closed Calais.'

He thanked her and sought the exit as fast as he could, which was easy as there weren't many people.

His mind buffered. Adela would be taken to St Thomas's hospital, where they would wonder why she had died without having the virus. If a post mortem was carried out, they would deduce she had been prescribed statins, but had not read the instructions. No foul play could be considered.

If they saved her, at least Maureen would have died by accident. With only Adela left, he could work on her to change her will in his favour. Boring. He would have to come up with another plan to get rid of Adela. Right now, he was going to his studio to celebrate by drinking half a bottle of whisky, and to make a list of what he would change in *Firecombe* after throwing out the tenants. The mobile in his breast pocket jingled. His office? A mobile number appeared on his screen. He put the phone against his ear.

'Hello?'

A voice he knew well shouted, 'Iggy!'

'Aunt Maureen? I didn't know you had… you could use a mobile phone.'

'You left me stuck in the lift. Mr Tran heard me shout. He opened the lock on the apartment door using a bamboo skewer and helped me out. He gave me the phone and explained how to use it. He wants me to call his kids, twice every day, and speak to them. As they are not able to go to school, he is worried they'll fall behind with English. You and Adela must be halfway to Paris by now. What's going on? How could the two of you leave me like this? I could have died, stuck here.'

Outside St Pancras, a sudden shower sliced the air. His beloved cord jacket would be ruined. The further Iggy sprinted in the rain to find a taxi, the more upset he became about the jacket.

SHANGHAI BALLOON

'Director-General Zhang, you sent for me?' The twenty-eight-year-old woman in a smart Ted Baker long-sleeved dress and high-heeled shoes waited for the head of the Shanghai Investment Bank to give her his attention.

Fanli was third out of four directors in the international bank, unusual for a young woman, but then she had graduated from Yale, and been awarded a doctorate from Harvard in financial trading. Gender equality was much spoken of in China and, on the surface, she appeared to be integrated, her position respected. However, she was conscious of disquiet at her seniority among older male colleagues.

'Our motto in the Shanghai Investment Bank is *Our growth is your growing*,' were Director-General Zhang's opening words.

Fanli scratched her forehead, which upset the uniformity of her shiny dark fringe. 'I know that, Sir. I was the one who introduced the motto when I started working for you, four years ago. It is appropriate. We have grown and not let down our shareholders, or our customers. Do you want to see the latest figures?' She attempted to pick the prepared file from her Ted Baker signature tote bag.

Zhang shook his head. Fanli started to wonder why the Director-General had asked to see her. She glanced at her smartphone – 08:15, which was 19:15 the previous day in Chicago.

'Our bank building,' Zhang said, after a short tense silence, 'is thirty-two floors tall, but narrow. It was like that when we moved in.'

She could not risk failing to speak to Rachel Jackson in Chicago, which gave her only forty-five minutes to make the call.

'As we have grown, it has forced us to hire more employees. Our premises have not expanded with us.' Zhang was obviously narrowing down on why he had called her to his office.

Impatient with the slow unveiling of the subject of her convocation, Fanli thought about the phone call. Businesswomen in America had more say than their Chinese counterparts, so Fanli would have to be more assertive with Rachel than was her usual style.

'We could move to a larger building,' said Zhang. He watched her face for any reaction to his words. She forced herself not to blink. 'But of course, this would risk bad feng shui. And established banks do not move premises like fly-by-night financial companies. Our constant address creates trust in our solidity. Besides, we are in the prosperous city district of Shanghai. Our logo, our headed paper, the gold lions in front of the entrance door...' He touched his temples fleetingly with the tips of his fingers.

'I agree.' She tried a smile, while still thinking about Rachel Jackson in Chicago.

'That is the reason why I have proposed to purchase the building to our east side, and join up with it,' said Zhang, 'thus retaining our address in the right business district, and with our gold lions still in place.'

Fanli said nothing.

'When I brought it up in the board meeting, you were against this idea,' continued Zhang. 'Not respecting my proposal, you came up with ten thousand objections and convinced others to side with you, undermining my authority. Your vehemence brought most of my board members onto your side. You, a woman.'

Fanli finally blinked. 'Besides the mundane problems of evicting all the tenants and paying them compensation,' she replied, 'there are serious construction issues, and unpredictable costs. Linking the two buildings would require deep foundations to be built. The pressure of our building leaning against the shoddily built one next door might result in the need to practically rebuild the existing one. The floor levels are unlikely to match. The height of the next building is two floors lower than that of the bank. The typhoon resistance would have to be recalculated. Those are just some of the many potentially costly problems.' She took a conscious breath. 'If I may be so bold as to add, this is not meant personally. It is merely voicing reservations concerning the project, Director-General.'

Director-General Zhang frowned. 'Apart from being irritatingly bold in whatever you do, you are making me look small and unintelligent in the eyes of my peers, while not coming up with an alternative proposal. It is condemnable, Director Chu. I can only take this as a personal attack on my position and person, something no Chinese businessman can tolerate from a woman, especially not from one in an inferior position. I am the Director-General and you...' he paused, looking her up and down, 'are a third director in a skirt. What do you know about walls linking buildings?'

'I am more than willing to talk to a geological surveyor and an architect,' replied Fanli, 'and let them come to you with the practicalities, in an effort to prove that my subservient observations, Director-General Zhang, are not malicious in any way. They will be men, and qualified in what I merely dare hint at.'

'Yet another plot to expose my own person to the ridicule of inadequacy to more people.'

Ignoring his old-fashioned Chinese ways, Fanli said, 'There are no more than about ten metres between the buildings. Just room for a narrow road and pavements either side.'

Zhang looked around his office, trying to figure out the extent of that distance. He obviously couldn't, therefore he suggested, 'Let's go up on the roof and look at the project from that perspective.'

Fanli picked up her Ted Baker bag, which contained the Consolidated Statement of Comprehensive Income for the first six months of the year, which she had spent hours the previous night preparing in case the Director-General asked for it, and slipped her mobile into the bag's outside pocket. Together, they left his office, she respectfully a few paces behind him.

Walking along the executive corridor on the eight floor, a Chinese lucky number, the scent of his expensive hair dye reminded her that the Director-General was born and bred in Shanghai, while she came from Guizhou province – another thing which Zhang found hard to accept in her. In Guizhou, teenagers rode ponies bareback, and mothers let their babies waddle around without nappies for the dogs to feed on their shit, which reduced nappy-washing and fed the dogs at the same time. Fanli had come a long way – but, once from Guizhou, always from the province. Sometimes, she even felt guilty for wearing Ted Baker, who probably designed his clothes for the bodies of women from more sophisticated backgrounds.

In the lift, they rose to the top floor, which was temporarily unoccupied as it was undergoing refurbishment. Fanli followed Zhang up some steps to a door, which led to the emergency staircase. Zhang took out a key he had brought, giving away the fact that he had premeditated this roof visit.

The seldom-used metal door squealed. Climbing the staircase, Zhang's shoes rang on the textured metal. Fanli placed her feet with care, so that the heels of her shoes did not get stuck in the lace pattern of the treads. They reached a concrete platform which signified the end of any further ascending in the building. No other employee of the bank had any reason to have ever been up there.

In the ceiling above them was an access lid to the roof. With a hook on a rod, Zhang pulled down a metal ladder. Halfway up, he could reach a wheel which he started to turn. Slowly, the heavy lid above him moved to the side on rollers. He stepped up and out onto the roof. This was harder for Fanli in her tight dress; she had to crawl over the lip and away from the hole. The runs in her torn tights rushed up and down her legs like insects. She put down her tote bag and struggled to her feet, under a shelter over the trapdoor.

'When we bought this building, I was taken up here,' Zhang admitted. 'There was a storm, I remember. Rain fell through the trapdoor right into the building. I had them build a little shelter over the hole.'

Fanli thought it resembled a miniature carport.

'Access to the roof is strictly forbidden, except for maintenance men with special permission from me,' said Zhang. 'You see, the periphery is not made secure in any way.' He straightened up and gave Fanli's legs a quick glance. Nothing was said as he picked up her bag and handed it to her. Where they now stood, two tiny figures on a rectangular flat roof, almost the highest in a collection of skyscrapers in the vicinity, Shanghai's morning activities in the streets below were reduced to a mere rumble.

A breeze teased her page-cut hair. His hair was treated with a substance which kept it stuck close to his scalp. This exposure to the elements rendered Zhang chatty.

'Once, a body fell onto the roof from a Cathay Pacific airplane. A stowaway had climbed into the wheel casing and fell out when the wheels were retracted after take-off for Los Angeles.'

'How did you know the body was up here?'

'The airline called the mayor's office, and they called me.'

Turning in a circle to orient herself, Fanli located the blue of the sea.

He pointed and said, 'There. That is east. If we move closer, I can show you the building I propose to buy and link with. Perhaps you would be so kind as to take pictures, ideally showing as much of the gap between the buildings as possible.'

Having reached the east side and stopped safely short of the edge, she only saw the upper floors of the neighbouring building. She realised he was asking her to advance right to the edge.

'I have to get onto my stomach to take pictures down into the canyon.'

'It's up to you,' Zhang said, having stayed further back. 'It is in your interest to convince the others that mine is an unviable suggestion.'

On all fours, Fanli crawled towards the infinity edge. There was nothing in the way between the roof surface and a plunge off the building – no rim, no safety railings. The east building was two floors shorter than the bank. Every apartment facing her had a balcony. From her elevated position, she could see the rubbish people kept on their balconies. It seemed to Fanli even more unrealistic to join the two buildings together. She could now also see further down into the gap, and took pictures, her trembling hand holding the mobile phone above the abyss, while armies of hot ants were running through her veins which, she knew, was called vertigo.

Zhang was making her do this as a humiliation.

Enough, she decided. He had had his go at watching her crawl around like a legless worm. She took a last picture and crept backwards until she felt safe. The embarrassing contortions had to be made again in order to stand up. Why had she dressed in the tight-skirted dress this morning? Perhaps there was a pornographic side to Zhang, although she had never worried about that with him.

Straightening up with as much dignity as she could muster, she picked the phone from the ground and shook her fringe so that it fell tidily. Zhang was no longer on the roof. Fear cramped her stomach muscles. When she realised that the heavy, insulated trapdoor was back in place, the blood rushed to her head. She ran to the lid. Its fit was tight. With her shoe in one hand, she banged on it most inefficiently. She started to shout Zhang's name, louder and louder, and the breeze took the words with it.

She sat down on the rim of the trapdoor and concentrated on bringing her breathing under control. Then she tapped Zhang's mobile number on her phone. A blue message read, *Number disconnected*. Only yesterday she had called him successfully.

Far away, high above her, flew a commercial airliner. It made her think of the man who had fallen out of one. Director-General Zhang would now be back at his desk. He would not be able to concentrate on anything but her, left helpless on the roof. Soon, it would be midday. He would go to the canteen for his jasmine tea. Others would mill around, greet him with respect, kowtow to his ideas. Not like her, who irritated him. She had been hired before Zhang's arrival at the bank. He had found

200

a female number three director and could do nothing about it.

Fanli sat under the little carport. She had missed the call with Chicago. It was so annoying, but she tried to push the thought from her mind. She took from her bag the financial statement she had prepared, and went through it again. In the capital and reserve figures, she had deducted the loss account wrongly by almost two million. She searched in her bag for her pen and altered the number, adding her initials to the correction. Any moment now, Zhang would be sitting at his desk and would open the plastic container containing the dumplings his wife made for him for lunch to eat with his jasmine tea. With his personalised chopsticks, he would bring the first to his eager mouth. The belly full, his disposition would improve and he would definitely relent, come upstairs, roll away the lid and tell her that it was an accident, that the trapdoor had just closed over him and that he had gone to get a technician to help her down.

It became two, then three o'clock in the afternoon. The lid underneath her remained inactive. No sound penetrated it. She decided that Zhang was now acting criminally. She would go to a lawyer and press charges. She knew one, one she had dated, not as lawyer but as man friend. They had seen each other regularly for two years, enjoyed eating in restaurants and talking business. Fanli's married sister and mother saw a lot of promise in this. However, the day they pushed the friendship a step further by sleeping together, the relationship broke apart irreparably.

Checking her watch, she saw with disbelief that it was now close to four in the afternoon. In two hours the bank would be closed. Perhaps Zhang had called for assistance with the trapdoor's mechanics and was now on tenterhooks, worrying about her. The technical department was always slow to respond, and the mechanics were bored and conceited; they put things right in the end, looking down at one unpleasantly. All that was needed was to fix the crank wheel, or even just push the lid across by force; surely they could work that out? With just a crack open, she could manage; at least there would be the possibility to communicate and hand items up to her. She was getting thirsty.

'Five o'clock. For God's sake!' Pink ribbons appeared in the darkening sky. The workday was almost done. Zhang could not possibly leave her up here all night. The wind got up. What if it started to rain? The little shelter over the lid would not protect her, if the rain was driven sideways by the wind. Zhang would look out of his office window and see the rain wash against the glass. He would jump up, throw his hand against his head. 'Director Chu!' he would say out loud and rush down the corridor to the lift. He could not hate her that much, not personally. They had had a business disagreement, as there are so many everywhere, every day.

She lay her ear against the lid and concentrated, but the insulation was compact and efficient.

'Hello!' she shouted. Nothing. She jerked her head round at a sudden grating noise behind her. A large, dry leaf was being swept across the roof by the breeze. It ended up caught against a pile of building material on the west side of the roof, which she now noticed for the first time as it was covered with a tarpaulin the same grey as the surface of the roof.

She went to investigate. If she had to stay here a few hours longer, she might as well make herself more comfortable, if possible.

The tarpaulin was partly rotten at the seam. Lifting a corner of if to peek underneath revealed an empty lychee tin. There was a broom with a worn-down head, an off-white plastic bowl, some breeze blocks and bricks, and several sacks of sand, now solidified to concrete.

It had become so dark that the roof looked like a different landscape, with what light there was coming from the many windows being lit all over Shanghai. People had lives down there, comfort, food and water.

Zhang would be on his way home. The entrance to the bank was on the west side of the building. If she leant over the rim far enough, she could probably see her colleagues leaving. Perhaps she should throw her handbag down to attract someone's attention? Many would know it was her Ted Baker bag. Or yell like mad? However, her voice would be drowned in the cacophony of the traffic. Besides, she did not have the nerve to lean over the rim that far; the mere thought of it activated the vertigo ants.

Her handbag? She stopped and pondered. Why had he permitted her to take her handbag along? Women and handbags belonged together. If he had planned to trap her up here, he would not have wanted her to have her phone with her. On the other hand, he needed her to have her phone to take pictures and, if her handbag had stayed behind in her office, it would have been noticed that she had gone missing. She decided to ask for a million American dollars in compensation, once the jury had charged Zhang with kidnap, or even attempted murder.

The battery icon on her phone was way down. Why had she not worried about that first?

The country people of Guizhou survived with little, her grandmother used to say as she clawed sunflower seeds out of a ripe sunflower head. She had insisted on the name Fanli for her first granddaughter, Fanli meaning generous and loyal. Grandmother, sadly, had departed from this life.

It began to rain, and rain hard, the drops like angry tears. Fanli took shelter under the little square roof, but not before knocking the dust out of the plastic bowl and setting it up in the open to gather rainwater.

She tried calling Zhang again. Same thing. She called reception. When Miss Liao answered, Fanli identified herself as third director and urged Liao to listen carefully.

'I have been locked out, on top of the bank building.'

Liao giggled, embarrassed.

'This is an emergency. Send someone to open the hatch to the roof and help me down.'

'I don't understand your message,' said Liao.

'Never mind. Just tell as many people about this as you can, but not Director-General Zhang.'

Liao laughed again. 'Many have gone home.'

'Please help me,' Fanli shouted into her handheld device. 'I will die up here on the roof.'

'On the roof,' repeated Liao and laughed again, so hard that she hung up.

204

In a short time, Fanli's smartphone would run out of power. She called the fire brigade and explained her situation.

'We do not respond to crank calls,' the operator said. 'You should be ashamed of yourself, taking time away from people who are in peril.'

'Look, I am the one in peril!' she replied. 'I am locked out, up on the roof of the Shanghai Investment Bank building. I can't get back down and night is coming. Please send someone.'

'Just a moment.'

Fanli sighed with relief. They were taking this seriously.

'Are you still there?'

'Of course I am still here.'

'I checked on our map. Shanghai Investment Bank does not have a roof terrace. Is this a domestic dispute?'

'It's not a terrace, it is just a flat roof. Someone cruel pushed me up onto it, closed the hatch and left.'

'Maybe you should call social services.'

'Please help me. My mobile is running out.'

'Recharge and then call social services.'

'I am exposed to the elements. No food, no water, no electricity.'

'The Shanghai Investment Bank. I am surprised they don't offer that on their roof terrace.'

'It's not a... You know what, you are not worth the last of my battery power.'

In her panic, Fanli pressed the first contact on her address list – the restaurant from which she regularly ordered take-away to eat in her studio flat.

'Yellow Dragon,' the man at the till answered.

'Thank God,' she said.

'What will it be? My brother has just made fresh dumplings.'

'Listen, where I work is the Shanghai Investment Bank in Pudong. It has a flat roof on the thirty-second floor. Someone pulled me onto this roof and closed the trapdoor, and now I am up here alone and night is coming.'

'It is too difficult for us to deliver up to where you say you are.'

'Never mind.' She had to save the last of her power in the phone.

The wind changed direction, and the dry leaf was detached from the tarpaulin. It scuttled across the roof and, after a moment of hesitation at the infinity edge, it was blown over the rim and gone.

Fanli checked the rainwater in the plastic bowl and drank the small amount. It tasted of sand. She licked the inside of the lychee tin as far down as her tongue could reach, in case there was any sugar left. The fruits had been eaten months ago, perhaps even a year. Fanli took her shoes off, curled up under the little shelter, bent her right arm and put her head on it.

'Things will get better,' she said, and thought, *I just need to sleep a little to gather strength.*

The metal lid felt so cold and hard that it seemed to attack the structure of her bones. She pulled the tarpaulin off the pile of discarded material and folded it as best as its stiffness allowed. She kicked it into submission, before dragging it under her shelter to curl up on it. The material was coarse, smelled most unpleasantly and was grubby with brick dust. The thought that, in a rainstorm, she could shelter under it, pleased her inordinately.

'Thank you, thank you,' she shouted into the night.

Riding on this positive thought, she found the strength to start on an inventory of her handbag. Apart from the mobile, there was her pen, *Shanghai Investment Bank* stamped on the promotional item; she used it to sign her business letters. She could tear up the pages of the financial statement into square bits, write the word *Help* on them and let them sail down to the ground. However, being practically weightless, the wind would just blow them away. Even if they did get to land, someone clever could piece them together and discover the bank's secrets.

There was her lipstick, lash-thickening mascara and a small bottle of coral-coloured nail varnish. There was a packet of Kleenexes, and a narrow tampon box containing two. Best of all was a little packet of extra-strong mints. She shook one out and popped it into her mouth. Sucking it and closing her eyes, she pretended for a moment that she was back in her normal life in the modern studio flat, grazing the fridge and throwing herself onto the sofa to relax and watch the news, before washing her hair, laying out her clothes for tomorrow and going to bed – a soft, clean, warm bed, with her childhood teddy staring at her with his beady glass eyes.

'The army.' She sat up. They had helicopters, could fly over the building and see her wave. They also had harnesses to hoist her up into their aircraft. The euphoria died out as fast as it had ignited. She had power for only one more call on her mobile. Trying to find the right person in the military would be a drawn-out nightmare. Fanli called her sister in Hong Kong instead. It rang and rang, then she heard Sandra's voice.

'Please leave a message,' and the phone went dead.

The wind increased. Night had come fast, the sun sliding below the horizon. Hunger started to gnaw. That morning, she had skipped breakfast because she was running late. Tomorrow, someone sent by Zhang would rescue her, Zhang being too much of a coward to do it himself, or to apologise to her, or even ever mention this little incident between them.

Shivering, she curled up tighter. The stars were out. Her gold watch told her it was midnight. She needed to pee. The plastic bowl was not an option; it had to serve as a rain reservoir. She went to the southerly corner, where there was a gridded drain, and peed into it. On her walk back to the carport, which she decided to call *small house*, to her pleasure she found a piece of green plastic string caught in a metal cowl over an air vent. She untangled it, rolled it and stored it in her handbag.

She settled again. 'Stars, so bright and so close.' She found solace in talking out loud, as if someone were there with her to hear it, take it in and hopefully respond.

Director-General Zhang was by now home. She had once been invited to his house on the occasion of Chinese New Year. Zhang owned two Pekinese dogs, miniature versions of the golden statues at the entrance to the bank – deliberately planned that way. She had tried to communicate with the dogs, but they seemed stupid, with inexpressive bulbous eyes, and noses so flat and inbred that they snorted rather than breathed.

'How was your day?' Zhang's Singaporean wife would have asked when he got in, giving her back the empty plastic container which had held the dumplings.

'Fine,' he would have answered. 'I left a director on the roof of the bank to die.'

Unlikely conversation. Tomorrow, Fanli would shout over the side of the building to be heard. Unfortunately, the whole top floor was empty for refurbishment, and the work had been delayed. And then it occurred to her that the window cleaning contractors usually came around the middle of the month. Today was the tenth of June. They lifted their cleaners on platforms right up to the top floor. All she would have to do was grab her bag and step onto one, to be brought down to the pavement.

A few weeks ago, she had been to a temple and lit several joss sticks to Guanyin, Goddess of Mercy. Would she help her now and send the cleaners to do the windows tomorrow, please? Actually, today would have been even better.

She should ignore the pangs of hunger, and her anger at Zhang, and try to go to sleep.

Grandmother's ghost rose before her. The kind, white-haired woman picked seeds out of the flowerhead with her thin fingers, put them into her mouth and, using her tongue, she adroitly separated husk from pip, which she ate, the husk spat out. She pushed the net hammock in which little Fanli was to be put to sleep, a soft song falling over her dry, colourless lips.

Tears ran down Fanli's cheeks. Eventually, she dozed

off, shivering in her light sleep. One worry-dream chased another. When, finally, day grew, she felt immensely worn out. She sucked another mint, savouring its taste. She got up and stiffly walked to the east side and the apartment block she had photographed, pictures which Zhang did not have as they were on her phone. The lack of photos would make him decide to come up onto the roof this morning; he was a meticulous man.

In the early morning light, looking down at the top-floor balcony of the building to the east, two floors lower than the bank, she saw a tricycle. The occupants had a child. A sizeable bamboo cage was hanging from a hook. She could not make out what kind of songbird was imprisoned in it. A metal filing cabinet showed rust at its corners, and a shelf with kitchen appliances obviously not used regularly was covered by a transparent plastic sheet. Crouching down, through the glass of the balcony door she could see into the kitchen – not all the way, but half of a table was visible, on which were dishes, possibly with food in them. Best of all, she saw the forearms and hands of at least adults sitting at the table.

Fanli sprinted back to the builders' residues, searched for a while and picked up a small, solidified blob of concrete.

Concentrating on the east building top-floor balcony, she aimed and threw the concrete as hard as she could. It hit the birdcage, which started to swing violently, so much so that it risked coming off the hook. The balcony door opened and a man appeared. First, he steadied the swinging cage, then he bent and picked up the concrete projectile, before he looked up. What he saw was a woman doing jumping jacks on the roof of the bank.

Fanli stopped jumping up and down, and started to shout. The man held his hand behind his ear, indicating he couldn't hear. She turned sideways so he could see her move her hand to her mouth as if to eat, but then stopped. She did the same with miming to drink. Then she sank to her knees and lifted up her arms in surrender.

A woman appeared on the balcony. He pointed to the figure on the roof. Fanli took up jumping again, and mimicked eating and drinking. The couple on the balcony stared for a while, but then, to Fanli's disappointment, went back inside. Perhaps to call someone, or go downstairs and next door to the bank to tell reception, more likely. Sadly, they sat back at their table, for now the arms and hands moved again as before.

Fanli searched for another projectile, a larger one, and threw that. It landed on the balcony floor, but nobody came out. The next throw hit the birdcage again.

The balcony door was thrown open. She did her dance, her eating and drinking mime. The man shook his fist at her. She held both arms up to heaven, screaming for help. She saw him hesitate. The anger had gone out of him; he decided that something was not right. Fanli analysed his movements. But then he went back inside.

The table was cleared of dishes. One of them probably was taking the child to kindergarten, and the other going to work.

Fanli returned to her *little house* to sit and ponder. A seagull flew low over the building top, squawking. If Fanli prepared a little heap of concrete blobs, she could knock one of these gulls out of the sky. But then what? Eat it raw?

She knotted the string she had found yesterday around a brick. Daring to lie down right next to the rim of the roof, her eyes closed, she let the brick swing until it had enough velocity to knock against the window of the floor beneath. The window did not break; the brick had no effect. Nobody was in the room. Pulling the brick back up, the string tore, the brick tilted, the string unwound and, to her horror, the brick fell down the building. She pulled her head back and waited for a scream, an ambulance siren. Nothing.

By now, everyone in the bank would be at their desk. Hunger gnawed at her stomach. From time to time, she went to check whether the birdcage people had returned home.

She pretended to have given up on hoping Zhang would rescue her imminently. The real good things only ever sneaked up on one, wasn't that right? From Guizhou, she had applied to Yale, but with no serious hope of being accepted; she had no contacts or connections. She had been about to accept a place at her local university, when, out of the blue, an envelope arrived from the USA. She had got in! *So long ago*, Fanli thought, *so innocent*.

This new day on the roof was overcast, and rain was possible. At least this would provide her with drinking water and perhaps some to wash her body, at night so as not to be seen. She could even put on lipstick to make her feel better about herself. This thought caused her to start weeping, so hard that her shoulders shook.

The reassuring thought that humans could survive without food for many days, and that it was dehydration

212

which was the enemy, which she did not have to suffer, finally dried her tears.

The birdcage people were at the table eating. Fanli threw a new concrete blob. It hit the birdcage again. This time, the woman appeared. Fanli hopped around, pretended to eat and drink, and sank to her knees, arms spread out. The man came onto the balcony. He unhooked the cage and carried it into the kitchen. *He anticipates that his cage will continue to be hit, unless he does something about the mad stone-thrower*, Fanli analysed. He would have to act. His wife was the cowardly type who would try to hold him back from doing something about a deranged woman on top of the Shanghai Investment Bank building. Was she not storing electrical cooking appliances on her balcony, rather than using them? What about letting her child use the tricycle in the play area?

By midday, moisture blankets wafted in from the sea and, shortly afterwards, it started to rain, large drops pelting down. Fanli pushed the Ted Baker bag under the tarpaulin and put out the plastic bowl to catch water. She took her dress off and her underwear when the rainstorm was at its worst, and had a natural shower, making sure she stood in the centre of the roof where nobody could see her nudity. A sharp neon zigzag cut through a dark cloud. An idea shot through her. She deliberately went to stand, clearly visible, almost like a Chinese shadow puppet, on the east side of the roof.

Luck was with her. The man had come out on the balcony to add more plastic sheeting over his wife's cooking appliances. Most probably sent by her to do so.

He turned round and froze. *He's seen me.* She mimed despair, her arms splayed across her naked breasts. He signalled back to her with a barely noticeable wave.

Another lightning zigzag inspired her to fall to the ground as if hit, her outstretched arm protruding over the rim of the roof. She had hurt her hip, but the important thing was that the man got the message that something was seriously wrong. She peered over the edge and watched him carefully. She could tell from his involuntary body movements that he was close to panic. Working with men, she had learnt to ignore what came out of their mouths and pay attention to how their real emotions leaked from their bodies. The man on that balcony cared for songbirds. He was unhappily married to a woman who only ever cooked him basic food, no matter how many modern electric appliances he bought her as presents.

The storm had passed. 'Surely the birdcage man has gone to the bank reception desk,' she said out loud. There, Miss Liao was not taking him seriously. Probably, she laughed at him insultingly. This was giving him doubts about what he had seen. He would return to his flat and do nothing more.

By midday, Fanli was proven wrong. Mr Birdcage had brought a nautical-looking rope with a metal ball at one end. He prepared to throw the rope across the gap between the two buildings. She was sure he would not have enough room to swing the rope. And, indeed, when he threw it, it flew a few metres, lost momentum and fell back against the east building, hitting a window in the flat beneath him. The breaking of glass pinged in the air.

'Sadly,' she said to her invisible, mute roof companion, 'this man is unpractical.'

After sucking on an extra-strong mint for lunch, Fanli got into position to watch the east building. The neighbour with the broken window was now on Mr Birdcage's balcony, an older man. Clearly, Mr Birdcage had explained the rope and the metal ball, and then pointed up to the bank roof. Immediately, Fanli started up her jumping jacks and mime of eating and drinking.

Both men, after watching for a while, went inside and did not reappear.

In the afternoon, a large seagull landed on the flat roof. When it became aware of the human under the shelter, it twisted its head left and right.

'Quite adorable,' Fanli said to it. 'Hey, you, I don't feel like eating you raw any longer. Come and visit me from time to time so we can chat. At least you are alive and can squawk.'

The seagull opened its beak wide and bent its head. It vomited the food it had eaten, and then took off. The moist heap it left behind was made of barely digested pieces of fish. Half a head showed, the eye still intact. One scoop at a time with her debit card, Fanli scraped up the vomited mess and fed it into her mouth. It was food.

Exhausted, she returned to her folded tarpaulin to rest. Four people knew she was up here: Zhang, the birdcage couple, and the older man with the broken window. Two days ago, it had only been Zhang; yesterday, the birdcage couple; and now broken window man. She had made progress; the gods were on her side.

When she woke up, it was evening. She attempted to count the stars for a while before they became blurred.

The next day, Fanli found it difficult to get up and function. Her body seemed to have given up emitting hunger pangs. In their place, a lassitude had overtaken her. By the time she crawled from her *little house*, Shanghai down below was again in full working mode, the bank beneath her busy.

Zhang could not possibly be so inhumane as to just go on as if nothing were amiss. It had now been seventy-two hours since he had left her up here. He would tell those who asked where she was that he had given her a few days off; that she had fallen ill with pneumonia, the measles; that she had twisted her ankle, dislocated a shoulder; that she had had a car accident, had been abducted. Whatever, his anger towards her had had ample time to subside. If he had a criminal record, he would never have been hired as Director-General and live an orderly, domestic life. What would make him decide to save her would be the special board meeting he had certainly called today, at which his proposal to buy the east building would be approved. Then, he would repent and rescue her, finding a plausible excuse for her absence. She would swear never to say a word, if he let her eat his lunch dumplings, all of them.

He had exposed her to three nights on the roof – that had to be enough, even for the most deep-seated anger. He prided himself on being an international magnate, while at the same time repeatedly complaining to the canteen manageress that the water was not hot enough for his jasmine tea leaves, making her cry in the backroom. Director-General Zhang was not a murderer, just a normal man. Being accused of inflicting bodily and mental harm on one of his directors would destroy his career, name and family, including the pair of stupid Pekinese.

★

Fanli drank from the plastic bowl, its coarse rim repulsive. Today had to be Thursday. Her elegant watch only showed the time, not the date.

If Zhang did not come to his senses, then she had the option of the people in the east building. She filled her stomach with water. It fooled her body into believing that food was in it, at least for the time being. Sudden diarrhoea indicated that the seagull fish medley had been the wrong thing to eat. The smelly mess Fanli dropped near the drain was luckily downwind. Rain would wash it eventually down the drain. Further weakened, she dragged herself across to the east side of the roof.

On Mr Birdcage's balcony was action which she guessed concerned her; it lifted her spirits. A small table had been installed, and an apparatus placed on it. The old man from the flat below waved to her, almost expansively. The men fiddled with the thing on the table. The wife appeared at the balcony door, only to step back immediately. After a while, both men waved, trying to indicate that they would do something clever to reach her. She held her breath. A projectile came her way, a black rubber ball. It landed close to her feet. Quickly, she grabbed it, and realised that a line was linking her

217

now with the balcony – two lines, in fact, as it was a loop that ran through the bubble and back to the balcony again.

The operation was not finished; the two men pulled at the line, and she saw that something was clipped to it and rising towards her. All she had to do was hold on to the ball. Slowly, in spurts, the item approached. It was a metal claw with three teeth, and a piece of paper stuck to it with a message: *We used a line thrower. Hook this anchor somewhere safe on your roof.*

She smiled and felt the unused muscles in her face. As there was nothing on the rim into which to hook the anchor, she walked it to the pile of builders' materials and secured the anchor claws behind a pile of bags containing solid concrete. She gave the men a thumbs-up.

Then, to her excitement, another item was pulled up the line. It dangled and swayed, but made its way to her. She had to lift it over the rim of the roof and unhook it. It was a pink plastic child's basket. On the closed lid was a picture of Hello Kitty. She lifted the lid. There was no food in it, damn it, but another piece of paper. People who had food had no idea what hunger was like. *Why are you on the roof? Bank reception does not want to know about you. Are you being punished by the bank or are you a criminal?*

Fanli's disappointment was as borderless as the roof she was standing on.

She turned the paper over, ran to her bag, clawed out her pen and, in anger, wrote, *I was left on the roof by mistake. Please send me food.* She pulled on the line, and the Hello Kitty basket travelled back over the canyon between the buildings.

Fanli watched their reaction when they read her missive. *Food. I need food*, she attempted to mentally communicate to them. It was now getting so dark that she could not see what they were doing, but the Hello Kitty basket made it back. One small moon bun was in it.

'When I could eat a horse,' she said to herself.

Ah, and what she had taken for a paper napkin was another note. *My wife does not give away her food. She believes you are bad. You took your clothes off.*

Fanli cried, until she realised that she was wasting precious strength. Then she wrote on the reverse of the note, *I have some money to pay for food*, and sent Hello Kitty on its journey.

In her purse she had 150 yuan, which was about the equivalent of 25 American dollars, and some change. All of a sudden, the deprivation she had suffered and lack of calories made her so dizzy that she fell in a faint to the ground.

It was dark when she regained consciousness. No more food had come her way. She was facing a fourth night. Tomorrow morning, she would eat the moon bun. It was something to hang on to.

After a night of turning and suffering, the magical day with food arrived. She ate the bun standing up, with view of the ocean. It was stale and chewy. The red soy paste filling had dried up. The autumn equinox, for which the bun had been made, happened nine months ago. Mrs Birdcage had probably found it at the back of a kitchen drawer.

At midday, the pink basket reached her roof. The

note inside said, *Send the money first and then my wife might be willing to part with some of her food.*

Fanli placed 30 yuan in Hello Kitty and fed it down. It went slowly, because she had so little physical strength left in her arms to pull the line.

Taking her bra off, because it had become too large for her shrinking breasts and twisted around her upper body, she sat, tailor-fashion, near the rim, waiting for the food she had paid for. Emphasising this positive moment in her current situation, her thoughts went to her sister who, in the last call from the mobile, had asked Fanli to leave a message.

Lingling was three years younger and three times better informed about life than her elder sister. Why had she not been able to answer the phone? She was an artist painter. And her husband had taken her to live in Hong Kong, from where he sold copies of oil paintings by the old masters. The copying took place in a warehouse in Kowloon. Lingling, who had had high expectations of being recognised for her art, gave up on that, to specialise in copying hands and feet from the originals. Colleagues specialised in torsos, landscapes, etc. Westerners bought the canvases, which were rolled into a tube and sent to them by post. It was understandable Lingling had chosen to paint feet; she was familiar with her sister's feet. They had kicked her nose often enough. The girls grew up sleeping in one bed. Older and not fitting next to each other any longer, they had slept head to toe for many years. Fanli smiled up to the stars.

Her thoughts reverted inevitably to food, yearning for fresh, warm, cooked food – a dish of duck with almonds, ginger shreds marinated in rice wine. At that New Year's party in Zhang's house, they had served pheasant in lime-zest sauce, and hand-made noodles.

Shortly after seven o'clock in the evening, the Hello Kitty basket safely crossed the canyon. Never had she anticipated opening a present with more nervous tension. A medium-sized plastic beaker had been sent. It contained cooked rice with a few sprinkles of soy sauce. There were a few green peas, and one slice of cooked carrot, nothing more. Worth about one yuan.

Please go to the police and tell them I am exposed on the roof against my will. If you do this I will give you a lot of money. I work for the bank. She added fifty yuan and sent Kitty back to the balcony.

*

The next day arrived, grey and dull. The extremely modest rice dish had had little impact on her extreme hunger. Even the gull's vomit had contained more protein. Surely, for the extra money, Mrs Birdcage would make an effort to send more and better food. She had a child to feed and knew the importance of nourishment.

Fanli yearned to shower and clean herself. The plastic bowl was now half-full. But there was no soap. And no toothpaste to clean her slimy teeth. She would pay for those later. Food was the priority.

Fanli went to watch the balcony and the arrival of Hello Kitty. To her utter dismay, the balcony was empty. Everything had been taken away, including the birdcage, the tricycle and the kitchen appliances. The table was still there, the line-throwing apparatus back in its box. That was the end of communicating, shot through her hurtfully. But no – the feeding line on which Hello Kitty travelled was still in place, on their side fixed over the hook from which the birdcage had been taken, and on her side anchored behind the concrete bags. Relief swept through her like cool seawater over hot sand. *But why did they empty the balcony last night?* she asked herself over and over manically.

Perhaps the woman's mother had died suddenly and they had to... They were afraid they would get into trouble with the law sending food to the next roof. He had cancer and had lost his job months ago, and they could not pay the rent any more. She could not bring herself to give food away, because she was mentally deranged, and the pressure of the mad woman on the bank... Fanli savoured the carrot slice on her tongue. She had kept it for breakfast.

As the day advanced, the strength of the sun increased and hers waned. Today, she remembered, was Saturday; management met at midday to discuss the previous week's business. Sandwiches were ordered in, and tea offered. It was always for her to provide the figures, which she put together with the help of the accountant and the strategist on Friday afternoon. Fanli pulled the report from her bag and checked it again. Looking at numbers made her feel that her life had not collapsed. She had contributed to the profit account. Obviously, not these last six days. She was an efficient worker. Once released and fed food, she could catch up.

Fanli pulled in her breath. Mr Birdcage was on the

empty balcony. Was she starting to hallucinate? Or did the spirits send him? There was nothing left on the balcony to justify his presence. He raised his face up to the bank building. She waved.

He went to the table where the gun had been, but now even the box was gone. When did that happen? He had only hired the equipment; that made sense.

His wife had left him and taken the child with her. Why had she taken the kitchen appliances? Probably to sell them. She was that kind of mercenary person. Good riddance. But what would Mr Birdcage do without her? How could he help Fanli, unpractical as he was?

He acknowledged her with a little wave, his arm close to his body. She mimicked food going to her open mouth. He disappeared in the kitchen and almost immediately came out again and put something into the Hello Kitty basket.

When she lifted the lid, she found the plastic beaker was half-full of rice, uncooked hard grains.

'I hate you,' she yelled in her disappointment, and tears dropped from her eyes.

He smiled and waved again before leaving the balcony, satisfaction about the great gesture he had just made for a low-down criminal written all over the back of his unpleasant, purple T-shirt.

If that rice were steamed, it would amount to a good portion of food. Uncooked, not even birds would eat it. But it was food. That was so irritating about it. She put a handful into the lychee tin the builders had left behind and put it into the sun to warm the water in it. *How long will that take?* she wondered.

She tore off the last page of her report, struck

through the final paragraph and wrote at the bottom, *Turn the page.* On the back, she wrote, *Dear important man owning a lovely balcony flat, thank you for the rice which is a most generous gift. May I suggest you put a pan of water on the stove and heat the water until it boils, and then add two, no make it three handfuls of rice, and let it boil until the rice is larger. Then put it into the beaker and send it to me. I know you can do this as you are an extraordinarily clever and practical man.*

'It hurts to have to do that,' Fanli said to her invisible friend.

Day seven, Sunday. Only a small group of employees would be working in the bank below her.

Trying to see into Mr Birdcage's kitchen, even crouching right down, head on the roof surface, she could not tell whether the man was boiling rice. Hello Kitty was in his court. She drank so much water she felt like a barrel.

Shortly after that, something happened to her mind. She could not see the sea any longer, and the buildings in the foreground seemed to be made of soft rubber, which allowed them to distort and sway drunkenly. *Do you see that? Do you see that?* Her fantasy friend did not answer. Fanli fainted.

When she blinked and light penetrated again, she knew she had just been granted a time of bliss. She had felt no hunger, no pain; no memories burnt her brain: utter dark bliss.

She rose dishevelled, surprised, disoriented. Then she noticed the handle of the Hello Kitty basket at the periphery of the roof, trying to get over the edge. She ran to catch it. Things were getting better. She would survive.

In the basket was the beaker into which rice noodles had been forced, uncooked and mostly broken. There was no note.

'Men are crap. Men like you should have been strangled at birth. Men like you do not deserve to breathe fresh air. Men like you... Asshole!' she finished her rant.

Mr Birdcage had long left his balcony. *Asshole* she had shouted, something she had never done before. In assholes it was warm; thermometers were stuck there. Vaginas, too, were warm and moist. Fanli pushed several noodles into her vagina and sealed them there with one of the tampons. She sat, immobile. Beggars can't be choosers.

*

During the next week, Fanli and Mr Birdcage came to some sort of mute agreement. She sent him money, and he provided her with uncooked rice and noodles. Several more times, Fanli let herself faint because it was so pleasant. One day, she found a clove in the rice which must have fallen in unnoticed. She savoured its flavour, sucked it for hours. Once, she found a curled-up spider amongst the noodles. That was less pleasing. What Mr Birdcage was sending her was obviously old food.

Fanli ran out of money. She looked forward to the moment she would not wake up after a faint. Despite receiving no money, every other day Mr Birdcage still sent uncooked rice and noodles, alternately. She asked him for soap, and back came the beaker half-full with washing powder. Fanli had an unusual shower that day and felt great, certainly lighter as she was now extremely thin. Other effects of malnutrition were a tremor in her hands, and eyes which seemed to blur or dim.

And then Hello Kitty did not come back for four days in a row. They were hard days. She cried a lot. Mr Birdcage seemed to have left the apartment. The old man below never got the glass replaced in his window. He, too, seemed to have moved out. And so had others; she could tell from the few lights on during the evenings. Director-General Zhang must have managed to convince the other directors to buy the east building. The tenants were starting to move out. She, Fanli, was doomed.

*

Two weeks later, though, she was still alive. Her body resembled one of those three thousand-year-old mummies found in a dig, which could divulge clues about an ancient civilisation.

The Ted Baker dress had been expensive, but it deserved that price tag. It was hanging on her emaciated body, but the colours had not faded nor had the cloth deteriorated. If Ted ever envisaged an endurance test on his goods…

She had stopped getting up, and used the last of her strength to write a letter to her sister, telling her how much she loved her, telling her that to die was not really such a scary thing, once one set one's mind to it. She put the letter into the handbag and closed the zip.

And then a miracle happened.

It had been a breezy day from the start. Clouds

sailed in the sky, and there he was, a man, a European with a round, pink face. He had blue eyes and smiled so widely that his teeth showed. Fanli was taken aback. He approached her, his head continuously smiling and bobbing. It made her laugh. When his face came right up to hers, she shied away a little; but then, delighted that she was not alone any longer, she reached out and caught his face with both her hands. His skin felt warm and soft. She hugged him; she kissed his smile. She smiled back into his blue eyes. She told him how hard it had been for her. He kept smiling and leaning against her.

Evening came, and she held onto him because the wind was getting stronger and threatened to take him away from her. As Shanghai softly drifted into evening, she sat on the roof holding on to the European visitor. For an hour or more, she whispered to him all that had happened since Zhang left her on the roof. He moved his head. He understood. He made squeaky noises when the story was particularly bad. But his smile never failed.

Then, for another hour, she told him about her work and promotions, and even her time at university. The early morning light was starting to spread when Fanli was telling the European visitor about her grandmother and her childhood.

She asked him for his name, but he did not have to spell it out. He was Mr Happy. She told him about Mr Birdcage, who had no idea that rice and noodles had to be cooked. It was rather sad that a grown man took so little interest in what his wife was doing for years and years.

Fanli attached the string of Mr Happy to one of the stanchions of the shelter. She slept most of the day, but happily. Inside her, she knew that evening would come and she could talk with Mr Happy some more. He had all the patience in the world. His smile was infectious. She fancied him. More than that, she was in love with him. The endorphins produced when a woman is in love work overtime.

★

She lay unconscious. The lid under her moved sideways, and a man squeezed through the gap up onto the roof. He was a surveyor, preparing the joining of the buildings. When he found the woman prostrate on the floor, he called out in fright. She had a pink birthday balloon tied to her ankle. He turned and yelled down into the bank for help. After prodding, the emaciated cadaver moved an arm. He put his ear to the reeking figure's chest. A heart was beating.

Others climbed up. Director-General Zhang was not one of them.

★

Fanli arose from a deep, dark place.

'She is awake,' a woman said.

Fanli wondered who was talking, and to whom. Clearly, there were others around her. How did they get onto the roof? Fanli opened her eyes. Everything was different. She was floating on lotus petals. After a while, she dared looked again. A hospital room, a soft pillow under her head, a soft cover over her body. She tried to

228

lift her arm, but a tube ran to it from a plastic bag on a hook.

A face came in close over hers. And it was not smiling.

'Can you hear me?' the nurse asked. 'What is your name?'

'Fanli Happy.'

'Happy, as in Miss Happy?'

'Where is Mr Happy?' Fanli asked. 'I need to talk to him.' Panicking now, she began to shout. 'Please, don't take Mr Happy away from me. Please!'

'The pink birthday balloon,' said the nurse. 'She was brought in with it tied to her ankle.'

'Of what importance is that? The patient is dangerously undernourished.' Matron was not impressed.

'Happy,' shouted Fanli.

'When they brought her in, I untied the balloon and put it in the bathroom,' said the nurse.

'Leave it there,' ordered Matron.

'The patient seems distressed without it.'

'It's a children's birthday balloon called Mr Happy.'

'I don't know about that,' said the nurse, but she went to the bathroom and brought the balloon back, holding it by its string. Fanli tried to sit up, but the drip line restrained her.

'No, no.' Matron pushed her back down. 'No rash moves. You have three ports in you.'

To the matron's surprise, Fanli reached out, caught the balloon and brought it close to her face. She kissed the taut, rubber skin. And then she whispered to the balloon, and her toes protruding from the cover moved as if in sexual arousal.

'The doctor is about to get here to check on you,' said the nurse. 'He will not want a pink balloon in his face.'

'You don't understand,' said Fanli. 'We are in love.'

'It is said to be normal after a prolonged lack of food,' said the nurse. 'Ghandi, who fasted for twenty-seven days, talked nonsense afterwards.'

'The doctor is here,' said the matron. 'Hide that balloon.'

Fanli held onto the head of her Mr Happy. 'I need him. He saved me. I love him.'

The glass door slid open. The nurse grabbed the balloon and pushed it under the bed.

'No!' protested Fanli.

The doctor checked the monitor. 'Do not increase the dose. We have to build up the body slowly, very slowly. I would like to examine her. Can we get that bed down a bit?'

The nurse pressed the button to lower the hospital bed. While the doctor worked blue rubber gloves over his fingers, the bed kept going down.

Fanli lay still, tears rolling out of the corners of her closed eyes.

'Why is she crying like this?' asked the doctor.

'She is in love, she says,' replied the nurse.

There was a sharp, loud bang.

The doctor jumped back from the bed. 'What was that?'

'Don't worry, Dr Chen,' said Matron. 'There was a balloon under the bed. It popped.'

'You have killed him!' Fanli twisted around in the

230

bed. 'We talked all night. I need him. You have killed him. You are murderers.' Fanli was so agitated that, on the monitor, the heartbeat line became erratic and the alarm beeped continuously.

'She is having a heart attack.' Dr Chen pulled the glass door. 'We need the crash cart in here!' he yelled.

HAIRY LEGS

In The Hospital Chapel

'God's will,' said the hospital chaplain, as Schubert's *Ave Maria* marked the end of the funeral service for a three-day-old infant. Justin slipped the bible into the drawer of the pulpit at which he stood.

With deliberate gentleness, a nurse in uniform came up to him. 'That was lovely, Justin,' Betty whispered, tears bathing her eyes.

A pathologist lifted the tiny white coffin off the stand and carried it into the backroom, from where it would go down to the basement in a special lift – the basement in which were located the morgue, the autopsy theatre and the incinerator.

Someone had opened the double doors of the chapel, which led back into the concourse of the large hospital. After gathering their belongings and their courage, the two dozen or so mourners filed out. The mother of the baby stumbled over the leg of a foldable chair. Instantly, Betty was at her side, propping her up and escorting her through the door, before returning to Justin who was pulling on his overcoat.

'I have to perform a service of this kind far too often,'

he complained. She agreed with him by way of a deep sigh. Betty was an NHS-registered discharge nurse in the maternity unit of the hospital, while Justin had an MA in theology from Cambridge. The two had known each other for over ten years and had been engaged for the last two, but their efforts since then to organise a wedding had always been foiled by something: work commitments, her father's illness, overbooking of venues. It did not really matter; they were committed to each other. They had met during a hospital chapel funeral just like this one – a nurse who normally assisted mothers taking new life out into the world, and a priest to console mothers when that new life was taken from them just as it was beginning.

Everyone had left the chapel. A janitor was collecting the flower displays to go to the elderly wards upstairs. Another closed the double doors and turned off the lights. Betty went to the backroom to grab her bag. Work was done for the day. It was five o'clock on Friday in late June. The turnstile behind them, they stood in fresh air, undecided in front of the main entrance. Further down, at A&E, an ambulance emitted its last squeal before coming to a stop.

'A bite to eat?' Justin suggested.

They walked to his Hyundai in the staff car park, while she unburdened herself. 'In the second half of pregnancy, the mother developed pre-eclampsia. The midwife team did everything they could. A lengthy birth procedure was too tough on the baby, which was already weakened.'

He let her talk about pregnancy and births, because

234

he knew how passionate she was about it. He also knew how it irritated her to be trapped in the secondary role of discharging nurse, a role she described as teaching the mother to latch the newborn onto nipples, handing out leaflets about how to care for nipples, and then carrying the mother's overnight bag out to the new father in the drop-off car park where he took over, dismissing her as if she were a hospital porter.

★

Justin did not know what had happened two years ago. Betty had accompanied a father out to his car, while the birth-giving mother was kept in the maternity unit. The man could not understand why his wife had given birth to a dead baby. Handkerchief against his face stifling sobs, he walked next to her with a slight stoop. At his car, he was so shaky, he dropped the key fob. She had to pick it up and give it back to him. In a moment of pity, she suggested a cup of tea before he drove home, which was met with, 'I'll never put foot back into that hospital. They're all incompetent charlatans, butchers, murderers in white coats with grand attitudes.'

Unbuttoning her white coat, Betty suggested the Tea Cosy on King Street. After a short, uncomfortable drive with a weeping stranger, she found the tea room was closed. It was Monday. In front of the door with the notice in the window, he entered a second phase of anger.

'Olivia is forty-one. It was her last chance. *My* last chance. We tried everything for years. At home is a nursery all prepared, yellow with a gigantic stuffed giraffe…' His grief prevented him from going on.

'With time the pain will lessen, and you'll find a consoling mechanism sets in. The brain does that for us.'

'I couldn't give a monkeys about consoling mechanisms. Having children is preserving our species.' He dared look at her. 'Those nincompoop gyno doctors and midwives. My baby daughter got stuck in the narrow tube. I know what I'm talking about when I say narrow. Now take a whole baby… They could have blown oxygen up the vagina. But no, they watched a machine printing zigzags. I am going to sue the hospital.' He took a deep breath. 'For a lot of money.'

'Best you go home and be on stand-by when the natal unit contacts you to pick up your wife.'

'I can't go home. There is the giraffe.' Puffy eyes pleaded with her. 'If you came with me and explained why she had to die?'

He was a nice man. Pity for him made her behave in a grossly unprofessional way.

The first thing he did after entering the semi-detached house was to close the nursery room door with a mighty bang. A little teddy bear came off its nail. Then, in the unaired living room, he opened a whisky bottle at the drinks trolley and started pouring.

Betty felt the burn against her lips and only sipped tiny dribbles, regretting her impulsive behaviour which had landed her in a stranger's house. Could it be excused? Sitting on a sofa, she started to explain what had caused the death of the foetus during birth. Still at the trolley, he listened at first, while drinking. His sobbing had subsided. Rearranging the bottles, he became inattentive. Eventually, he came to sit on the armrest next to her. Shortly after, he caved into the seat on top of her lap, some of his whisky spilling on her shirt.

In a bedroom decorated in black and white – generous silver plumes, or perhaps ferns, printed on black wallpaper – on smooth black sheets, she let him have his way with her. In hindsight, the little sips she had taken from the whisky might have added up. She had not been able to answer his big question satisfactorily, and he was not a man with a philosophical side to him. Black sheets, and a glass and fake-brass drinks trolley?

He had grabbed her, owned her the way Justin never did. She luxuriated in the body contact; the coupling act felt smooth and natural. With Justin it hurt. She felt thrilled that she was experiencing sex as a pleasure. A real woman had lain dormant inside her all this time. When he pulled out, tears slid from the corners of her eyes. A unique and secret magic moment of her life had just come to an end, and she had enjoyed it like a shameless hussy. Nobody would ever know about it.

*

Certainly Justin had no idea and would probably not believe it – his plain dependable Betty jumping into bed at two in the afternoon with a total stranger.

He changed gears in his Hyundai, and she tried to keep chatting the way she used to. In moments as familiar as this, she was able to suppress the sinister guilt she carried around inside her. To fool Justin, she talked about babies dying during gestation, and those dying at birth, and those who only lived a very short time. He had to remind her to put on her safety belt, because she was carried away.

With every case, Justin thought, she seemed to get more involved and, if it turned bad, she took it as her own traumatic loss. So much so that she grieved for others, and seemed to withdraw from him. For some time now, she came up with excuses not to have sex. Justin was starting to get impatient about it.

They reached Grantchester and walked to the pub near the river, which was a safe place because it had been their picnic meadow early in their friendship. Now the day was overcast, as was suitable for mourning after such a sad send-off. Betty could not let it go. 'That poor mother in the chapel today; her milk had just come in, soaking her blouse. Her hands twitched, reaching for the warm body of the baby she had carried inside her for a full term.'

'Tea or coffee? Perhaps you would like a hot chocolate?'

'A beer. Get me a beer.'

'Betty, is that sensible?'

'Who cares?' She fiddled with the condiment set and looked as if she was about to burst into tears.

He made the decision for them to have chicken nuggets with chips and two glasses of red wine, which would count as supper.

'Come on, Betty. Humans die in hospitals: babies, grown-ups, old people. I have to give them funerals while they lie, still and unhearing, in a coffin on the stand. When I chose theology, I knew this would be part of my job. But eighty babies a year? I am a robot hospital employee and not a proper vicar with a church and parish. And you know what is worst of all? I am forty-five years old.'

Betty looked at him with some surprise. He had just delivered an emotional outburst, which she had always assumed was her prerogative.

The wine was brought to the table near the window, overlooking the meadow which reached down to the River Cam.

By the time they had finished their food, dinner guests were arriving, so he ordered two desserts – his favourite, crème caramel – to be served in the garden.

'I am doing something which I have not told you about.' He hacked into the burnt-sugar lid with the point of his spoon.

She waited for him to go on, and he confessed that he had started to look around for another position. He bemoaned the fact that it seemed impossible to find a church which would offer a rectorate to a forty-five-year-old man without specific experience in the field. 'Still, I have not given up.'

He paid the bill and they left the pub. On the way to the Hyundai, his mobile purred. He answered, and she let him walk ahead and concentrate on his caller.

'Yes!' He raised both hands in a gesture of delight, the mobile phone in one of them. 'I have been offered a job.' Immediately, he amended it to, 'We have been offered a job.'

Betty looked frightened.

'And it is not in the Shetland Islands or the Outer Hebrides.'

'So where is it?'

'In a village called Stockfield in Northumberland.'

She scrolled on her phone. 'I found it. The village is near the Tyne, but Google Earth shows hardly any buildings. Just fields and a few farms.'

'The real thing,' Justin enthused, 'a congregation of honest, hardworking, down-to-earth people. You will be the vicar's wife, helping me look after them.'

It had never occurred to her that he might make such a career change. There would be a village vicarage. They would have to be married and not live in sin.

'I would have to learn how to bake,' she said. 'There is always baking involved, church fêtes, village charity events.'

He nodded. 'I guess so. Isn't that great?'

She made a sour face. 'I don't want to be the minor character in the big play, the way I am as discharge nurse. I want to be recognised as a proper midwife.'

'There probably will be mostly home births. The closest hospital is…' He was now searching on his phone. '… in Newcastle, about forty miles from Stockfield.'

She twitched. 'Surely not Newcastle. There must be a natal unit closer to Stockfield. What about Berwick-upon-Tweed?'

'Miles away. What is your problem with Newcastle?'

She said nothing more. She lowered her lids over her eyes for a moment. Her brain had not been kind to her and let her forget the tragedy she had suffered, alone and in secrecy. There was a well-established

240

birthing unit in the Newcastle hospital. She had chosen it because it was far away from Cambridge, and because a senior midwife she had trained with was working there. Their friendship had made it possible for Betty to have an abortion two months after the big mistake on the black sheets with the weeping man. Although there was no trace of toxoplasmosis in Betty's blood, she had convinced the two doctors that, during the first month, she had contracted the illness after eating uncooked meat. Toxoplasmosis, as the name indicates, poisons the blood; during early pregnancy it is greatly responsible for brain damage in growing foetuses. Once the doctors were convinced that a termination was in the best interest of the baby and the mother, it was a fast procedure, and one overnight stay.

'We'll probably drive to Newcastle regularly to buy things. It is a big city. You will get to like it.'

'I will never like it,' she mumbled, still suffering from the grief of the loss. Every pram she looked into brought back the clamp-like pain. Every toddler she heard giggling brought tears to her eyes. In all those years with Justin, she had hoped to become pregnant, get married and start a family. But no. Sod's law. One sperm on one occasion fertilised one of her eggs. Heaven punished her for her behaviour. The devil had something to do with the whole thing. That much became clear to her. The devil would never let her find peace in herself again. The devil made sure Justin could not get her pregnant. Her only chance of holding a baby in her arms had been destroyed in Newcastle. The hospital with a tall incineration chimney. Up that chimney… No tears would ever erase the cruel truth of what had happened.

★

Three months after their chicken nuggets in Grantchester, Betty and Justin were driving north, trying to keep up with the removal van. Everything they owned was stored in the *Andy Able Movers* vehicle, except for jewellery and important documents, which were in a box on the backseat of the Hyundai.

'He is driving way too fast,' Betty said.

'Maybe he wants the journey to be over. I do.'

'Our furniture must be getting thrown around.'

'I hope not.' Justin overtook a car to advance faster. 'They wrapped our dining table in a grey rug and strapped it to the wall of the vehicle. I watched them do it.'

'I am getting nervous,' she admitted. 'We've been driving for more than two hours. Where are we now?'

'We're in Yorkshire.'

'Your new job is rather north on the map of England. It is getting more and more agricultural.'

'Yup,' is all he said and changed gear.

★

Just after they passed the village sign of *Stockfield*, they saw a fox dash across the road. Betty clutched Justin's arm.

'Oh no, oh no! The movers' van has hit it.'

Andy Able Movers stopped. Justin slowed down. Betty chewed her thumbnail. The body of a red-pelted fox lay

242

on the verge. The driver of the van came out and walked back to it. With one kick, he propelled the body into an overgrown ditch.

'Stay in the car, Betty. Close the car door and calm down. There is nothing we can do.'

'The fox might be alive, suffering,' she said. 'We need to get it to a vet. I hate our van driver. Hate him. This is such an upsetting thing to happen at the entrance to our new village, a bad omen at the start of our new life.'

'Country foxes cross the road all the time. Some don't make it.'

'Still, it is bad luck for that to happen to our fox in our village,' she grumbled, not yet appeased.

'Let's go and find the vicarage.' They drove on, Betty still craning her neck, trying to see something of the fox in the ditch.

'Here we are.' Justin's voice had risen an octave. 'Vicarage it says on the entrance post. Vicarage it is.'

Andy Able was already parked on the gravel in front of a good-sized Victorian house, standing all by itself up a mild incline, just before the church it served. No other dwellings were nearby. The hateful driver and his colleague sat in their seats like toads, eating out of foil and drinking from cans. It was by now well past lunchtime.

The red-brick façade of the vicarage was double-fronted, with bow windows on the first two floors, and two peaks to the slate-covered roof. The roofers had fixed ornate peak finials and ridge cresting. As there were already carved gable decorations and scalloped soffits, the vicarage looked over-decorated, as if the builders could not stop themselves from embellishing. They had wanted to create a remarkable house to go with a four hundred-year-old church, but their decorative additions made the house outstanding in an odd way, giving it a faulty physique rather than the intended effect. This had probably been done in the last years of the nineteenth century.

Betty walked alongside the house to have a look at the back garden. There was no fence between the cultivated garden and the large field beyond it, which was being ploughed. Along tramlines moved a green tractor with yellow hubs pulling a plough behind it, metal blades digging sideways into the earth to leave furrows, while the gigantic, deeply-profiled tyres gripped the soil as they slowly rotated. She noticed a woman testing her way unsteadily over the ploughed earth, as if her shoes were not up to the challenge. The tractor stopped; the woman increased her clumsy moves to reach it. The man in the driver's seat and the woman below him talked for a while, before the tractor moved on and the woman returned to the edge of the field. It was a Thomas Hardy sight, Betty thought, and realised the tractor was now heading her way.

Quite close, the driver jumped out and lumbered up to her. Sticky earth coated his work boots. His age was difficult to make out with the facial hair along his cheeks, surrounding his mouth and prolonging his chin.

'Hello,' she said to the agricultural figure and gave him a generous smile. They should get acquainted, as they were obviously going to be neighbours.

His hairy chin was jutted shortly towards *Andy Able Movers* visible in the driveway behind them. 'You're the new ones,' he said, and she liked his voice.

'I am almost Mrs Halsey, a midwife, and the man coming towards us is the Reverend Justin Halsey.'

The farmer rubbed the skin of his neck, skin which looked red and raw. He did not pick up on the 'almost', but to her surprise mentioned her midwife role.

'I'll tell Charlotte you being a midwife. That's helping a pregnant woman to make a baby.'

'You could put it that way.' Betty gave a little laugh.

He remained serious and went on, 'The woman I was just talking to is knocked up.'

'Is the baby yours?'

'My mother might help, I guess, but the farmhouse is small, and I haven't told her yet.'

'How far along is she?'

'Nobody must know about it.'

Betty was just about to say, 'They'll find out sooner or later,' when Justin caught up with her.

'No-one is in the vicarage,' Justin complained. 'There is no note on the door. I have written to the dean twice during the last two weeks asking him to email me a list of members of the church committee, names of people in the village I will be dealing with, a plan of the services to be held and other helpful tips. I heard nothing. He knew that we would arrive around midday today. Nobody is here.' Only now Justin seemed to take breath and acknowledge the presence of the farmer. 'Who is this?' Justin asked his wife.

'Neil,' the farmer interjected, and then added, 'The Rev buggered off last week. Took his missus with him. She's off her rocker.'

'Speak English, please,' said Justin.

245

Betty felt Justin's shudder of irritation at the same time as dealing with her own. 'We've been driving all this way and now we can't move in,' she explained. She looked from Justin to the farmer.

'It's not locked,' said Neil. 'We don't lock houses round here.'

Meanwhile, in front of the house, the movers had found the house open and had forced a wedge under the entrance door to keep it gaping. At present, they were struggling to carry the new Italian dining table tilted on its side. It was part of an expensive dining set, for which Betty and Justin had saved months.

A pair of crows shrieked, before taking off from the roof of the house. In the top-floor window, a person – a man in a high-collared black coat and a top hat – looked down at Betty. The figure had a powerful impact on her and she stood, deeply affected. Her hair bun had come apart during the long drive and was now bunched in loose strands, held up against the collar of her padded anorak.

'Someone is in the house.' She pointed with a shaking finger. 'He is at the window up there. Look!' she insisted.

Of course, when the men looked up, all they could see was the sun's glare bouncing off the window pane. Behind it, nobody showed.

'We'd better go in first and tell them where to put our things,' Justin suggested. The movers, told to hold their horses, approved. They let go of the table. It hit the pebbled ground with a crunching sound. Betty raised a cry of protest, but Justin led her past the porch and into the dark, square hallway.

'I am afraid things get damaged in moves,' he added.

When she checked back over her shoulder, she noticed Neil's stocky silhouette in the light at the open door behind them.

'It is strange and wonderful to walk into my first vicarage,' said Justin happily. 'I came to assume this would never happen to me.' Taking both her hands, he made a few dancing moves before forcing her to turn around herself and ending up with his arms crossed over. 'I should have carried you over the threshold into what is our first house, and not a flat in Cambridge.'

'I am not a virginal bride, and this brooding house belongs to the Church of England,' Betty replied. Within herself, she was thinking, *I am a woman who has sinned and murdered a child.* To Justin, she added, 'Besides, we are not alone. A nosy farmer with muddy shoes is watching.'

'You will be a bride soon,' said Justin. 'We are firmly booked for a civil marriage ceremony back in Cambridge in three weeks' time, whether your father can come or not.'

Betty had found out that she was pregnant, on the day Justin had first set a date for their wedding. A devilish conspiracy against her. She had used her father's health as an excuse to cancel and to get away to Newcastle for that gruesome termination.

Two years had passed, and honest, straightforward Betty had become a tortured woman, burdened by a dark secret. Unaware of all this, Justin was just now announcing a new date for their wedding.

'Thank you for doing that, darling,' she said, opening a door which led into the kitchen. 'It was time to legalise our, our...' She searched for the right word.

247

'Love,' he finished for her.

She was already at the kitchen cabinets, inspecting the insides. 'This kitchen is pretty amazing. OK, it is on the old-fashioned side, but that is quite trendy these days.'

'Will you marry me in three weeks' time?'

'Don't be absurd.'

'An Aga.' He patted the dark-green gloss enamel. 'Quite a beast. Can you handle it?'

'I'm able to handle you,' replied Betty, 'and therefore my answer is yes, Reverend Halsey of Saint Barnabas, Stockfield, I will marry you.'

Justin bent under the kitchen table, which was pushed against the wall. And then, with his foot, he manoeuvred a wire cage, larger than a shoebox, closer to him.

'What is that? And there is another one at the entrance to the pantry.'

'A walk-in pantry. How lovely…' Betty disappeared inside it.

'Multi-catch rat traps,' said Neil, who had rather creepily followed them. 'It can hold up to eight.'

The men heard Betty moving things around in the pantry.

'Neil,' Justin began in a new, caring, country vicar's voice, 'tell me, Neil. Have you been in this house before?'

Neil nodded. 'When it's empty.'

'Are there rats in the vicarage?'

'No.'

'Then why are there two multi-catch traps for them in the kitchen?'

'You have to ask the fruitcake, but she's gone.'

Justin scratched his eyebrow, while nothing further was said. From the pantry came more noises, as if Betty were making a nest for herself.

In the meantime, the movers had brought the table into the dining room adjacent to the kitchen. Along the table edge, the wood had been bruised in places, and a long, triangular splinter had come off in the careless drop onto the gravel. Two-by-two, held awkwardly using the armpit as a clamp, the eight dining chairs were carried in, the dining room door being savagely kicked open with each delivery.

Betty clustered the chairs against the table, eager to make the dining suite look complete and welcoming. It worked. The generously sized room showed off the Italian table and its eight chairs. Above it hung a lamp the previous occupant had left behind, one which would never be fashionable no matter how much trends changed. The heavy curtains, too, had been left hanging either side of the bay window, which looked north towards the garden and Neil's half-ploughed field. In the winter, it would be cold in this room, especially as there was only one cast-iron radiator to provide warmth.

Neil, who still followed them, obviously taking on the role of their guide, stepped forward when Betty fingered the curtain material.

'She made the curtains,' he said, almost simultaneously with Justin declaring them ugly and having to go.

Through the grime-covered window, Betty saw the tractor abandoned in the upheaved earth. She turned and faced Neil. 'Will we get the pleasure of seeing cows next to our garden? Sheep, perhaps?'

'It depends,' he finally answered. 'If the new Rev stays put, maybe our sheep.'

She stepped further into the bay window. Somewhere, out there, had to be the mother in the small farmhouse Neil had mentioned. Betty shrieked as her right hand became caught between sticky pieces of cardboard.

'What's the matter?' Justin stopped investigating the radiator's thermostatic valve.

'My hand is stuck in something a child must have made.' She tried to shake it off her hand. 'Why would that be left behind on a windowsill?'

Before Neil could react, Justin pitched in. 'The fruitcake, right?'

'It's a fold-together glue trap,' Neil said. 'They are on all the sills downstairs.'

'They work!' Betty had to pull hard to peel the cardboard off her skin.

'Spiders, roaches and crawlies get caught in it,' Neil explained.

In the downstairs cloakroom, where Betty had gone to wash the glue off, she noticed that the water supply worked, but the plughole in the sink was blocked with expanding foam. And the tall corner cabinet was full of woodlice.

On the first floor were four double bedrooms and a small, oblong bedroom. On the second floor were three more rooms. Opening the doors, one by one, she fully expected to come across evidence of occupancy.

Perhaps it had been a man in a black hoodie? A wide-open house was an ideal shelter for a homeless man. Perhaps she had imagined it, upset by the nasty cawing of crows.

The bathroom was surprisingly large, with an old bathtub squatting on lions' paws. When she turned on the hot water tap, it gurgled and spewed air, but no water came. Standing on tiptoe, through the small window Betty could now see what had to be Neil's farmhouse, a two-up two-down built onto a large barn – or rather the other way round. On her way back down to the first floor, on which were the only rooms they would furnish and use, Justin's face appeared from the landing above, where she had just come from. *How?* she wondered. *How could he get up to the second floor without passing me on the stairs?*

'I'm just going to see the church,' he said and then added, 'There is a problem with the master bedroom. You'll find out.'

The master bedroom made up the width of the house, a bow window facing south to the front, and a large casement window to the north, overlooking the fields, with an en-suite shower room to the side. In the room stood the previous occupants' four-poster bed. It was probably carved from oak or walnut and was heavily cornered. The geometrically panelled roof was supported by four bulbous columns. The curtain poles were fixed right under the roof. The mattress had been taken away.

'They couldn't move it,' explained Neil, looking chuffed to be left in sole charge of Betty.

'Somebody managed to get it into the room,' she said. 'Surely, it comes apart. If necessary, we can saw the wood into bits. I'm not going to sleep in someone else's marital bed. Our mattress is unlikely to be a fit. Justin would want to close the curtains around it, and I need air to breathe.'

When she checked the bunched-up bed curtains at the head end, she realised that they were made of heavy chains which, disturbed by her, started to clank. She pulled her hand back.

Perhaps the previous vicar and his wife were perverts? A blacksmith must have fixed this chain curtain to the bed. Neil kept reminding them that the *missus* was mad. Betty felt she could sense the disturbed woman's presence; she had definitely left behind an influence over the house. It was confirmed by every new, unnerving discovery. It was not so much that this woman had aroused a ghost, but rather that she had been the initiator of unbalanced spiritual and physical interaction. Possibly, a woman with a sick psyche was able to create an unhealthy aura. Betty had, for a while, contemplated psychiatry in the nursing college, but decided against this idea after a visit to a mental hospital.

She had to weaken the negative spell in the vicarage by remaining strong and healthy in body and mind. Easily, the negative vibes of the house could seep into her. Sensing this danger, she knew she had to protect herself, fight it even. There were no men in black at windows, and Justin must have found another way to go upstairs.

'Is there a second staircase in the house?' Betty asked Neil, who was looking at himself in the tall mirror the movers had already brought and propped against the master bedroom wall. He patted his sideburn. He was proud of his facial hair and obviously spent time looking after it. She did, of course, not tell him that growing so much hair was a sign of shyness and wanting to avoid contact with people.

'It's a house with inner rooms.' With a final check of his face, he tore himself away from his reflection. 'I'll show you.'

Betty had never heard of inner rooms.

'Right here.' Next to the bunched-chain curtain, Neil pushed against the wall, and with a creak a rectangular section gave way, revealing a narrow door in the wallpaper of large, black lilies. He opened it enough for her to step forward and look in. It was dark because it had no window, a dust-covered confined space with an atmosphere of its own. A rough-hewn staircase led upstairs from it.

'Only up and not down?'

'The space downstairs is the walk-in pantry.'

Courageously, she ventured into the inner room and looked around. In a corner stood an old-fashioned sewing machine table with a pedal. Neil said the *fruitcake* had made the dining room curtains. Obviously a long time ago, as by now many layers of cobwebs were wrapped around the machine. Holding her breath, Betty started to walk up the wooden treads. Cobwebs shivered in the air disturbed by her presence. There was no handrail, nowhere to hold onto except the wall on which, with fright, she noticed the imprint of dirty hands, fingers spread. Looking closer, she counted six fingers on one hand. And the same imprint three steps up, still with six fingers. Now she found herself in a windowless space identical to the one she had just come from. She turned round and went back down to the master bedroom.

The sun suddenly shone into the room. This was natural, positive and reassuring. Betty had to concentrate on this, and deny the dark forces the power to play their evil games. She opened the south-facing window and took a few, deep breaths, until she felt the oxygen put things right in her tense body. Her eyes roamed over a soft green landscape in which were patches of darker woods. The River Tyne snaked through it all. Neil came to stand next to her, so close that she thought she could hear his heart beat.

'Nice view,' she said, pointing. 'There is a large property over there.'

'A posh pile. It belongs to Arabella Davenport and her daughter, her daughter…'

She waited for him to say it.

'… Charlotte. She lives in the cottage.'

'I see,' Betty said, not seeing the picture at all, except remembering that the secretly pregnant woman Neil had spoken to in the field was called Charlotte. 'Your pregnant woman friend?' Betty sensed the conflict within him. Charlotte and Neil needed help with the pregnancy. She could help. It would be her first midwifery job. 'Has Charlotte had check-ups at a maternity clinic?'

'She can't. Her mother must not find out.'

'Is there a husband, or father, living with them in the posh pile?'

'Davenport is a big cheese. Spends most time in Dubai. Look…' His fingers curled. 'I would like you to look after her till the baby is safely born. I can pay, if it's not too much. Arabella, Charlotte's mother, drives to Newcastle shopping every Friday morning. Maybe you could go to the cottage then? I'll give you Charlotte's mobile number. You have a pen?'

She did not. Betty had left her smartphone in the glove compartment of the car. She looked around the bedroom and opened the top drawer of the bedside table, which she had first to disentangle from the chains. The small drawer was empty except for a slim book. *Practical candle-burning rituals.* She pulled the wooden knob of the cabinet underneath, the space for the chamber pot. A plastic storage box was in it, fitted with an airtight green lid. She prised off the lid and instantly dropped the box.

'Dead rats! And, on top of their decomposing bodies, a crucifix with a brass Jesus.'

'Close the bloody box,' ordered Neil. 'It stinks.'

She pushed the lid back on and held out the box to Neil. 'You take it with you, please. Throw them on the compost heap or bury them. Just take them away.'

'She always gave me the dead rats, too, and said the same. I have to burn them, you know.'

'What was her name?'

'Elizabeth.'

'That is my name.'

*

In The Posh Pile

Arabella went from the main house to the cottage. Charlotte, who opened the door to her, wore her long blond hair tied at the back into a ponytail.

'Mother,' she stated the obvious.

'Aren't you going to invite me in?'

'Sorry, Mum. It's just that the place is a mess.'

'I only need a few minutes of your time.' Arabella peered past her daughter to see inside the living room, which comprised the whole of the downstairs of the cottage, except for the small kitchen and narrow bathroom built as add-ons.

'If you're looking for Neil, he is ploughing up the east field to plant potatoes,' said Charlotte. 'He is working hard to grow a new type, cross-inseminating Jersey Royals with Maris Piper. It is not easy.'

'How frightfully exciting.'

'Mum, what do you have against Neil?' Charlotte asked, hurt.

'Do you have a large piece of paper and a sharp pencil?' replied her mother. 'They are potatoes. What's complicated about that?'

'The special ones can be named after royalty.'

Arabella, bored with the potato conversation, changed course. 'A new vicar and his wife have moved into the vicarage.'

Charlotte had nothing to say to that.

'I wonder how long it will take for the wife to become mental?' said Arabella. 'There are rumours going around the village about the vicarage.'

'Neil said they are fiction.'

'Charlotte, dear, I don't think it is appropriate for you to still frequent Neil.'

'We have history. And I have my reasons.'

'You can do so much better, darling. We're lucky

Neil did not propose marriage. All you need to do is lose some weight. You look chubbier every time I see you.'

'Neil isn't refined, but his heart is in the right place.'

'Potatoes,' Arabella said theatrically, which brought the conversation about Neil to an end.

★

In The Hamilton Corporation Conference Room

Edmund Hamilton stopped at the door to the brightly lit conference room. He wore a suit and a new white shirt, the collar as stiff as cardboard. His dark chestnut hair shone, vitamin-enhanced and pampered. At the end of the oval table sat his father. The Hamilton Corporation was by now a vast empire that justified an impressive conference table, and permitted Edmund to dress expensively.

Hamiltons' real estate property portfolio ranged from luxury residential properties to financial centres all over the globe. To this was added a whole skiing village in Switzerland, a luxury three-masted yacht in the Caribbean, five-star hotels in New York, Paris and Hong Kong, and an island in the Seychelles, besides a fleet of executive airplanes. With a manicured hand, Hamilton Senior held a file; the other drummed on the cherry wood tabletop.

'Why the conference room and not your office?' asked Edmund.

'Why not?' With a rare smile, Hamilton pulled out the chair next to him.

'Is it going to be our style now to invite everyone to

lunch from whom we buy property – an attempt to make them feel better about our low offer?' asked Edmund.

Hamilton looked at his son, long and hard. 'I negotiated the deal with the Church of England five years ago. Our corporation has subsequently been described as inhumanly benefiting from the downfall of others.'

Edmund fiddled with one of his gold cufflinks, a present from his father together with the Jaguar F-Type.

'By the way,' Hamilton added, 'I had the lawyers transfer the Church of England contract solely into your name. You are young and better suited for it. I found them tough negotiators. Too many exclusion rules are in the small print. Thou shalt not alter the outside aspect of the vicarages, nor shalt thou erect any buildings on the ground without the Church of England giving their consent, and it goes on. Three times more commandments than the original list.

'With the purchase of Stockfield Vicarage, I intend to make a showcase of our considerate approach. Hamilton Corporation, the real estate people who care. The loss of that Victorian beauty near the River Tyne will be particularly tough for the vicar who has just taken up the post. I was thinking of a farewell lunch organised in the vicarage. We need a picture of me shaking hands with the vicar in his costume for the article in *The Spectator*. After that, you will be in charge and can deal with those bible thumpers.'

'Thanks, Dad.'

'Don't thank me. It's small fry. Hardly worth our time. At most, a dozen vicarages a year.'

Edmund nodded. 'Hence the lunch in the vicarage.'

258

'What are you talking about?'

'You feel guilty and want to clear your bad conscience by lunching with a man of God.'

'Nonsense. One old vicarage, four new dwellings in its place.'

'I don't like it. I'll take over the vicarage project in my own name, but that's all.'

'Thank you, son. You'll go to heaven. Imagine all those winged nude angel boys turning you on.'

Edward frowned. 'You promised me, on my dead mother's head, that you would never, ever, bring anything to do with anything like that up again.'

'Wear your asshole with pride. You've got only one,' Hamilton said.

'You have no feelings. You are a crude, calculating old geezer.'

'How could you say that when I go out of my way to be generous with vicars?' said Hamilton. 'I am even going to offer caviar.'

'I need to go away at once and live somewhere where you're not.' Edmund's voice was unstable.

'Yep. Marry a fat Guatemalan with five children and live in a pallet-made shack. She won't mind that you're gay.'

With loud scraping, Edmund pushed the chair away from the table and got up. With a forced, detached gait, he walked out of the conference room, not without first righting the framed print of the Hamilton Corporation yacht ploughing through rough seas.

★

259

In Stockfield High Street

Betty and Justin walked down High Street. It was one of those rare occasions when they shopped together. Betty had convinced Justin that they needed to buy candles, sturdy white candles, a few red candles and, ideally, one which was made with black-tinted wax. She had wanted his support in the hardware shop. The vicar of the village would be sold good-quality candles, which she needed according to the bedside-table book about chasing the devil from one's home.

'If we have blackouts, it doesn't matter what colour the candles are, does it?' Justin did not entirely trust her since they had moved to Stockfield. At times, she caught him watching her with a frown on his forehead, his expression calculating.

They passed the tea room called *T-4-2*.

'Don't look,' she ordered her husband. 'At the table near the window are Neil and Charlotte.'

He immediately looked. 'So what?'

'There is so much you don't know.'

'What are you up to now?'

'I have been hired as midwife, my first job. Finally, I will be able to apply my spatulas.'

'You don't have spatulas,' said Justin. 'You are a discharge nurse and there is no shame in that.'

'I walked away from my job in Cambridge with a midwifery kit, and two home delivery packs.'

'Stolen.'

'NHS property which serves the NHS purpose,' said Betty. 'It does not matter where in the country, as long as it is used for its intended purpose. I will live up to it. You've had several Sunday church services. Now it is my turn.'

'It is still theft.' He remained stubborn about it.

They walked on, safely past the police station and right into the lion's mouth.

'Excuse me,' said a well-dressed middle-aged man, accosting Justin. 'The lady over there tells me that you are the vicar of Saint Barnabas church.'

Justin did not react well to this. 'If you need anything, come and see me Sunday in church after service.'

'My name is Hamilton of Hamilton Corporation.' The man's tone clearly implied that the church was beneath him. Instead, he introduced the young man who had joined him, after buying a local newspaper in the corner shop. 'My boy, Edmund d'Aubrey Sinclair Hamilton. We're in Stockfield to assess the local property market, especially the area you live in.'

'Why?' asked Betty.

Hamilton gave a short laugh. 'I like women who are direct. Nothing is going to happen for a while,' he said. 'First, geological reports have to be scrutinised, and environmental studies commissioned. Vicarages are being sold by the Church of England, which needs money in the kitty. You'll hear from us again in about six months' time.'

'I hope not,' muttered Betty, after Hamilton and his long-named son walked away in their pointed leather shoes.

Arabella, who had enabled this unpleasant encounter, was shouting and waving from the front of the butcher's shop.

'What now?' Justin bristled. 'This is why I don't want to come shopping in the village.'

'It's a small place,' replied Betty. 'Everybody meets everybody all the time.'

'Can we go home now?' he asked like a petulant child.

'Not yet. Arabella is steering our way.'

'Aren't they splendid, father and son?' the tall woman gushed. Her red swing coat matched the colour on her lips. 'My husband knows Hamilton, of course, him being a developer and hubby a banker. I had no idea Hamilton had such a handsome son, who is number two in a billion-pound company. Why are they here looking around Stockfield? What did Hamilton say to you?'

'Nothing worth repeating,' said Justin dryly.

'I saw you talking. You have to tell me. It's for Charlotte's sake. Edmund Hamilton would be the perfect match for my daughter.'

'Excuse us, please.' Betty brushed her hand over her forehead. 'I have a headache coming on.'

'You have to tell me what they said, Reverend Halsey,' Arabella insisted.

'They said they would be back in six months' time,' replied Justin.

'You make it sound like a threat.'

'It is a threat. Property crooks like those two itch to turn generously built houses into modern flats, frogmarching vicars out of residences, which they had to maintain on their small salaries. That's what this is all about.'

Arabella had never experienced the vicar so passionate

nor verbose outside his church. His wife looked sickly pale. Arabella swung the front panel of her coat over her shoulder. 'Six months is a long time. Much can happen.' She turned and went her way.

'Six months,' Betty repeated. 'In a pregnancy, that is two out of three thirds.'

Justin, head down, set off back home carrying the bag with the candles.

★

The Eviction

A letter came from the dean with news that was so bad Justin had to hide it from Betty. This was easier than he had anticipated. Betty was deeply involved in doing midwifing for a young woman who could not to be named. He knew she was in her element the day he watched her disinfect metal forceps and spatulas in boiling water over the Aga stove. The unwelcome image of a witch at her cauldron came to his mind. Betty was finally happy and in her element, and now they had to pack up again and leave a vicarage which historically went hand in hand with the church.

The dean had offered to relocate them to a small bungalow on the other side of the village. Justin had been there to visit a retired widower. All the houses were small and pebble-dashed, with courtyard gardens and wheelchair-adapted access. With terrible clarity, he understood that, working from such an undesirable place, his status would be diminished, probably even in the eyes of God. He would be a pseudo-reverend,

263

rather than the committed man acting in the temple of his God, with his bed and bread in close proximity. Undermined, eventually he would lose heart and leave. And then what?

At St Barnabas, to where Justin had run in panic, he gazed at the church quietly, until his heart calmed down, before entering the porch. He pushed open the carved-oak door. Once inside, he closed it behind him, waiting for the latch to click. It was the noise made by latecomers disturbing his sermon. On a narrow table, Justin gathered the leaflets about the history of the church, built in 1650, and shook them into a neat pile, before walking down the aisle between the rows of pews. Parents of brides had sat here, frightened widows at the funerals of their husbands, couples and godparents with infants in lace. In only seven months, it had all become so familiar to him. He was a matter-of-fact practising clergyman.

Now, as he faced the altar, covered in an embroidered cloth with just the polished chalice standing on it, a deep-seated flicker of passion for religion, dedication to purity and to what was holy and good in men, overcame him. He brushed tears from his eyes.

If only Betty could share what was the deepest truth in him. She seemed to move through life like an empty vessel, eager to fill it with her self-made belief in spiritual danger, the existence of evil, certainly welcoming ghostly thoughts. To his dismay, she often voiced them: the devil had occupied the vicarage and was trying to ensnare her, ensnare Justin. She imagined Satan in black feathers on the roof, screeching, or with furry legs scurrying across the floor. Calculating spiders crouched in webs in the corners, and the devil even showed himself at the upstairs window. When thunder rolled over the fields of Northumberland, she heard Satan growling; when someone had an accident, the devil himself was at the scene, grinning. And this woman was married to a man of God – his better half.

Justin sank to his knees in front of the altar. He joined his hands and lifted them. God was the one who was everywhere. His glory swept dark shadows out of the way. His benevolence encompassed every creature with love, even those with long, pink tails and eight legs, rustling and weaving in dark corners.

Justin's eyes moved up to the tall, narrow, stained-glass windows. In the one to the right-hand side, old and bearded Saint Barnabas was depicted in nature. From his kneeling position, Justin saw the vegetation and earth around the saint's naked feet with clarity. Justin gulped. What he had taken for rocks were furry brown rodents, the size of large rats. Their teeth, showing white in the glass, were about to bite the patron saint's feet.

'Muskrats!' Justin exclaimed in disbelief, and his voice produced an echo under the vaulted ceiling behind him. How could he not have noticed this before? Doubt crept into him as he stood up and made his way out of the church. Had the rocks cut by the artisan been turned by Betty's devil into vicious rodents, ready to torture the saint?

Breathing heavily, feeling the hurt of God's taunting, Justin returned to the vicarage.

'While you were gone, the Hamilton man and son came to the door,' Betty informed him.

Justin made the stupid move of checking his wristwatch. 'It is not six months yet.'

'Apparently, things have moved efficiently. They've offered to organise a goodbye lunch for us next Wednesday.'

'The last supper,' Justin said, barely audibly.

'They are willing to order caterers to bring food, and to invite the people we want to attend.'

'People in the community who will benefit Hamilton Corporation.'

'Don't get angry right away,' said Betty. 'I said I would do the food.'

'Financial greed, the exploitation of so-far-untouched beauty, undermining ordinary love and kindness.'

'Why are you talking so loudly? A lunch party. Isn't that what we bought the Italian table for?'

'You don't understand,' he said, and she turned away from him, hurt.

★

The Goodbye Lunch

Edmund drove his father up to Northumberland in the new Jaguar I-Pace. On the backseat was a bunch of flowers in a cellophane funnel. Hamilton reached out to press the button for music. Edmund pressed the same button to stop the music.

'This lunch at the vicarage was your idea,' Edmund said. 'The generous idea behind it made you feel good, but now we are on the way to actually having to do it. You saw the type of people who live in Stockfield?'

'That's why I invited Arabella and her daughter,' replied Hamilton. 'Davenport, who would have been useful, is unfortunately still in Dubai.'

They finally passed the Stockfield village sign.

'I need to pee.' Edmund parked on the verge and opened the driver's door.

Hamilton watched his son walk along the ditch and then stop and pee in that familiar male peeing position, stiff legs, pelvis pushed forward. Hamilton liked the sight. His son was a he-man. The gay thing was just a phase. His son would go far. His son would be rich and intimidate people. His son was a Hamilton.

Edmund shook his penis and zipped up. They drove on.

'You won't believe this,' Edmund said. 'I have just pissed on the skull of a dead animal.'

Hovering at the open door of the vicarage, Arabella, in black silk trousers and formal black jacket, came to life. 'The Hamiltons have just driven up in a sleek Jaguar. Now, listen to me, Charlotte, I want you to seduce young Edmund. He is the one for you. Trust me, I know. I also know that you can do it.' She stepped back into the dark of the entrance hall.

Edmund turned the engine off. Hamilton tiptoed across the weed-infested pebbles in an effort to protect his new shoes from chaffing. He looked up at the dark March sky, hoping it would not start to rain before he reached the house. Edmund followed with the flowers.

Charlotte, standing at the open vicarage door like a misplaced statue, wore a calf-length skirt that had a tiger-filled jungle print on it. A silver-buckled belt separated it from the plunge V-neck blue cotton top. Her breasts, still plump, showed low in the top. Edmund, coming face to face with her, in a spontaneous move offered her the flowers which had been intended for the hostess of the vicarage. Surprised, Charlotte cradled them in the crook of her arm. Hamilton strode straight past the two of them into the house; Charlotte and Edmund remained under the porch. It was awkward, especially as Edmund realised his mistake with the flowers. He scratched the newly shorn back of his head. The front part of his hair was wax-peaked. He looked down. Her arms and legs were pale, the feet in sling-back sandals.

Arabella appeared again from the hallway. 'You two, take your time out here to get to know each other.' She saw the flowers. 'How nice, Edmund. What a gentleman you are.' She was gone again.

'I get it,' said Edmund. 'Quite a yenta, your mother.'

Charlotte moved closer to Edmund. 'If this scheming is supposed to work, you should have gone easier with the aftershave. Overpowering,' she said, sniffing. 'As for the artistic hair spiking…'

'Hair care matters,' he replied, defending himself, and patted his quiff with gentleness.

She hesitated, but then could not help plunging in, Charlotte-style. 'We're both single. It bothers them. They feel compelled to change that. We were invited here to seduce and fall for each other.'

'Unless you're Guatemalan and have five children, it won't work.'

'So far,' she said, shaking her head, 'we don't communicate.'

'You're right,' he said happily. 'We don't. I like you.'

Arabella, having sneaked back to check on progress, overheard the end of this conversation. She smiled, pleased with herself, and left them to it.

'Let's just ignore it and each other,' Charlotte whispered to Edmund. 'This is going to be such a boring lunch. I could not care less where the vicar lives. I don't go to church.'

'Suits me,' he said. 'My father forced me to come.'

'My mum is taken by your dad, big time.'

'You might have to tell her to get in the queue.' Suddenly, Edmund stepped further back from her. She watched him give his middle finger a quick lick before using it to draw over his eyebrows, exhibiting great unease at the situation they were in.

'Sorry you had to come here when you didn't want to.' She tried making him feel more at ease. 'You must have a lot of influential friends in London. Cool girls. Going out a lot.'

He puffed air from his nostrils. 'My mother died, and Dad does nothing but work, and when he doesn't, he makes me work for him.'

From inside the house, they heard the vicar urge the guests to take their places at the table. Reluctantly, Charlotte and Edmund joined them.

Hamilton was placed at the head of the table, opposite the vicar at the other end. On one side, against the wall, was Edmund, with Charlotte to his left. Neil, whom Betty had invited as their only neighbour, had not arrived yet, but would be sitting opposite Edmund, Arabella to his right and Betty to his left.

'There won't be pre-lunch drinks – too much alcohol,' announced Justin, who wore a tired suit for the occasion.

'Wrong,' boomed Hamilton. 'Edmund, get the box.'

Obediently, Edmund got up and left the dining room, clashing at the door with Neil coming in tentatively.

'Don't get me wrong.' Justin felt the need to defend this lunch. 'I planned to offer red wine during the main course.'

Hamilton was already filling the wine glasses on the table with the spuming *Dom Pérignon*, which Edmund had brought in a cool box. They all raised their glasses and toasted to a happy future for Justin and Betty in a new home.

'I hate champagne,' Charlotte whispered to Edmund next to her.

'I don't care.'

'That figures.'

'What does that mean?'

'I have no idea what we can possibly talk about,' she said, and then looked at the others around the silent table. 'They don't either.'

Hamilton, the only one still standing and obviously planning on presiding, started with, 'Folks,' in the American way, 'lunch is offered to you by the Hamilton Corporation. It is a gesture to say thank you, vicar, for having kept the people of Rockfield on the right path for so long.'

'Stockfield,' corrected Arabella, and grinned up at Hamilton just a tad too long.

Charlotte stole a glance at Neil and saw the usual

look of strained anxiety, his mind no doubt on the potatoes which were not performing as he hoped. She looked across at her mother, flushed while talking in an exalted voice to Hamilton about God knows what. The man's attention was somewhere else. She checked the calm, pale face of Justin, sitting at the end of the table under a framed print of a goatherd in a djellaba with the city of Jerusalem in the background. The vicar had an odd, musty smell about him, and seemed to have lost weight. Under his chin, the neck was folded in layers of dry skin. Perhaps feeling her scrutiny, he looked up, and the neck folds tightened.

'I'd better get more glasses for those who will want red wine,' said Betty.

'Communion wine.' Arabella tried to make a joke.

'Only if you're absolved of sin,' Hamilton winked at her. 'I am right about that, Vicar, aren't I?' Hamilton pushed the issue. 'Isn't drinking a sin?'

'Gluttony is,' Justin said. 'I guess drinking goes into that category.'

'You guess, and it is your job to know. In my company, I fire employees who use the words *I guess*.'

'I better go and see what Betty is up to in the kitchen.' Feeling under pressure, Justin left the room.

'What could a woman like Betty be up to?' Charlotte lifted her shoulders.

Edmund laughed. 'Your daughter is funny,' he said to Arabella.

'My Charlotte is amusing and socially well connected,' replied Arabella. 'She has lost a lot of weight recently. She can also prepare grilled oysters.'

271

'Now you're talking, lady,' mocked Edmund.

The vicar did not reappear. Arabella commented on it. 'While we're made to wait, Betty is giving Justin an earful of complaints for having to do this lunch for us.'

'She insisted on doing it,' said Hamilton. 'Who argues with a vicar's wife?'

'The vicar,' said Charlotte.

Edmund smiled at her, pleased, the corner of his mouth pulled up on one side. Neil looked confused, noticing for the first time that something was going on between Charlotte and Edmund, even though Edmund's hand had lingered on Neil's backside when they had collided at the door. It had been more than just an accidental awkwardness – more like groping: the groomed city boy considering the potato farmer for... Neil had to work out the *what* himself, and this pointless lunch was very much in the way of it. However, looking at Edmund now chatting to Charlotte about Tudor architecture, he had to say to himself, *Nah, no way.*

Justin returned from the kitchen, carrying a large tray with seven bowls containing lettuce shreds with prawns under a pink sauce.

'Tell me something, Vicar,' Hamilton said. 'There is an electric wire hole up there in the corner of the ceiling. When was the vicarage re-wired?'

'It wasn't.'

The guests all looked up at the hole.

'I see something moving in the hole,' said Edmund. 'Something black and hairy. It's trying to squeeze itself out.'

'Hot rolls, anyone?' Betty came from the kitchen, holding a basket lined with a napkin.

'Look.' Charlotte pointed. 'It has come out of the hole – a black spider!' she said with disgust. 'It is scuttling across the ceiling right over our heads. Upside down. How can it do that?'

'Betty,' said Hamilton, 'did you know you had a black spider living in the corner of the ceiling?'

Betty pulled the Italian chair back to sit. As if spurred on by a nervous urge to confess, she replied, 'You have just discovered the vicarage's dark secret. Evil is everywhere. It can walk upside down. It can disguise itself as a rat. The more you kill, the more rats there are. Dark ectoplasm flows from it all. It floats around the vicarage, up the hidden staircase backwards, its black leathery claw beckoning you to follow. Horrible.' She crossed her arms, and Justin just had time to pull the prawn cocktail bowl out of the way before her crossed arms landed on the table, her head on top of them.

'The house spider,' Justin said, as if nothing unusual had just happened, 'is almost certainly female, a night-time web-weaver living in the ceiling.' Looking around and getting no response from the guests, he added, 'An innocent animal, one of God's many creations.'

Betty's head shot up. 'God must have put this spider together late on the sixth day using up spare, hairy legs! On the seventh day, he met up with Satan, who asked him to make more of those lovely black spiders and similar animals who thrive in churches, or vicarages filled with naïve vicars.'

'Betty!' Justin barked at her. 'How about getting on with lunch, huh? I am a man of Christian faith.' In outrage, he jerked up from his chair, dislodging the print on the wall behind him. Jerusalem fell to the ground, the glass breaking with a dry crack. He contemplated the damage done to a picture which had hung long enough on the wall to imprint its shape.

Before Betty could respond, Justin singled out Hamilton; the vicar's neck stretched. 'You brought that on us. You and your fancy son. We had just found our feet in Stockfield and you are turning us out. Can't you build on free land, instead of demolishing historic buildings?'

'Farmland.' Neil, mute until this point, spoke up. 'No way. There isn't enough arable land left. Farmers already get the worst deal from the government, while food is getting short. The population is growing. Every female immigrant makes several children.'

'Babies,' took up Charlotte, staring at Neil. 'Is that what you mean? Babies are not unwanted population growth. They are adorable little people, hoping to learn to smile, explore life and be loved. It was a girl, by the way, and I wanted to call her Amelia. I wanted to hold her in my arms at least once. It wasn't allowed. The little body had to be given to research.' She then looked at Betty. 'It is your fault.' Charlotte was vehement, and reached across the table to grab Betty's arm. 'I trusted you to help me. You said you were a midwife. You said the placenta and umbilical cord were in the wrong place, and used tongs. How can you know without a scan?'

'I have more than twenty years' experience in the maternity unit of the best Cambridgeshire hospital…' replied Betty.

'As a discharge nurse,' Justin could not resist saying.

'You, shut up!' Betty stood up and disappeared into the kitchen.

Charlotte fell back against the chair. She had hardly eaten any of the prawn starter, which Justin now collected off the table. Her eyelids were pressed together and squeezed tears down her pale cheeks.

'I couldn't have known she is rubbish,' said Neil.

Justin left the table to hold open the door, as Betty came through with a pile of warmed plates. She went back to the kitchen, and returned with a large bowl of chicken, mushroom, boiled potatoes and French beans.

'I lost the child, too,' said Neil. 'Arabella does not like me. If she had been a bit more helpful, this would not have happened. There is a natal clinic in Newcastle where Amelia could have been saved. Her body ended up there, anyway.'

'Why don't you pass the food and help yourselves?' Betty suggested, concealing her anguish.

Hamilton used this moment to turn to Charlotte. 'You were pregnant and not married?'

'Talk to my mother about that,' she replied. 'She's sitting right next to you. She disapproves of Neil. Your son is a better deal.'

'You and Edmund?' said Hamilton. 'Don't make me laugh. I have big plans for Edmund.'

'There is a lot of hostility around this table,' Justin intervened. 'This is not what we hoped would happen.'

'Oh my God!' came from Charlotte. 'Spiders are tumbling out of the hole. Look, look, they are running on the ceiling.' She unfolded the serviette and put it on her head.

'They are not doing any harm playing on the ceiling,' said the vicar. 'Just ignore them.'

'Hard to ignore when the biggest one comes down to jump on my back.' Charlotte gave a shiver, pulled the serviette off her head, and then abandoned the table to watch from further away.

'It won't jump on you,' said Neil. 'It's not a jumping spider species.'

'Why was it flexing its legs in preparation, then?'

'Ridiculous,' came from Hamilton, who got up, squeezed himself behind Edmund and climbed on Charlotte's empty chair, a fork in his hand. The fork stabbed, but the prongs skidded on the smooth plaster, just missing the black furry body. Hamilton lost his balance and had to jump down from the chair. He landed clumsily. From the way he sucked his teeth, it was clear that he had hurt himself.

'Don't do things like that, Mr Hamilton,' Betty advised. 'The creature is evil and clever. If you wish to thrive, leave the spider alive.'

'You live in a diseased house,' said Hamilton. 'I can't believe the surveyor didn't say anything. Thousands of hairy insects live in the ceiling, and you did nothing about it. Your wife talks about rats. Ever heard of DDT, or Polyfilla? For starters, why don't you switch on the ceiling light?'

'There are no bulbs in the fittings,' admitted Justin, his hand shaking so hard he had given up pouring the wine. 'Betty and I only ever eat in the kitchen.'

'Hamilton Corporation has made the Church of England a decent offer for this house,' continued

Hamilton. 'We are going to hold back on it until such time as you get a certificate from pest control declaring the house clean. Don't smile so stupidly,' he snapped at Betty. 'This doesn't mean you can stay living here.'

'Dad, you're very rude,' Edmund dared to say.

'Mollycoddling such people will get you nowhere, Edmund. You'll find out when you're in charge of this job.'

'I would like to correct something said earlier.' Neil raised his hand as if he were at school. Surprised looks turned to the timid, hairy young man. 'A spider is an arachnid and not an insect. An insect has three body parts; the spider has only two. The head is part of the thorax.'

'You don't say?' Hamilton discarded the ineffective fork back onto the table. 'For this crap, I have cancelled an important board meeting. Edmund, let's go.'

'The spiders must come from the room above,' Edmund pointed out. 'Why not find out what is up there?'

'That makes sense,' said Charlotte.

Hamilton gave her a sharp look. 'Who asked you?' he said.

'Directly above us is our master bedroom,' said Betty. And quickly added, 'There is trifle for pudding.'

'Of course there is. It's the most basic and unimaginative English dessert for those who can't cook.' Hamilton limped to the door leading out to the hall.

'More arachnids are squeezing through the hole,' observed Justin, looking up. 'I don't understand it.'

One behind the other, the seven of them climbed

the stairs from the sombre hall. Neil, at the rear, was held back by Edmund, who hooked his fingers into Neil's belt. Neil stood rigid in heightened anticipation of what would happen to him next.

'Say,' Edmund started, when the others had reached the first floor and were out of sight and hearing. 'How do you grow potatoes?'

Surprised, Neil nevertheless explained. 'When potatoes get older, they grow knobs and, after that, a shoot. On the ridge of the ploughed furrow, you bed them in. The shoot grows and makes...'

Edmund smirked. 'You are coming onto me, aren't you? Knobs and shoots and beds.'

Neil wriggled free of the hold Edmund had on his belt. 'Look it up on Google.' Neil felt his embarrassment coat his head like a cap. He put his hand on the rail in order to join the others upstairs.

'Not so fast, farmer boy. Charlotte's mother wants to hook her up with me.'

'You have things; you're a city boy. I live with my widowed mother in a small farmhouse.'

'What is Charlotte like in bed?'

Neil objected to the question and went up three treads, before Edmund hopped up right behind him.

'You made her a baby, so there have been knobs, shoots and beds. I couldn't do that. I wouldn't want to do that.'

'Yeah,' said Neil without turning back. 'If I was wired like you, I probably wouldn't want to, either.'

'Arabella is a bitch, isn't she?' Edmund pressed on with this unpleasant conversation.

'Davenport is in Dubai. She is frustrated. Let's go and find out about those spiders.'

The two men climbed the rest of the stairs.

★

Conclusion

Betty's hand was at the door handle. The others gathered on the landing behind her. 'We have not used this room as our bedroom,' she said. 'You'll see why when we go in.'

'Then let's not dilly dally and do so,' Hamilton pressured. 'I made an offer on the house. This gives me rights.'

When she opened the door, the others walked in slowly. In the darkness, the large room looked sinister, resembling a torture chamber with the wooden frame and glinting chains around it. Hamilton felt along the wall near the door for the light switch.

'No bloody bulbs in the lamps in here, either. A torch. Do you possess a torch? You know, the tube with batteries, a light coming out of it?'

'There is nothing special about this room,' Betty tried to reassure them. 'Let's go downstairs and have pudding.'

'Part of this room is above the dining room. That's why we came up here.' Edmund brushed past the group and headed for the bedside table, which was pushed into the corner above the spiders' hole.

'I believe he's wrong,' Betty objected. 'Anyway, there are no spiders up here. I would know; I clean the room. Let's all go downstairs.'

Instead, they advanced further.

'Chains around a bed – creepy,' said Arabella, touching the iron links.

'The chains are to keep the devil from molesting the sleeping.'

'The devil?' Hamilton laughed at Betty.

'My wife is reading the wrong books,' said Justin. 'Folk magic, the evil eye, candle-burning, the antichrist. It's getting to her.'

'This lunch is getting more interesting by the minute,' Charlotte said. 'First there was one eensy-weensy spider and then the whole harem was on the ceiling. Now we have Satan rattling chains while vicars are sleeping…'

She was interrupted by the sound of a door slamming somewhere in the house.

'You see?' Betty grinned with her lips pressed together.

Justin, with large strides, went to the south-facing window and opened it. This did not dispel the stuffiness of the room.

'If nobody objects,' said Edmund, looking around for approval, 'I am going to pull the bedside table away from the wall, so we can check the corner behind it.'

There was the short, sharp noise of shattering glass. The mirror, tilted against the wall, was intact. It had come from outside, from the front of the house.

Neil took the initiative and leant out of the open window. Pulling back, he looked at Edmund. 'I saw some kids running away from your Jag.'

Edmund almost leapt out of the room. They heard him rumble down the stairs.

'They weren't kids,' said Betty. 'As little as the spiders are really spiders. If you stay here long enough, you will understand how *He* works.'

When Edmund returned, all energy had gone from him. He opened his fist and showed them a pile of diamond-like pebbles.

'What are those?' asked Charlotte.

'My windscreen.'

'There is council housing further down the road.' Justin felt the need to make things clearer. 'Kids from there cause trouble.'

'How could small children have the strength to break a thick windscreen?' Betty challenged.

'You have a point,' Hamilton took up.

'Satan's doing,' Betty almost sang.

'We are getting side-tracked.' Hamilton strode to the bedside table and lifted it up. He immediately put it down to one side. 'I don't think Betty is cleaning this room. Look at this mess.'

They went closer. Behind the bedside table was a mass of cobwebs, so thick it resembled the discarded veil of a bride. Hamilton tilted the table forward, and they saw holes in the back of it.

'Spiders are living in there,' he said. 'That must be their nest. I should have gloves to do this.'

'Stop!' Betty ordered him. 'You have no right to open the drawers. This is personal. It's *my* bedside cabinet.'

'I heard you say you and your husband did not use this room.'

Neil stepped in at this point. 'There are dead rats in the bedside table. Mrs Halsey did not close the plastic

281

container properly. Spiders suck meat out of their prey. First, they inject them with venom. The venom decomposes the meat of the victim. After that, the spider sucks up the mushed meat like a milkshake.'

'How disgusting!' said Charlotte and stepped back.

Hamilton, intrigued, knelt on one knee to open the lower cabinet of the bedside table. He pulled out a square plastic container with a green lid.

'Give me that.' Neil came forward. 'It has been my job for a long time to burn the dead rats.'

Hamilton handed the box to Neil. 'Strange things go on in this vicarage. Perhaps the devil *is* in it,' he said, attempting a joke, while pushing himself up into a standing position, not without wincing from pain in his leg. When Hamilton was upright and had found his aplomb, he turned to Edmund. 'You will have to deal with vicarages.' He gave a chuckle as he added, 'Good luck to you.'

'Take the box away,' pleaded Betty. 'Now. Please.'

'Ratcatcher of Stockfield, do as she says,' said Hamilton.

Neil hesitated. 'How many rats is it this time?'

'Many, many rats.' Betty made a wide move with her arms.

'It's spring,' replied Neil. 'Rats come into houses and barns in the autumn.'

'Don't you just like to listen to a dead rat conversation?' Hamilton tried to jolly Arabella, while Edmund rolled windscreen pebbles in the dell of his hand.

'How are we getting home without a windshield?' Hamilton interrupted his son's absorption.

'You duck, and I drive slowly,' suggested Edmund.

'Wrong answer, son. We have to find an auto glass repair place and probably a hotel.'

'You, Hamilton, can stay in my house, and Edmund with Charlotte in the cottage,' offered Arabella, 'until the car is fixed. I am sure neither of you will mind. Charlotte and Edmund are getting on so well.'

Edmund shook himself like a dog doused in water. 'Look, Arabella, this does not work for me. I'm engaged to Timothy.'

'Oh, you're so not.' Hamilton looked at his son with unchecked hatred. 'I'll make sure of that. Now, let's open that box and then go home. I need to know whether these are actually rats and not just Betty's demons. If they are rat cadavers, my offer for the vicarage will have to be lowered considerably. Rats carry the plague.'

Neil went to push up the corner of the plastic box, but found that it was not properly closed. Betty, tense, gripped Justin's arm. Neil peeled the lid off. Curled inside the box was the body of a tiny baby, still in the foetal position and starting to decompose. In its neck was a gaping wound, surrounded by dried blood.

'Amelia…' Charlotte whispered aghast and fainted against her mother.

'I am going to be sick,' said Edmund.

'Close the lid, it stinks,' said Justin.

Betty gave an evil laugh. 'The devil has BO. Once it gets up your nose, it stays with you forever.'

Charlotte, who had come to, started to weep. It was a monotonous sound, interspersed with slurry words. 'Things went wrong. This fake midwife told me I was losing too much blood. She reassured me she could put it right, would change the position of the foetus. Later, she said she had not succeeded, and that I had aborted it. According to her, she took it to the hospital for research. I was too upset to push things further. All I wanted to do was believe that my baby was an angel and in heaven.'

'My daughter went through a deep depression.' Arabella guided Charlotte to the bed, where they both sat down, Arabella stroking over the blond hair again and again.

A spider appeared from under the bed, heading for its food cupboard. Arabella jumped up and stamped on it, so hard the metal chains rattled. 'The dirty beast was making its way back into the cupboard.'

'My baby was eaten by Betty's devil,' Charlotte whined.

Hamilton was the first to compose himself. 'Betty,' he addressed the vicar's wife with gravity, 'you have lied about your qualifications. This resulted in the death of a human being, for which you are responsible. You hid the evidence and caused enormous pain, especially to the mother of the child. I hope you spend years in prison. You are a devil-worshipper, an evil woman.'

'Saint Michael, defend us in battle,' said Justin. 'Be our protection against the wickedness and snares of the devil. May God rebuke him, we humbly pray. And do Thou, O Prince of the Heavenly Host, thrust into hell Satan and all evil spirits who wander through the world for the ruin of souls. Amen.'

WOMAN ON BICYCLE

It was a foggy November morning in the year 1970. On the concrete balcony of a fifth floor apartment, in a brutalist building in Central Berlin, a young woman in a white apron brushed her long blond hair and gathered it with a rubber band. She pulled a hairnet over it. She had little space to move, as most of the balcony was taken up by an old chest freezer that did not fit into the kitchen of the apartment.

The girl's name was Marlene Seiler; she was nineteen. Her only wish was to become an actress. Even in primary school, the teacher had told Marlene that this ambition of hers could never be more than pie in the sky.

Marlene's mother, Adela, had failed to become an actress because of an unwanted pregnancy at the age of twenty-one. She had set out with determination to make her baby fulfil her own thwarted dream. From the fifth month of gestation, she named the baby Marlene after Dietrich – or, if it were a boy, Curt after Jurgens – while babbling about stardom to the unborn inside her. After twenty-six hours of labour, looking at the newborn placed in her arms, she gasped. Marlene was born with a cleft lip. It was a cavernous, triangular hole from the upper lip right up to the little nose. Marlene would never be the adored actress on the red carpet in Cannes, with her mother in the audience being photographed for being the mother.

'This can't happen to me,' the young, unmarried mother protested when she fully realised that her baby was handicapped. As a pushy, controlling person, having faced hard times during the war, the mother discharged herself from the maternity unit. 'This will be fixed,' she growled grimly, her daughter bundled in her arms.

*

Marlene bent over the balcony rim. The early fog had not been dispelled by the rising of the sun. An orange, sulfuric haze hung about the street lamps down in Engel Strasse. Up on the fifth floor, the noise of the traffic was muffled by the lingering fog.

Marlene posed one elbow on the concrete balcony rim. She brought her other hand up to rest it loosely at her neck, as she if was about to perform. Her blue eyes on the balcony wall of the next-door apartment, she quoted Goethe's *Stella*: 'Let me weep. I would that the day were over. My whole body is still aflutter.'

Marlene stopped. Despite several cosmetic operations to close the cleft, her lisp still played up when her mouth muscles got tired. With her finger, she patted along her upper lip. In the left-hand corner, where the lip curved up, the skin was numb, the tiny nerves severed. It would improve with time; that's what surgeons said to distraught parents.

The shrill siren of a police car jolted Marlene out of her thoughts. It sped down Engel Strasse and, instead of stopping in front of the building to arrest someone, drove on towards Franz Sturm Platz. Marlene sighed dramatically. Her parents owned and ran the Seiler Bakery on the ground floor, and sometimes served citizens who had close ties to East Germans who were of interest to the police. Head tilted back, Marlene drew the back of her hand over her forehead.

'It is not yet near day. It was the nightingale and not the lark,' she recited Juliet.

This early private time was precious to Marlene, who got up every morning before sunrise to help her parents. Her adoptive father downstairs started the day even before that, to heat up the ovens.

Leaning over the coarse balcony rim again, she could now see the grass medallion and two park benches of Franz Sturm Platz, where she had been taken in her pushchair as a toddler – vague, but peaceful memories. A less peaceful memory was from the age of ten, when her parents had stood on this balcony and sobbed. The East German army, who had rolled out barbed wire through the town, were, to everyone's consternation, actually in the process of building a wall. It zigzagged through the middle of everything, three metres sixty high, made of bricks and coated in solid concrete. They had bricked up the end of Engel Strasse.

It felt to her, then, as if she had been shut off from the rest of town, the countryside, the rest of the world. She felt that she would never have a normal life, certainly never fulfil her dream of having her name in lights at the top of the credits, the way her mother said it could be. The father had explained that the wall was there to stop people escaping from East Berlin, and she wondered what they had done to be imprisoned like the bears in the zoo. Some of these people had been regular customers in the Seiler Bakery and had looked entirely normal.

From then on, there was news in the *Berliner Tageblatt* about East Germans risking their lives, trying to climb over or tunnel under the wall. In 1962, a student was machine-gunned off the wall by the East German army. There was a photograph of him, bleeding to death at the foot of the wall on the east side, while someone on a ladder on the west side threw down bandages, water and medicine. Every customer in the bakery expressed their horror about it. The day after, the chief editor of the *Berliner Tageblatt* died in a road accident, despite light traffic.

Later, as a teenager, Marlene had often sat on the old, rusty, chest freezer on the balcony, watching West Berlin being rebuilt, with some bullet-riddled house fronts preserved as memories. To the horrors of war and the six million victims of the Holocaust had been added this savage, divisive wall, stifling any attempt at light-heartedness. Oppressed by this, she often had the urge to exteriorise her deep-felt feelings about the sad reality of German life, by acting it out. She had wailed in despair, mimicked agony, while the tweeting blackbird, perched on the Stalin Star on a building opposite Engel Strasse, was her only audience.

Now, on this late autumn day, almost an adult,

Marlene left the balcony and went back into the kitchen. First, she ripped a paper tab from the wall calendar on which was printed 11 November 1970. Then, she washed her hands before starting to make a sausage meat mixture, which she rolled out on a flour-powdered board and shaped into dumplings, to be boiled and brought down to her father in the bakery. He pushed them into dough pockets for baking.

The wood-framed wall clock told her it was five past eight in the morning. Her father, Hans Seiler, had already kneaded the dough for today's bread and traditional Berliner Pfannkuchen, jam-filled buns and the Seiler Bakery's very special sausage meat-filled pasties. It had been her mother's idea to fill buns with meat, so people working in offices could get a full meal with one meat and one jam bun, especially as she thought men were not so keen on sugary confectionery. It became a success, and the Seiler Bakery's buns were widely known. They were even mentioned in travel brochures about Berlin.

Since she had graduated from high school at eighteen, Marlene had applied herself, experimenting to find the most pleasing spice mixture for the meat, the right temperature and length for the boil, and in making them fresh every morning. It was a disappointing first year of her much-yearned-for grown-up life, in which she had pictured herself becoming an actress. Kneading together minced meat until the skin on her fingers became crinkled in an ugly, small kitchen was far from her desires.

Her mother, Adela, had had a tough life. The Second World War, which started before she was ten, had cheated her out of a carefree childhood and enjoyable youth. Born with blond curls and cornflower blue eyes, she had, over time, forgotten how to smile or laugh. Since her marriage fifteen years ago, she had sold bread and Pfannkuchen in the bakery.

There was one thing which still made her feel alive, though, and that was going to the cinema, and following with eager interest the fate of actresses depicted in magazines. Marlene was brought up to share her mother's only passion. At the age of three, in a dress her mother had sewn, it was intended that Marlene would become another Shirley Temple. At six, Adela took Marlene to see films, which the child did not understand. There were no toys, only her mother's escapism, with which Marlene became slowly imbibed.

Marlene was inattentive at school, her concentration being on learning the roles her mother chose, in dresses her mother sewed for her. It pleased her mother, but also gave Marlene a sense of self-worth. School, Mother told her, was for people without ambition or imagination. Adela had glowed with pride when Marlene was chosen to play the top role in a school play, which the secondary school master had written. Mother lived for Marlene's yet-untarnished chances of becoming what she had missed out on. Hans Seiler, often irritated by the agitation in his household, called his wife and daughter 'my two drama queens', and could not understand why they went to the cinema so often, sometimes seeing the same film twice, even on school days.

Huddled in their cinema seats, hot, sweaty hands joined when the film lit up, mother and daughter were transported into other women's lives, into experiences of unknown love in places different from Berlin. The limitations in their stunted lives, baking and serving narrow-minded customers, puffed away when Romy Schneider appeared. She had a glow about her. Actresses were given the freedom to explode with emotions; they were loved for it. But, in the staircase of the building on Engel Strasse, one was not allowed to do more than whisper. In the basement, when it was the fifth floor's day to use the washing troughs, the hung-up linen was often torn off the line and trampled on. The neighbour on the same floor, Frau Erb, and Mother said nothing. They bent down and picked up the linen to wash it again on the assigned day.

Adela had dressed her daughter in princess dresses from the moment the toddler could walk. She had hidden the raw scars on the child's face with sticking plaster. Adela helped Marlene look after her precious hair, bought vitamin-enhanced conditioners. Adela counted calories for her daughter, in case by some miracle some talent scout would notice her, the way it happened to people in magazines.

In mid-January, Marlene would turn twenty. Her parents would pay for her to go to university and study drama. Mother, who clearly had worked on her father to achieve this, had not been able to keep it a surprise. After Marlene had thanked them for their generosity and a place had been secured in the drama department, Adela sobered.

'You will rise to fame without me. The university enables students to get acting experience with a live audience, helps them onto the stage, Hollywood even. You will leave me behind and forget what we share, the films we have seen. You will become ashamed of me, a baker's wife in an apron.'

Marlene saw her mother's pain and, with a sudden rush of emotion, ran to her. 'We are doing this together. You can help me rehearse, and I guess there will be a lot of that. They will also want me to see as many films as possible. Don't worry, Mother. We will do everything together the way we have always done.'

Adela beamed on hearing this and, arms linked, the two of them went into the living room to read the latest *Der Stern*, which promised to reveal the real Simone Signoret.

Marlene reassured her mother once more. 'You are the most special person in my life.'

'And you will become a famous actress,' Adela replied, 'slender and shapely as you are, and with your long legs and fabulous blond hair.'

'Looks is not all, Mother. It needs a lot more. For the next three years, I will have to work hard at learning to act professionally, and finding my own style of portraying other people in a convincing way.'

Mother and Marlene spent the rest of the afternoon going through old copies of *Der Stern* to judge which star had the most allure. They deplored Vivi Bach, the blonde actress, who was also about Marlene's age. Vivi played with her piled-up yellow, plastic hair and a puffy-lipped large mouth most artificially. They moved on to Elke Sommer, who had the stage, the bright lights, the applause, success and fame served on a platter, holidaying in Italy and being cast straight from the street. She was made into a sex symbol and invited to Hollywood at the age of eighteen.

'Younger than I am,' said Marlene pensively.

★

The first day of university, Marlene felt overwhelming love for her mother, who stood at the door of the bakery in her white apron, tears drawing two silver streaks on her cheeks.

'I take this course for both of us, or else it is not going to happen.'

Walking past Franz Sturm Platz, Marlene declared, 'Now begins the story of a new blonde actress, one who used to pick daisies from the lawn in this park, before it was defaced by a high wall.'

The drama course covered more than just role-rehearsal, speech and projecting oneself. She had to take theatre history and stage production, including décor. Papers had to be written, and homework was expected.

Every afternoon, Adela waited with anticipation for Marlene's return, and was ready to help with homework, and comment constructively on the endless voice-training exercises. Marlene took the course seriously and worked with dedication. Sometimes, her mouth hurt so much that the lips would not work any longer. The parts she had to practise were all from classical plays.

Mother and daughter even went to charity shops and bought used hats and other props, to make the acting practices more realistic. Marlene, standing in the brown-wallpapered, brown-carpeted living room amid the brown furniture, had a golden radiance about her, as she soliloquised the part of Klara in Goethe's *Egmont*.

'Careful, my love, let nobody be awoken, least of all ourselves.'

Mother thundered in the role of Brackenburg, wearing a feather-enhanced hat. 'In God's name!'

'Indeed,' uttered Father at the door, before closing it hurriedly again.

Adela had problems when it came to analysing characters and their psychological progress through plays. 'Hans never progressed in any way through all the years I've been married to him.'

'It is about pseudo-analysis of characters, which are made up by scriptwriters,' explained Marlene. 'But they still need plausible motives for what they are asked to do.' She used Brecht's *Caucasian Chalk Circle* to explain how a character deluded himself with an unrealistic dream, which became a danger to those who were drawn into it.

Despite the homework, Marlene's exam monologues never received plaudits. Perhaps she was hampered psychologically by the cleft palate, even though wonderful cosmetic work had been done. Adela shared Marlene's frustration at not being able to better herself.

'What can you expect from a baker's daughter?' a student colleague once said, which hurt. Meanness born from competition made friendships with classmates impossible.

There was only Frau Augsburg, the elocution coach, to whom Marlene could talk freely, perhaps because Frau Augsburg had felt around in her mouth to help position the tongue in the right place. This had been an invasive move, but Frau Augsburg told Marlene that growing a thick skin was part of learning to act. To protect her mother's feelings, Marlene pretended at home that she was admired by everyone on her course.

'What's with supper?' asked Hans.

'I just don't have time today to prepare your meal,' Adela said dramatically, and reached for the copy of Schiller's plays which lay on the coffee table. She flipped through the drama of *Kabale und Liebe*, looking for the part of Ferdinand she had offered to play.

★

At twenty-three, Marlene graduated with mediocre results. *Works hard, but lacks self-confidence.* Marlene studied the report, but then said to herself, 'Stop explaining your sorry self. Shut up and act.'

Back home, Adela was disappointed. Marlene reassured her that, given the chance of a real role, she would be able to cope, shine even. The next step was to hope for the placement office to come up with an acting job. Weeks passed. Marlene asked herself, *Why would they give something promising to a young woman with sausage mixture on her sleeve?*

Modelling was a favourite way into film acting. Marlene had the figure, and forced herself to apply to department stores as house model. The best she eventually achieved was being hired in the cosmetic department near the entrance of a store. She had to sit on a chair, and someone demonstrated a French tress-making tool, plaiting her hair and undoing it again and again. Bored, she left after eight weeks due to migraine.

How had the famous blonde dolly birds made it?

'Introductions, darling,' said Frau Augsburg, whom Marlene still met from time to time in the Café Kranzler. 'And taking their clothes off. But the most important thing is to be in the right place at the right time. Having a rich baron father was, of course, hugely helpful to his darling, Elke.'

In *Get Carter*, Britt Ekland had established herself as a sex symbol in less than five hundred frames. She, Marlene, was definitely in the wrong place and fully dressed still. She did manage to get into a catalogue, being photographed in frocks for middle-aged women. The excitement at being chosen as part of a group sent to model on a cruise ship sailing from Bremen to the Caribbean made her burn a whole batch of sausage meat. Adela helped her pack and sewed her a black cocktail dress, regarding the cruise as the springboard to fame.

During the cruise, Marlene felt so seasick that she wanted to die.

After that disaster, nothing else helpful came her way. She continued training her voice and rehearsed roles endlessly. With the kitchen towel over her head, she acted mourning Isabella in Schiller's *Die Braut von Messina*, while mixing pork mince at six in the morning. At the age of twenty-five, she received some money from her uncle, Adela's brother, who was her godfather. With it, she could afford the Ellen Zimmer acting studio's advanced course, which promised to get her a first stage-part. She progressed to performing flawlessly the Lady

Macbeth monologue, her trained voice rising and falling as she gave emphasis to certain words, less importance to others, keeping her tongue in the position Frau Augsburg wanted it to be. The quality of her acting became sound; she managed to come across as self-assured.

She began an affair with the drama teacher, a minor film actor whom she thought it was worth losing her virginity to. However, sleeping with him was a waste of time, as he slept with each would-be starlet in turn, as she found out later.

The course turned out to be hours of voice projection, reading and pronunciation, while the months passed in the company of hopeless old cases still hoping to go somewhere with this.

She was finally cast in a vaudeville play, in a Berlin Keller theatre where timing of delivery was important. The local rag, in its review, said that, instead of being engagingly funny, she seemed desperately funny.

Shortly after that, she modelled in the lobby of the Esplanade Hotel for Baroness von Klimheim's charity event. Hanging around afterwards, she came across Larry Scott from Los Angeles. He was stocky, and bad at small talk, but showed off his familiarity with Hollywood. She pretended to be mesmerised by him. When he revealed that he was in Berlin to co-direct with Peter Hames, who had won an Oscar, she drank two more gin and tonics. She had heard that such a film was in the making.

After the third G&T, and with her adoring eyes on his, Larry invited her up to his hotel room, where she performed a shoulder-off move with the black cocktail dress while he watched, sitting on the end of the bed. In front of him, she struck a pose.

'Set down, set down your honourable load,' she began. 'If honour may be shrouded in a hearse, whilst I awhile obsequiously lament the untimely fall of virtuous Larry Scott.'

It amused him. When he started to take off his jacket and unbutton his waistcoat, she swept past him with a caressing smile and went out of the door.

He protested. She leant back in. 'I have no right to damage your reputation.'

Timing was everything. The next day, he sent her a cactus to the bakery with a note: *They only bloom in Hollywood.*

She kept asking herself: if she had slept with him, would she now be in Hollywood? Somehow, this small interlude changed things for her. She was now twenty-six and more confident. She had also found a way to hide any trace of scarring with make-up. Giving up the acting classes, she concentrated on projecting her confidence. She called Baroness von Klimheim, suggesting they meet to discuss a scandal concerning Larry Scott. Intrigued, probably because the American had seduced the baroness, the latter invited Marlene on the spot to a drinks party at her house.

Marlene was astonished how easy things became when one stepped over oneself and went for it.

To make the most of the opportunity, she dressed with care for the event. She had learnt enough about projecting her own image to choose sophistication with an element of kittenishness, to appear aloof but adorably innocent still, for those men who were self-assured enough to look beyond the obvious.

'Why a cactus?' the baroness asked. The American had obviously sent her real flowers.

'I guess, my refusal to give in to his charm was interpreted in a prickly way.'

This worked with the baroness, and Marlene felt that she had just gone up a ladder and not slithered down a snake. The proof of this came when the baroness made an announcement to the group they were standing with.

'I have a mind to introduce our Marlene to Knauf.' She did not divulge who Knauf was. Everyone else knew.

About ten days later, Marlene received a printed invitation for dinner at the baroness's Schloss.

Felix Knauf turned out to be a surrealist film director. He was tall and judgemental about people, and had the greenest eyes she had ever seen in a man. His trousers were, most oddly, held up with wide, embroidered braces.

'I was invited here to meet you,' he said to Marlene over the dinner table, not without a tinge of mockery.

'Maybe I was invited as a lab rat, to test your dedication to the absurd,' she replied. 'My profession is making Seiler buns, and I have never had a role in a film, not even in the background, despite Ellen Zimmer's acting studio.'

'You are a lot more than that,' said Knauf. 'You remind me of Rita Wegner, who also studied at Ellen's. The school's methods will pay off, especially with their emphasis on classical theatre.'

'Surrealist as you are, I am surprised you value the traditional style.'

'Someone who has never studied Shakespeare has no right to come to me and ask to be in one of my films. For this is what you are after, isn't it, little lab rat?'

'So,' she said slowly, 'in your films, actors wear codpieces and tights?'

He laughed out loud. 'You have just put your finger on what I am currently after. I apologise, but confess to thinking *film* all the time, inspired by many things, even in my dreams.'

Aping him, she quickly replied, 'I too apologise, but admit to thinking of becoming an actress all the time, starring ideally in one of your films, even in my dreams.'

★

When Knauf and Marlene met a second time, by themselves in a hotel bar, to celebrate his Cannes Palme d'Or for short films, he told her he was casting for actresses in his next full feature film. She sat up straight, shook her blond hair and growled at him with perfect teeth.

He slowly closed his eyes, while a smile spread on his handsome face. 'It's not about a zoo, although you have just given me a thought to pursue. Thank you.'

'A tiny, eensy-weensy role. Pretty please?'

'I have considered you,' he said encouragingly. She waited, frozen in her pose. 'You are wrong for small roles. I intend to give you an important role. The script for it is not yet written. Will you be my wife?'

She nearly fell off the chair. 'Is this play-acting or real?'

'That is the first thing you will have to find out for yourself and then handle, without cheating or asking my two previous wives for clues. They were both actresses.'

★

Felix Knauf and Marlene were married in the registry office in Berlin. It was spring. She wore a flowery dress her mother had sewn. Felix arrived twenty minutes late, riding on a trained ostrich led by its handler, the bird wearing a bride's veil on its silly head. In their wake were press photographers.

The next day, a picture of Felix on the ostrich was on the front page of the *Berliner Tageblatt*. It made it around the world. She wasn't in any of the pictures.

At this, the most inconvenient moment, her uncle asked her to help out in the bakery again, as her parents could no longer manage the workload. She owed him – he had financed the Ellen Keller course – and there Marlene was, in her apron and hairnet, yet again ripping paper tabs off the calendar on the wall, before digging her manicured fingers into the meat mixture.

She avoided conversations with her mother about the marriage with Felix. Surrealism was an invisible enemy between the couple. He was an artist and, in his head, creating relentlessly. As there was no room left for her, she became neglected and frustrated.

Adela guessed that things were not going well, when Felix told her he didn't like Seiler buns. With a puckered mouth, she told her son-in-law that he was a snob and not at all what her daughter deserved.

Marlene imagined that he would retort with, *Why didn't you find her a butcher's son?* Felix didn't. He never did what one expected.

'The German Film Commission has chosen me to make a surrealist film to present at the next Cannes film festival.'

'So what?' said Adela, responding as expected. 'Germany is not that big a country. What is surrealism, anyway?'

He took her question seriously. 'It is producing incongruous, imaginary or shocking effects in film, often by unnatural or irrational juxtapositions and chance effects. It should reach the subconscious of a person. Freud and Jung initially developed this idea.'

'Mind-blowing,' said Adela, who privately thought her daughter had married an idiot.

'Precisely,' said Felix, pleased.

Adela brought him a bun, and he pretended to like it. However, in the double bed that evening, Felix rolled away from Marlene again.

'Not now,' he grumbled. 'I need to track a new thought.'

'It has been months since you touched me,' said Marlene. 'You never listen to what I am saying, either.'

'It doesn't contribute to my visual compositions.'

'Not everybody lives up to your surrealist genius level. Some of us need to remain realists without the *sur*.'

'Not funny. Just leave me be. I need to be creative right now.'

'A woman's needs ignored lead inevitably to strife and war.'

'Very Nordic.'

'The woman I meant is me.'

★

Felix was even too busy to help her find their own apartment to rent, and so the couple moved into the small roof apartment in the same building which housed the Engel Strasse bakery. From a smaller version of the same, narrow, concrete balcony, married Marlene could at least still see Franz Sturm Platz, the grass and the benches, on which nobody ever sat any longer.

Marlene tried out a female ruse on Felix. 'If you give me a role in a film, I will sleep in the alcove. If you give me a role in a film, I will not talk to you for three hours after you get up in the morning.' She gave a toss of her loose hair.

It did not work, and tension grew dense in the small apartment with triangular eaves pinching head space. Not even Adela made it up the stairs any longer.

A retrospective article in *Film International* criticised Felix's work. First, he was depressed, and depression turned to anger. He blamed Marlene for undermining his creativity – her pestering concentration on him, and the marital enslavement which forced him to wash dishes and put out rubbish.

After a shouting match in which he slapped her, true to her threat of strife and war, she packed her suitcase and walked to the Hotel Terminus, a 2-star self-catering hotel with cooking facilities to share on its three floors.

She was making herself a cup of coffee in the kitchenette, to go with the box of Seiler buns she had brought, when a middle-aged man in striped pyjamas walked in and asked her to make him a coffee as well.

'I am not your maid,' she put the arrogant man in his place.

'Do you know who I am? Max Goldbaum? Who won the Golden Bear for this year's best film at the International Film Festival in Berlin.' He puffed out his ample chest.

'My husband has a Palme d'Or.'

'And who would that be?'

'Felix Knauf.'

'Now you're talking, lady. Let *me* make coffee for *you*. Oh, and you brought Seiler buns.'

'Before I say anything more, I have a right to know what you are doing in your pyjamas in this kitchenette.'

'I've just left my wife and have nowhere else to go. You?'

'I had a gigantic argument with Felix and wanted to make a point.'

'You shouldn't have left. He is a genius in the revival of the surrealist genre.'

'You are welcome to go and live with him. How would you describe your genre?'

'Expressionism.'

'Sounds just as painful to live with as surrealism.'

'Can I take you up on your offer?' said Goldbaum. 'I am dying to meet up with Felix. If we worked together, giving expressionism an injection of the surreal, we could make a winner.'

Marlene left Goldbaum in the kitchenette and traipsed back to her room. Sitting on the cheap bed, she realised that her daring attempt to punish her husband might have backfired; perhaps it was going to please him. Looking out of the small window, she saw Goldbaum leave the hotel and walk up the street, carrying a black briefcase in which she knew were scripts. Felix would be delighted and grateful, if he knew she had met Goldbaum. She decided to stay the night in the hotel, because she had paid for the room. Returning home the next morning would be early enough.

★

Subdued, the next morning she returned home, and trudged up the stairs back to their flat. Inside, Felix was scribbling on a notepad. She closed the door behind her. He looked up shortly.

'Hi,' she said, but got no response. Just then, the doorbell rang. Felix dropped his pen.

'It's probably Max Goldbaum.' Felix's voice was ringing with excitement. 'He called last night. He is big. An international celebrity. It was inevitable that the two of us would get together one day.'

'Only thanks to me.'

Max walked in with a huge bunch of roses in one hand and a bottle of champagne in the other. He handed the champagne over to Felix and put the bunch of flowers on the table. With hands free, he came over to Marlene and hugged her.

'You clever, clever girl.'

★

Marlene heard her mother's puffing on the staircase. When she opened the door to her, Adela almost tumbled onto the rug in the entrance space.

'I've just seen Max Goldbaum...' she said, short of breath, 'under his umbrella with his black case walk past the bakery window.'

'He came here to work with Felix on their new project: *Woman On Bicycle*.'

Mother and daughter tiptoed to the closed living room door. Marlene put her ear against it.

'What are they talking about?' whispered Adela.

Marlene pressed her head closer. 'A new set design, which costs more than the budget.' She listened again. 'Oh, they want to copy the arches under the Brandenburg Gate.'

'Whatever. The important thing is that auditioning must have started.' Resolutely, Adela opened the door and pulled Marlene inside with her.

Max finished his argument before reacting to the women's presence. 'The columns have to be strong enough to support the weight of a man.' He looked up. 'What are these women doing in here?'

'We've come to audition,' said Marlene, with a rabbit-tooth giggle.

'Doris Day's trademark giggle, not suitable for our film. Over to you, Felix. They're your women,' said Max.

'The casting is already over,' replied Felix.

'What about the woman on the bicycle?'

'Her part is purely symbolic. Filmed in high contrast, it is to trace one mental thread through the storyline.

The cyclist only appears from time to time, sometimes wrapped in smoke, cycling against wind, dressed in different costumes. She will be the end of the film, cycling into the distance, leaving the film's quintessence to be worked out. About twelve minutes at twenty-four frames per second in total.'

'We don't care about the length,' Adela spoke up for both of them. 'Do we, Marlene?'

'Don't make this into something it is not.' Felix felt he needed to clarify. 'They are just takes of a woman cycling. No dialogue. No credits.'

'I want to do this. Please, Felix. I know I can do this,' Marlene urged.

'I can do more than do it,' said Adela. 'I would add depth to it.'

'Actresses,' sighed Max. 'Unless we write in a tandem, why not let them each convince us why they should get the part?'

Looking uncomfortable, Felix agreed, and his mother-in-law and wife seemed to embrace the idea.

Age before beauty, thought Adela, who decided to go first. With a performative hand gesture, she began, 'Not knowing the story, I can offer competence in whatever situation, thanks to my maturity. I used to cycle during the war, when petrol was rationed. No-one should ever forget about this. Knowing my son-in-law Felix, the film is intellectual and thought-provoking, which the image of an older woman cycling could convey more pointedly. The young like frivolous films and want the film director to do the thinking for them.'

When it was Marlene's turn, she began by looking

at both directors slowly and smiling at each in turn with big eyes.

'At our wedding, you, Felix, offered me a role in one of your films as a present. I'm still waiting. Am I not an attractive blonde with blue eyes in her twenties – the German ideal?'

'Let's not go anywhere near Hitler,' said Felix. 'What else?'

'I have a degree in drama from Berlin University and a diploma from the Ellen Zimmer acting school,' continued Marlene. 'Surely my mother, a fifty-year-old, is not what you are looking for?'

'Excuse me,' Adela had to put in. 'What about Therese Giehse in *Mother Courage*? Much, much older than me, Giehse turned Brecht's film into a big classic, portraying the hardship and depression of a woman during wartime. I personify a woman who lived through a war. Berlin people can identify with that in me. I should be the one chosen to cycle.'

'What about men?' Marlene kept fighting. 'I can be an object for their sexual dreams, which is a necessity in films nowadays. I should be the one chosen to cycle.'

Felix decided. 'I choose Marlene.'

'Because she is your wife?' said Max.

'No Max, because it is the right choice.'

Marlene put her hand on Adela's forearm. 'I'm sorry to take this away from you.'

'Darling, I am not at all that sure I can still cycle.'

Marlene murmured, 'Thank you for saying that.' She turned to the men. 'I need this role. I would shrivel and die if you did not give me this break. I have spent

308

my whole life working towards it, given up everything else for it. If I never get a chance, I will end up despising myself.'

'Don't be so melodramatic,' said Adela. 'You *have* made it, in a way. I can say to everyone I meet, my daughter is married to the famous film director, Felix Knauf.'

'I have already disappointed everybody by being born with an ugly hole in my face,' said Marlene. 'I need to be someone in my own right.'

As if exhausted by this outburst, Marlene sat down and remained very quiet. They realised that, if it *was* despair, it was a deeper pit than they could imagine. Frightened by her intensity, Max tried to dissuade her.

'Look, my dear, you will just be cycling. Not even ringing the cycle bell. And there will be no close-ups.'

'Because of my scars?'

'Scar is the right concept,' Felix intercepted. 'Well done. Your sporadic appearances symbolise the mental scar, the fissure, running through the story.'

★

One early January morning, the two directors began filming in the centre of Berlin. It was chill, damp and dark. Heavy clouds obscured a waning pale moon. The location chosen was a street of bleak and dreary concrete apartment blocks, crowded against each other. It had been closed to traffic.

'Perfect,' exclaimed Max, as the cameras were installed. Against a wall leant the silver bicycle.

Marlene was asked to sit on a high stool. She had been dressed in an ample white tulle ballgown. When Nina, the make-up girl, finished and held up a mirror, Marlene saw on her face lots of foundation and strong eyeshadow. Max then insisted on a dark lipstick – altogether, a creepy bride on a bicycle in lugubrious surroundings.

The cameraman fussed, wanting the beam of the bicycle headlamp to be more powerful, in contrast to the dark canvas.

'We're not doing Gothic,' Max approved. 'We want a camera obscura effect.'

The bulbs were changed. Marlene's hair was rolled into a bun and pinned at her nape. A strand of white-blond nylon hair, interwoven with red velvet tassels, was clipped to the top of her head, falling into her face.

While the process of preparing her progressed, the two directors in the dark beyond the beam of light simply watched, unsmiling, their creative minds elsewhere.

Marlene felt manipulated and left out, the way she had felt in the department store when offering her good hair simply for a device to be demonstrated. Now, two major cinematic creators were designing every move she had to make – a dream come true, although a mute one, after all her hard work to learn roles and overcome her deformity.

The gaffer – or general dog's body, as he called himself – set up a smoke machine three metres in front of the bicycle. It would be pulled backwards as the bicycle advanced, dispensing puffs of white smoke. Marlene was told to get onto the bicycle. Nina held the meringue tulle train behind her to protect it from the grime of the road.

Up at a window, an old woman was watering her geraniums, water starting to drip down.

'Shit,' said Max. He shouted upward, 'Hey, lady, stop watering flowers. We are making a film down here. If you want to be in it, come downstairs and join us.'

The window upstairs closed with a bang.

'If I were to put together all the frames of people we have filmed, just to get them out of our way, it might be worth something,' Max mused.

Suddenly, Marlene felt nervous. There was a tingling of discomfort in her nape, where she felt the clip stuck not into her hair but her scalp. The unfamiliar make-up made her feel as if she wore a mask. The lipstick tasted of black olives. The sombre surroundings did not help, either. Turning her head, she saw her shadow and that of her bicycle, grossly enlarged against the façade of the apartment building. Its heavy front door was slowly pulled open. A white-haired woman appeared, her walking-frame planted step by step ahead of her. On the handle of the frame was threaded a green plastic watering can.

'Will you make me look pretty?' she asked, lifting her face.

'She is perfect,' gloated Felix. 'Let her pretend to give the woman on the bicycle a push.'

'You're right,' Max agreed. 'We can raise the smoke machine, and the white tulle petticoats will slowly amalgamate with the white clouds. The old goat's face behind will be transformed into a phantasm as she lets go of the bicycle and vanishes into the background.'

311

Marlene had performed on stage at university and in Ellen Zimmer's school. Stage fright was hardly excusable now. She had no speech to deliver. She had to cycle in short spurts the way they directed it. She pushed her backside up onto the saddle, before putting one sandal-clad foot in white cotton socks on the pedal. Further down the road, lights on tripods with open stable-door flaps blinded her. Puffs of white smoke into which she would cycle played around her in swirls. Behind her, she heard the breathing of the old woman, ready to pretend to push.

'You won't ride over my feet, will you? I have five bunions.'

'Ready, everyone?' Max called out. 'Instructions clear? Marlene, you cycle down the road towards us slowly, and stop gently when I raise my arm. Everybody, still now. Smoke a notch up.'

'Sorry, no.' The cameraman stood in front of the full-on spotlight. 'Too bland. I want only two-point lighting on this one.'

While the gaffer removed the spotlight, Max ordered Marlene not to smile. A serious expression of concentration was required. 'OK?'

The cameraman checked around him. 'Take one.' He clapped the slate.

Marlene took the handlebars and pushed down on the pedal, putting on a sad expression. Her knees rising slowly up and down, she cycled down the street. The old woman, blinded by smoke, had long let go. Marlene's sandal slipped on the pedal, which twirled and started making a noise.

'Cut!' shouted Max.

It had to be done twice more. The last time, the old woman gave up and disappeared into the house, forgetting to take the watering can with her.

Unruffled, Felix wanted to do the take again, with green fluid added to the smoke. Max concurred. By now, many of the petticoats had rips.

The slate clapped again. Marlene set off. The smoke now had an unpleasant smell; she had to cough. As directed, she turned the corner at the end of the street, cycling slowly into viciously green clouds. The coughing persisted. She was forced to stop.

'For God's sake!' exploded Max, who had sprinted down the road after her. 'Dawn will ruin the light. Cough as much as you must, but keep cycling. From now on, you have consumption.'

'Brilliant.' Felix caught up with them. 'That can work.'

The directors decided to go back and do it again. From up on the balcony, the old woman shouted, 'Hello.'

'Please, somebody shoot her,' joked Max.

Felix gave Max's chest a hand flick. 'Make-up for consumption? What do you think?'

'Yep.' Max shouted for Nina to change Marlene's make-up from dramatic dark to sickly pale, with dark red around the eyes.

Nina came running with her case. 'Hold still.' She attacked Marlene's face.

They had to redo the take twice more. Marlene realised how little she had known about the painful, frame-by-frame putting together of images in cinema acting. The January sky above them lightened. Felix and Max announced that the last and most important part of the filming would be next.

★

They gathered in a small children's play area off Eberts Strasse, near the inner city gardens and close to the Brandenburg Gate. Both gate and garden had been walled up in the East, a worn wall which, over the years, had been decorated with graffiti and advertising stickers. It was not far from Engel Strasse. Tea-and-biscuit time was over, and so was going to the nearby restaurant to use their toilets – for which the restaurant owner had been offered a role as an extra.

The directors gave new directions, sitting on a children's seesaw, an image which the cameraman felt so inspiring he could not stop filming their alternate rising and falling. The smoke machine had been replaced by a wind machine, to be pulled backwards on the same trolley. Marlene, already dressed behind a pop-up screen, emerged in black leather trousers, a black roll-neck pullover, and black boots. Nina had changed her sickly consumption make-up to sophisticated, subdued pale, enhanced with a diamond coronet and dangly earrings, which clashed with the biker outfit.

'Too basically explicit,' commented Max, pushing himself up on the seesaw, deck shoes pressing into the wood chips on the ground. 'The visual immediately regresses from object to personal identification. We don't want that.'

314

Felix, having been forced down on the plank, held it down by squatting on it and looking up at Max, legs dangling in the air.

'It's too linear,' he said. 'We need a visual lure.' He released the pressure and Max came down to the ground with a thump.

'Excellent,' voiced Max, pushing himself up again. Watching Felix go down, with a grin he said, 'I knew we could work together. Lure, you said. We need a very long, narrow scarf. Blood red.'

'Blood red,' repeated Felix.

'We don't have one,' said the wardrobe mistress.

'Then get one.' Max held out his hand to be helped off the seesaw by the gaffer.

'Now?'

'No. In ten years' time.'

'Yes, Herr Goldbaum.' She started to run out of the playground towards the road.

'Taxi,' he shouted after her. And then, even louder, 'Red!'

★

The wait for the arrival of the scarf seemed long. They were by now into the afternoon. They sat on benches. They engaged small children in conversation. They bought ice cream from a van. Nina seemed to relish the break, engrossed in a book entitled *How to Antagonise People*.

The wardrobe mistress returned. 'No long red scarfs anywhere. But,' she calmed down her breathing, her hand against her chest, 'I found a red silk sari, and with my scissors…'

'Taj Mahal,' said Felix dreamily. 'We could include…'

'There will be no Taj Mahal in *Woman on Bicycle*,' said Max. 'Snap out of it and hold the ends of this sari.'

The scissors cut through the four metres of red silk.

★

They watched Nina wrap the red scarf around Marlene's neck, then made her sit on the bicycle while the gaffer tried out wind strengths on the machine. Only when Marlene struggled with breathing, and the scarf ends fluttered a long way behind her, was he satisfied.

The script dictated that the Berlin Wall should appear to end, as the symbolic cyclist rode along, and that the Brandenburg Gate, which was actually in East Berlin, would be revealed as open between West and East. For this illusion to work, they had massively enlarged photographs of the view through the gate, and fixed them against the wall where the view would have been visible had the wall not been in the way. In the same way, five cardboard pillars had been built to match the real ones supporting the gate behind the wall. They were erected in direct line with the photographs, if the camera was set up in the right place. All that had to be done after that was to cut the film to conceal the bits of wall which should not be there.

Marlene would cycle into the wind, in front of the photographs on the wall and the fake pillars, the red scarf ballooning behind her.

Waiting for the camera to be positioned, she noticed someone in a group of onlookers giving her a timid little wave. It was Frau Erb, their Engel Strasse neighbour, who had recognised her.

From the East came a military voice through a loudspeaker. 'Move back! Move back! This gate is protected heritage.'

Angry shouts followed, indicating that the guards were annoyed about the filming so close to them, and perhaps puzzled by the pillars.

Marlene heard her mother's voice shouting. And there Adela was, standing next to Frau Erb on the lawn. Driven by curiosity, she was creeping closer to the filming action.

To Marlene's dismay, Adela approached her. 'You look pale and exhausted, darling. Let me take over.' She pushed her daughter off the saddle.

'What is my bloody mother-in-law doing here?' Felix wanted to know.

'It's too much for Marlene,' replied Adela. 'She is not up to it. I am going to take over.'

'No, Mother. You are not,' Marlene hissed.

'The cyclist through the story aged,' continued Adela. 'Normal. She has now become me.'

'When did you become a film director?' shouted Max. 'Go back to your Pfannkuchen.' He was so angry, a vein showed pulsing on his forehead.

Some onlookers had come closer. 'Where are the actors?' I brought my autograph book.'

'The actors will be filming in a studio,' replied Max. 'Get out of the way.'

'So, is this cycling just the fill-in between the real story?' asked Frau Erb.

'Not if I am doing the cycling.' Adela, her chin up, looked about her.

'Mother, please go home. I'll see you when we are finished here.'

'Marlene, if you are going to do this, you must make sure you stand out. Rebel a bit. Come up with something more dramatic than just pedalling.'

Just then, Felix announced that things were in place for the final filming. 'You are in the way. All of you. Please leave now.'

'Let's wrap this up!' Max shouted.

Marlene was on the bicycle again. The slate clapped. She set off and cycled along the graffiti-covered wall. The wind machine against her was strong. Soon, she would reach the fake Brandenburg pillars to her left. The wind was increased. The scarf tugged at her neck. She had to hold on to the handlebars tight and shut her eyes at times.

She pushed down on the pedals, the wind machine being pulled backwards in front of her faster to maintain its distance, the flame-red Indian silk flying behind her.

'Your daughter looks like an exotic bird, flying in front of the gate,' Frau Erb said to Adela.

Marlene projected forward on the bicycle and immediately back, before falling off. She lay twisted on the ground.

Max and Felix cursed.

Adela smiled. 'Good girl. She brought some drama into the dull scene. I told her to animate her role.'

The cameraman ran to the fallen figure, still filming. He was filming the people closing in on Marlene on the ground. He even took portrait shots of Marlene's face, until a first-aider with a Red Cross armband bent down to check the fallen figure.

'That is your doing,' Felix said to Adela.

'If you had let me ride the bicycle,' she replied, 'I would have first thrown both arms into the air before falling off, and let out a scream for people to remember.'

The first-aider stood up. He wiped over his forehead with his arm. 'The young woman is dead. The scarf caught in the spokes of the bicycle and strangled her.'

From Adela came a scream, which the people on the scene would remember for the rest of their lives.

'Cut!' shouted Frau Erb, who had got into the spirit of things.

GRAMERCY PARK

Officer Ray was speeding up Second Avenue in his NYPD Chevrolet Impala, when the dispatcher came on the car radio.

'Proceed immediately to 21st and Third – Gramercy Park. Young Lenny needs back-up.'

'Can't oblige,' said Ray, and reached out of the car window to plant the magnetic siren onto the roof. Instantly, he was transformed into a beast of noise and danger.

'Deputy Commissioner says the situation in the park is apparently getting out of hand,' the dispatcher insisted.

'I'm tailing the Puerto Rican who just shot and wounded the corner shop Sikh. Get someone else.'

'I'm just following orders. Suggest you do the same.'

Ray felt the urge to swear copiously, but foul language clean-up week had just finished in the Department. Five hundred and thirty-five sworn-in officers had been made to attend lectures.

The dispatcher had cut communication.

The villain had been running on the sidewalk, dodging obstacles and people. Ray should have parked anywhere and given chase on foot, taser ready, but he had lost the man because of the call.

Ray performed a U-ey in the middle of the four-lane avenue, dodging by seconds the ambulance on its way to the wounded storekeeper. Resigned, Ray drove back down towards Precinct 13, Manhattan South-East.

'Yes, Sir. I'll do anything you say, Sir. It's no trouble at all. Fuck you, Sir,' he said to the dead car radio.

Gramercy Park was a private green oasis between 21st and Third. It had a history of glamour, of wealthy people a long time ago having bought the land, shared deeds. To use the park, they needed a key. To get a key, they needed to live around the park. To live around the park, they had to be rich. It wasn't a crime hotspot. Neither was it a patch which offered police officers promotion or a ribbon.

Often, a rookie straight out of the academy was given park duty for a while, to learn the ropes. Lenny was one of them. Ray decided to put a good face on the job, and sort it out in minutes. Helping out a colleague in trouble had its own merits.

'After that, I'll go back up to look for the Puerto Rican scumbag.' Aware again of his swearing, he repeated, 'The gentleman with a bullet in his gun and a twitchy trigger finger.'

He left his Chevvy halfway up the kerb on 21st. The park, surrounded by tall railings, looked peaceful and under control. People strolled on pebbled paths, children played, dogs sniffed. Only the sudden flutter of a disturbed pigeon drew his attention.

The tall, iron gate had been left ajar for him. Ray strode into the garden. Lenny crept into view from behind a bush, shoulders up.

322

'Thanks for coming to help,' he breathed.

'My pleasure,' joked Ray. 'You really got yourself into a tight spot in here with all the shooting and knifing going on. Has the statue been toppled by terrorists?'

'The statue is of Edwin Booth, a famous Shakespearean actor,' said Lenny. 'Installed in 1918, six years before Gramercy Park Hotel was built.'

'They should have made you park guide, instead of moving you from traffic to crime.'

'I was told to familiarise myself with the turf.' Lenny was obviously the earnest, meticulous type, trying too hard to go by the book, too hard to get it right.

Ray tried another way to get a grip on Lenny. 'Know the patch, observe what's around you, be ready to act at all times.' He went on, 'For instance, that man over there on the bench, near the pond, is about to choke on his deluxe deep-filled prawn sandwich. What were you so freaked out about to call the Deputy Commissioner for help?'

'All right.' Lenny swallowed Ray's sarcasm. 'The guy who is not eating a prawn sandwich is actually the actor, Billy Cochran. He comes in here often. Perhaps to pay tribute to the statue. I'm going to ask Billy for an autograph. Remember him in *A Bad Lot*? The bit where he stands on the roof, just been shot, arms out, shouting, "Once upon a time a beautiful woman loved me".'

'You do know Billy is gay?' Ray attempted to tamper down Lenny's exuberance.

Ray stepped out of the way of a small girl on a scooter, which was skidding on pebbles. He had a go at the new clean and polished language of communicating. 'I have to be aware that it might be understood as an insensitive question, but why have I been asked to help out here?'

'Check them out at three o'clock,' Lenny whispered conspiratorially. 'The man with a kid in a stroller, not the old woman.'

Slowly, Ray turned his head. A man in his forties, wearing a collared shirt, chinos and sports jacket, sat at one end of a green park bench. In front, facing him, was a child strapped into a stroller. At the other end of the bench sat an elderly woman of African origin with short, white hair. She was neatly attired in a coat over a dress.

'And?' said Ray. 'A dad is taking junior to the park. The boy is playing with a kaleidoscope.'

'That's not a kaleidoscope. It's a can of beer.'

'The guy is a bad father.'

'What you can't see from here is the handle of a knife sticking out of the guy's belt at the back. Knife possession – that's a 10-10 K. He is not just a bad father, see.' Lenny was satisfied with his observational skills. 'And, besides the concealed weapon, it is a crime to give alcohol to a minor.'

Ray shook his head. 'If I told you a few stories about my old man...'

Lenny's voice had risen. 'For the record, I have started writing things down on my pad.'

The two police officers watched as Bad Dad on the bench twisted sideways to engage the white-haired woman in conversation.

'Have you seen *The Night Gang*?' Ray asked Lenny.

'The film for kids?'

'Gulimor uses his sword to move asteroids out of

324

the way – a sabre with the head of a silver snake with red fangs.'

'So?'

'Look at the handle of Bad Dad's plastic knife stuck into the belt.'

On the bench, Bad Dad was edging closer to the old woman, who began gesticulating and shouting. The two of them had got into an argument.

'Disturbing the peace,' said Lenny. 'That's already on the list on my pad. That, and threatening behaviour.'

Now they looked on as, suddenly, Bad Dad slapped the elderly woman, quite hard.

'Assault.' Lenny's pen was busy on the jotting pad. 'Racially aggravated.'

'Why isn't she just walking away?' wondered Ray.

At that moment, as if she had heard him, she got up to leave, but the man pushed the stroller to block her way. She tried to turn to the left, but the buggy was blocking her feet. The same happened when she turned to the right. When it looked as if she had made it, the stroller was pushed into the back of her legs. One of her shoes came off.

'Outrageous,' commented Lenny. 'You see now why I asked for back-up?'

'I guess now is probably the moment we could intervene.'

'Probably? Could?' Lenny stared at Ray in disbelief.

Before they made a further move, Bad Dad picked up the woman's brown lace-up shoe, ran with it to the pond and flung it into the water, before sitting back down on the bench.

'Theft,' triumphed Lenny. 'Disturbance of natural habitat.'

The two cops confronted the criminal. Ray spoke up first. 'Officer Fitzgerald, NYPD. Is there a problem?'

'You jolly well know there is a problem,' the woman interjected. 'You have been watching the behaviour of this insane man. How he got to be in charge of a child is beyond me. The boy is drinking beer and has pooped his pants.'

'My first arrest,' Lenny whispered to Ray, who was wiping saliva spray off his ear.

The toddler tossed the can out of the buggy.

'Littering.' Lenny put pen to paper.

'I need my shoe,' the old woman insisted. 'It's my best pair. I am not rich. Not like those who live round here.' Her head made a rotating move. 'I'm the cook in number fourteen East 22nd.'

Lenny, familiar with the location, suggested they fetch the park attendant.

'The water will have ruined the leather,' whinged the cook.

'I'll go,' offered Bad Dad.

They saw him cross the pebbled space and then, on the spur of the moment, sit down on the bench with Billy Cochran.

The child started to cry. 'Abandonment,' said Lenny.

Ray sighed, bent down, picked up the beer can and gave it back to the child.

In the distance, the park attendant was visible. Lenny hot-footed to him. After a while, both of them returned, the attendant carrying a long pole with a metal claw at one end.

'Where abouts?' he wanted to know, bad-tempered.

'Over there,' pointed the woman.

'More like over here,' corrected Ray.

The warden dragged the pole through the bottom of the pond three times. Plastic bags emerged, but no shoe. 'There's so much stuff at the bottom. In the winter, we lower the water and can get at it.'

'How can I function with only one shoe till winter?' complained the cook of number fourteen.

'You won't dredge up wisdom from the bottom of a pond, if you don't already possess it.' Billy Cochran had joined the group at the edge of the pond, Bad Dad in tow.

Bad Dad took the pole from the park warden. 'May I?' His fingers curled around the wood. 'I seem to remember where it landed.'

'Sank, you mean,' said Billy. 'And all that under Edwin Booth's nose.'

'A massive honker, which could be very much in the way.' Bad Dad gave Billy a shy, daring look, as if he might have offended with that remark.

There was something going on between Billy and Bad Dad from which the others were excluded. Moving between the box hedges, holding the long pole vertical, Bad Dad reached the statue. He looked up, aimed and, with a hollow ringing noise, the metal hook hit the bronze nose.

Lenny wrote down *Defacing monuments*. Edwin stared ahead, his long nose still intact, the strident sounds of Manhattan not far away, as always.

'This is the moment we take him in,' said Ray,

and took Bad Dad by his arm, with the reglementary correctness he had been recently lectured on. Lenny was left to push the child in the stroller behind them.

Reception in the 13th Precinct was manned by Rufus, a cop who had to work sitting down – two bullets had pulverised his knee cartilages. Recognising Ray, he became animated, as if he were still in the game.

'The Puerto Rican didn't get caught. That grocery shop has been hit three times this month.'

'I need Maggie to interview, and Sue to babysit.'

'Done. Room three.'

*

In the blandest of rooms, Bad Dad was made to sit in a chair at a table. A woman in police uniform, with tied-back hair and fat ankles, came into the room. The tiniest of gold nose studs caught the light. She offered Bad Dad her hostile smile, before pulling out a chair and sitting down across the table from the suspect. Ray and Lenny remained standing.

'Name?'

'Hadrian.'

'Like Hadrian's Wall?'

'Everybody says that. It is annoying.'

'If you're worrying about the child while we have this little chat, he is being looked after by a colleague of mine.'

Hadrian said nothing and avoided her eyes.

'Are you the father of the little boy?'

'No.'

'Who is the mother?'

He hesitated for a while, before saying, 'My wife.' And added, 'I guess.'

'Does she know you took the child to the park?'

'She sent me to take him.'

'Despite the fact that you said you were not the father.'

'I am the father, if you like.'

'The woman you were harassing on the park bench, is she known to you?'

'She is exactly the sort of busybody old trout who makes my job difficult.'

'Your *job*?'

'My job is being husband and father.'

'That is the basis of family life.'

'It's almost impossible these days to land something worthwhile,' said Hadrian. 'Booth with his big nose might well smirk down from his plinth.'

'You gave a baby beer to drink.'

'He is not a baby any longer.'

'How old is he?'

Hadrian hesitated. 'One and a half. Two, perhaps.'

'You don't know?'

'I don't remember what she told me. Normally, I try to avoid kids and pets.'

The door opened, and Sue pushed the stroller with the boy into the interrogation room. 'I managed to clean him up. Now he is hungry. He should go back to his mother.'

'Where does his mother live?' Maggie continued.

'Number fourteen East 22nd.'

'The same address as the cook on your bench?' said Lenny. 'Interesting.'

'Same house, but my... my wife only rents the upstairs apartment. Cook works for the people downstairs.'

'We need a motive for the suspect to have acted the way he did,' Lenny quoted from his rule book.

Maggie pushed her chair closer to the table. 'What is the name of the mother of the toddler you took to the park?'

'Angela.'

'Are you in a relationship with Angela?'

'No.'

'Did Angela give birth to the toddler?'

'I believe so.'

'Where is the natural father of the boy?'

'In Honduras.'

'What you do for a living?'

'I'd rather not say. I promised.'

'That won't wash with me. There is a list of infractions you committed...'

'A long list,' Lenny amended.

'For some of them, you'll get a fine to pay,' added Maggie.

Hadrian's shoulders sagged. 'That's all I need.'

'What we need from you at the moment is to be less obtuse,' said Maggie. 'Otherwise, we have to add obstructing an investigation. That often carries a hefty fine.'

'Will you arrest me?'

There was silence in the ugly room apart from the sound of Hadrian's breathing in and out.

'Look,' he suddenly spoke up. 'I'll level with you. I was harassing the black woman because I want to be arrested. I neglected the needs of the child because I want to be declared unfit as a parent. I want to get a fine from the Gramercy Park Owners Association and refuse to pay it. If you don't detain me, I will have to go back to the park and throw the old woman into the pond. Maybe then, the mental health department will intervene and lock me away.'

Lenny looked at Ray and shrugged. The older policeman said to Hadrian, 'You want my opinion? You're nuts!'

'Good,' said Hadrian happily. 'Finally, I am getting somewhere. I worked hard to prepare for this show and to get it right.'

Ray snarled, 'You premeditated this little show?'

'Most actors can't find employment,' responded Hadrian.

Puzzled, Lenny contributed, 'Gramercy Park is dedicated to an actor.'

'Playing Shakespeare a hundred years ago, he did not have to become a jobbing actor to pay the rent.'

'What's a jobbing actor?'

'One who is so desperate, he needs to accept any job going, no matter how vile.'

Ray felt the interview was drifting, and wanted to make some progress. 'What does this have to do with your criminal behaviour?'

'I want to be arrested. I want to be put into a mental institution. I want to be led away by Social Services.'

Lenny and Ray looked at each other. They both shook their heads.

'My current employer,' Hadrian went on, 'is Angela, the mother of the boy. I have to play her husband twenty-four-seven. Plus act as doting daddy to the child. I have to walk arm in arm with her in town. The dame doesn't want people to find out that the man she married left her for a broad in Honduras. I wash, iron, clean and shop. Yesterday, she forced me to cook lasagne, because that is what good husbands do. I have to lie in bed next to her and imitate orgasm noises, to reassure the child in the next room about the stability of the family.' Hadrian took a deep breath. 'I can't stand it any longer. Capiche?'